PRINCESS
and the
PLAYER

The Last Guy (w/Tia Louise)
The Right Stud (w/Tia Louise)

Strangers in Love Series

Beauty and the Baller

PRINCESS
and the
PLAYER

ILSA MADDEN-MILLS

Published by Montlake, Seattle

www.apub.com

Amazon, the Amazon logo, and Montlake are trademarks of Amazon.com, Inc., or its affiliates.

ISBN-13: 9781542038461 (paperback)
ISBN-13: 9781542038478 (digital)

Cover design by Letitia Hasser
Cover images: © Friends Stock, © Elina Leonova / Shutterstock; YUBO, Tetra Images—David Engelhardt / Getty Images

Printed in the United States of America

To the handsome player
I married twenty-three years ago . . .

Chapter 1

TUCK

"To Tuck, the oldest wide receiver in the NFL! Happy birthday, old man!" Jasper says as he raises his glass of Dom Pérignon.

"Still kicked your ass in the gym today, quarterback," I say as he and Deacon clink their glasses with mine. "You puppies dream of being me when you're thirty-five."

"True, true. You're a legend on the field," Jasper says. "In fact, you're so old I bet you still have a Blockbuster card."

I grunt. "Jesus, that's lame—and wrong. I grew up on HBO."

Deacon, our running back, refills our glasses as our limo moves smoothly through Manhattan traffic. He chuckles. "I'm not going to make any jokes about your age because I sincerely feel bad for you, but think of it like this: You're one year closer to wearing a big ole diaper. Better yet, you'll be wearing it while you watch us play."

Jasper cackles as I roll my eyes. These young guns are twenty-seven and consider me old, which is sorta true in the football world. Most wide receivers peak in their midtwenties, then decline by 50 percent each year after. Somehow, I've lasted fourteen seasons. I have had two ankle fractures, a broken wrist, four dislocated shoulders, and a groin injury but still keep coming back and playing my heart out.

They start whispering, and I eyeball them, wondering what they have planned for tonight.

They surprised me an hour ago when they showed up at my place wearing black masks and killer suits. They gave me a mask—only mine has a shit ton of feathers on it. Judging by their excitement, I'm surprised they didn't insist I wear a sash and a crown.

I sigh. Usually my birthday is a somber event, and I either hang at home with my current girl or go to the Baller. I drink a few beers and eat a slice of chocolate cake. That's the tradition.

I gaze down at the scars on my fingers and knuckles, glossy and whitened over time. My birthday is also the day my father died ten years ago. These guys don't know that. Why would they? I keep my personal stuff close to my chest.

Whatever. Fine. No matter the dark shit going on in my head, I can roll with a surprise party. It's not a stretch to put on a smile. I've been doing it since I was a kid.

"You all right there, Tuck?" Jasper asks as the limo pulls to the side of the road and stops.

"Yep," I say as we get out of the car. "So what's this big surprise? Where are we going?"

"Oh, it's nothing special," Jasper murmurs as he and Deacon share a sly glance, then giggle like frat boys.

Uh-huh.

One of the feathers from my mask sticks to my mouth, and I spit it out.

Sure, I'm a carefree guy. Some might even call me a party boy. But *this*—this shit is just weird.

Jasper tosses an arm around me, obviously the organizer of this shindig. He's dressed in a tailored navy suit, and his frizzy white-blond hair is twisted up in a man-bun. His eyes twinkle. "Trust me; you'll love what we have planned. I can't tell you because I want to see your face when we get there. It's going to blow your mind."

I glance around the dark alley we've entered. There are no shops, lights, or people. A rat scurries off to the side. "If a clown jumps out from behind that dumpster, I'll kill you," I growl. "Birthdays are prank-free zones."

"For the third time, there aren't any clowns tonight!" Jasper lifts his hands. "I wouldn't do that to you, Tuck!"

"Clowns should be murdered," I add. "Wanna know who invented clowns? A psycho, that's who."

They burst out laughing, most likely recalling their last prank, where they tossed a "synthetic partner" female clown—with tits and a vagina—in the locker-room shower with me. I wrestled that monster to the ground and threw her out.

Guess I deserved it. The month before their prank, I took out a Craigslist ad as a hot woman looking for men to give her anal and left their cell numbers. Their phones blew up with calls and voice mails for days.

Jasper grins. "There's no tricks where we're going. Just beautiful women—"

I halt. "If you're taking me to a strip club, I don't do those anymore. Remember the redhead? The one who stalked me—"

"Yeah. She had some serious boundary issues. What was her name?" Deacon asks.

"Lollipop," I mutter with a groan. "Still can't look at redheads without flinching."

I went to a bachelor party where she was a stripper. I tucked a hundred in her bikini top. Didn't even get a lap dance, but she got obsessed, sent weird letters, and then showed up in cities where I was playing. Once she smashed the windows on my Porsche. The final straw was when she confronted me outside my apartment building. She was arrested and sent to jail. The Lollipop Incident may have happened a few years ago, but the trauma lingers.

3

"Here we are," Jasper announces with a hand flourish as we stop at a metal door outside a ten-story brown building. Blackout shades cover the windows, and if there's a club inside, I can't hear it.

Jasper knocks, and a peep door slides open. He whispers a password, and the entrance creaks as we step inside. Red carpet leads us to a two-story foyer dimly lit with Victorian-looking sconces. Ornately framed portraits cover the interior walls, scenes of fancy people from long ago.

The man who opened the door sweeps hooded eyes over us. With auburn hair, he's tall and well built and wears a black tux with tails. "Membership card, please," he says in a haughty British accent.

Jasper pulls out his wallet and flashes a card at him, then nudges his head at me and Deacon. "I've brought two guests that the board approved last month."

He bows. "Ah, yes. Welcome to Decadence, gentlemen, the premier club of New York. I see you have your masks—good. I'm Brogan, your guide during the orientation. We wish you incredible delights and pleasures in our playhouse. Tonight's our fairy-tale theme. Let us begin. Follow me, please."

Hold on . . .

Delights and pleasures? Playhouse?

What the actual . . .

Ah, shit . . .

I raise an eyebrow at them. "A sex club. Seriously?"

"Oh yeah, baby!" Jasper says as he pumps his hips. "There's gonna be a hot time in the *old* town tonight."

I shake my head at him. "Dude, is this place even legit?"

"Totally. The mayor sponsored me," he says as he tugs me along the hallway. "It's got a steep membership fee, seventy-five thou a year, plus a vetting system. They run background checks, credit scores, you name it. We have the masks so no one knows who we are. There aren't any Lollipops here, so let that thought go."

"I managed to stop thinking about her, but thanks for reminding me."

He smirks. "You could be a mechanic or an accountant or whatever. That's the cool part. Pretending to be someone else."

"I see."

"I usually say I'm a personal trainer, you know, because of my great body. Anyway, tonight everything's on me—drinks and the entrance fee. You're welcome." He does a bow like Brogan did at the door.

"How much was it for us to get in?" I ask.

"For special guests, five grand each, so ten."

"Damn," I say. Sure, we make millions a year, but that's pricey for a birthday.

"Whatever. It's my gift. I've been several times and . . ." He kisses the tips of his fingers. "Amazing. And you're worth it. Don't cry about it or anything, you big baby."

I grunt. "You're the drama queen. I'm the bad motherfucker. Get it straight."

He chuckles. "Which is why we get along. Yin and yang. Peas and carrots."

"I'm dying to see what it's like," Deacon says as he rubs his hands together. "Don't wuss out on us, Tuck."

These two are obviously foaming at the mouth to bring me here, and Jasper spent a lot of money on this. I exhale. Why not? With a few more drinks, I might even forget the demons in my head.

I put on my fake smile and spread my hands. "Is there cake?"

"There's a food area with a huge buffet—" Jasper says, then cuts off as a voluptuous woman in a see-through mermaid outfit appears in the hall. She sashays toward us, murmurs a husky "Hi," and then disappears.

"Who needs cake when sexy Ariel is here?" Deacon breathes. "Did you see her tits?"

I did—great rack—but I'm craving cake. I eat healthy twenty-four seven, and I've been looking forward to cake. Wait a minute; I'm thinking about sweets instead of tits. Jesus. I *am* old.

We step into Brogan's office. After handing over our cell phones and signing numerous consent forms, we get a rundown about the different parts of the club—some are just for regular socializing, and others are "play" areas. He informs us that some floors have themed rooms for privacy—or not. Each room has a bed, condoms, lube, toys, and hand sanitizer.

Wanna be a pirate? Cowboy? Biker? Vampire? It's here.

Jasper leans over to me and whispers, "I could have gone with a nice bottle of bourbon, but I wanted your present to be unique. I love you, man. For real." He sniffs and waves his hand like a swooning woman. "Now I'm all misty. You like it, the club? Please like it."

Sure, I'm down with people exploring their sexuality. To each their own kink—I don't judge. I've done my own crazy shit—a few threesomes, maybe a foursome (I really can't recall)—but that was in my early days of the NFL. These days I prefer a girlfriend.

Did I want to come here tonight? Nope. It's not part of my tradition.

"Stop torturing me," he begs when I don't reply. "Tell me you love it. Come on. Please, please, *please*."

"God, stop with the whining. Fine, fine, it's cool. Awesome. My mind is blown. My dick is hard. Plus, I've always wanted to wear a mask with feathers."

"I hear your sarcasm and choose to ignore it. Is it weird that I bought a glue gun and stuck more feathers on it? I fucking loved jazzing it up, so don't lose it, yeah? It's a memento of our friendship."

I huff out a laugh. "You seriously need to stop buying shit online."

"Never. I would have told you I was a member, but it's kind of like *Fight Club*. There *is* no Decadence Club."

"Right."

"We were *never* here. We *never* walked down that alley. The mayor *is* not a member. You never *saw* Brogan. Hmm, I wonder if I could fake a British accent." He clears his throat. "Ahoy, matey, how the bloody hell

are you? Wait, let me try again—that was my pirate impersonation."
He clears his throat. "Hiya, mate. Fancy a cuppa?"

Smirking, I hold my hand up for him to be quiet, keying into
Brogan. Apparently, Deacon was the only one listening.

"Before you touch someone, ask, and before you join an orgy, ask.
A simple tap on the shoulder will do," Brogan says in a somber tone.

I roll my eyes. No thanks. I'm here, but I'm not touching anyone.

Brogan gives us name tags. Jasper writes in Prince Personal Trainer,
Deacon chooses Prince of Princes, and I pick Prince Player. Brogan asks
if we'd like to hit the locker room, disrobe, and wear towels around our
waists.

I rear back. "Whoa, now, hang on. I'm drawing a line. My dick does
not swing free in a club."

"Same," Deacon mutters, cupping his groin.

Jasper huffs. "Pussies. Fine by me. We'll stick with the suits. We do
look good—am I right?"

I guess we do. I'm in gray, Deacon is in black, and Jasper has the
navy. It's going to be hard to pass as a mechanic in a five-thousand-dol-
lar suit, but whatever. Happy freaking birthday to me. "There better be
cake," I tell them.

After Brogan declares we're ready, we go through double doors and
head upstairs to the second floor, pausing on the balcony that overlooks
the downstairs bar area. Deemed a social area—no full-on sex allowed,
just petting—it's like a regular nightclub: people dancing, a naughty
fairy-tale movie flickering on one of the walls. It's not gritty or dirty like
I expected; the vibe is glamorous, with chandeliers hanging from the
ceiling and an oval swimming pool in the center. Long black couches
line one wall, where couples make out while others stand and watch.
Nothing I haven't seen in a regular club.

Following the signs posted, we walk down another staircase to reach
the floor. A few men are dressed like us, but most of the clientele went
all out: guys in white jackets with gold tassels and lapels; women in

princess costumes—some skimpy, some floor length with big skirts. As for the men in towels, I salute them for their bravery.

"Oh my God, Snow White is here" comes from Deacon as a woman rises from one of the couches. She's wearing a yellow miniskirt, white thigh-high stockings, red heels, and a headband. Straightening her mask, she makes her way over and asks Deacon if he'd like to dance.

"Uh . . . ," he says, throat bobbing. "I'm here for a birthday. God, you're so pretty . . ."

"Go on; we'll be fine," I say and nudge him her way. Deacon is the shy one and sometimes needs a push.

"Why didn't she ask me?" Jasper asks, frowning as they disappear on the dance floor.

"Come on, pretty boy; there's plenty of women for you. Let's get some drinks." We head to the bar.

A woman slams into me, her chest colliding against my arm. She'd been in a rush, and the impact sends her reeling. I catch her before she falls and tug her up to my chest. "Whoa there. You okay, sweetheart?"

Breathing heavily, she raises her face, a glittery white mask covering her upper cheeks and most of her forehead. Her eyes capture mine, and I linger on the striking aquamarine color, the irises outlined in thick black.

Petite with her hair in a haphazard updo, she's wearing a floor-length white dress. There's a tiara on her head attached to a veil. "Great costume, Princess Bride," I say after glancing at her name tag.

She jerks away. "It's not a costume, and I do not want to have sex with you! Pervert! Get away from me!"

I drop her arm like it's hot, and she storms off, weaving as she clutches a bottle of tequila.

"Excuse me! I was trying to help!" I call back, brushing at the liquor she spilled on me. "And I didn't want to have sex with you!"

A few people around us who saw the incident chuckle. She flips me off over her shoulder as she stumbles around the people on the dance floor, then disappears into the throng. The *audacity*. Women adore me.

Jasper laughs. "Making friends already, huh? Maybe you've lost your golden touch at thirty-five. Damn, you're almost forty!" He legit looks horrified.

"Five years away, asshole."

He gets his "I have a great idea" face. "Remember how you and Ronan used to make bets?"

"Hmm." Ronan was our former quarterback before Jasper—and my best friend. A few years ago, he retired after a career-ending injury and moved to Texas. Now he's married, and I miss the hell out of him. In our younger days, we'd make bets about who could get the most girls at a bar. I won 99 percent of the time—I can be charming when I want—and I may have bragged about that winning streak to Jasper.

He raises an eyebrow. "We should continue the tradition. I bet you can't get Princess Bride into you. If you can't, then I'm going for it. I do love brunettes."

"Good luck. She's rude and short."

"Tuck Avery only dates tall girls," he says mockingly, then slaps cash down on the bar. "This is yours if you can do it."

"A dollar. Impressive."

He gives me a smug look. "It isn't about the money. It's your competitive streak. You, my friend, love a challenge."

"Nope. Not interested." I shove my hands through my wavy golden-brown hair. Longer than usual, it falls around my shoulders. Since training camp started, I haven't made the time to get it cut. Now we've started the season, and it's the last thing on my mind.

Jasper hands over one of his extra hair ties, and I put it in a low bun. Behind the bar are plain black ball caps. I pay for one and turn the cap backward and slip it over my head. I check my appearance in the mirror behind the bar, rubbing the heavy dark scruff on my face I've let grow. Mechanic?

"You *want* to do the bet. Say it," Jasper says, bringing me back. He beats his fists on the bar. "Do it, do it, do it!"

"Stop acting like a moron."

"Ah, you're scared you don't have what it takes! First you wouldn't wear the towel; now you're running from an itty-bitty challenge. You're old as dirt! Live each day as your last, man—that's my motto. You might die tomorrow, am I right?"

"Maybe." I pretend interest at the people in the pool.

"Carpe diem, Tuck! Seize the day—and the princess!"

"Dammit. Why are you such a prick? Game on, quarterback," I say with exasperation as I roll my eyes. Why not? What else is there to do?

He pumps his hips. "Yes, yes, yes, my man is gonna try for the end zone! A true player in action!"

People turn to look at us, and I chuckle. "You're a child."

He raises his glass. "To Princess Bride and football!" We clink our Dom bottles together.

Deacon comes back to slam shots with us, then takes off to check out the BDSM dungeon with Snow White. Several women stop to chat with us, and I feign interest as my gaze searches for Princess Bride.

A few minutes later, she ambles off the dance floor, her updo completely down. A strobe light flashes on her, and it's hard to tell if she's attractive with the mask, but the dim light shows creamy pale skin and plump rosebud lips.

Excitement buzzes over me as I gaze at her. My competitive streak is ready. Plus, no one calls me a pervert and gets away with it. She *will* worship at the throne of Tuck tonight. I'm not sure how, but I'll play it by ear.

A tall man in a towel follows her. I ignore him, focusing on her as I smile at her wobbly approach, meeting her eyes with my best smoldering look. She ignores me, plops down on the seat next to me, and then bursts into tears.

Well, this is unexpected—but it could work.

Mom always said I could make the rain vanish with my personality. I was her perfect slice of sunshine, and I smiled nonstop in those horrible days of childhood, pushing her blues away as I shoved down my own fears.

As long as no one peeks under the shadowy surface of me, all is well.

I smirk at Jasper.

In the bag, my eyes say.

Chapter 2

TUCK

The guy in the towel takes the seat on the other side of her, his barrel chest covered in dark curly hair. His name tag—attached to his towel—says Prince Rolex. He's wearing shimmery brown pantyhose.

"You have an interesting choice in men, Princess Bride," I murmur idly under my breath as I drain the bourbon I switched to earlier.

Prince Rolex says something to her as his finger twirls her hair. She gets off the stool and stumbles, her backside falling into the cradle of my spread legs. She uses my thighs as support as she finds her balance and jumps up to face him with clenched fists.

Her veil hangs over one side of her shoulder, and I stare at the deep V on the back of her dress. It's not one of those fluffy dresses that can stand up by itself—no, it is silky, hugs her curves, and glitters with pearls and sequins. She said it wasn't a costume, and I get it. It's a real fucking wedding dress.

On her back, from one shoulder blade to the other, is a winged tattoo draped in pink and blue roses. The right wing is slightly bent. I squint to read the script but can't.

I hear her mutter a distinct "No" to Prince Rolex, then, "Stay away from me, pervert."

I'm practically hanging over her shoulder as he leers at her with heavy-lidded eyes. My temper stirs, itching to rise, but I shove it down to see how this plays out.

"Come on, baby; stop playing hard to get," Prince Rolex says. "I've got everything you need. Let's go try that doctor room." He rubs a hand over his chest and pinches one of his nipples. "You need a breast exam. A thorough one."

"Not interested," she snaps. "How many times do you need to hear it?"

He grabs for her hand, and she jerks away.

"Hey, man, she said no," I call out sharply, but he's so focused on her that he either doesn't hear or he's ignoring me.

He puts a fat hand on her shoulder and grips her, making her cry out as she falls forward. I snatch her away from him as I wrap my arms around her waist before she hits the floor. Using gentle hands, I ease her behind me and out of his way. She barely weighs anything.

With one look at his red fingerprints on her shoulder, anger ignites. I shove his chest with my hands, and he tumbles back, loses his footing, and falls on his ass. "The lady said no. Those are the rules. Get the fuck out of here."

Several patrons flinch at my voice and back away as I look for an attendant. Not seeing one, I curse. Fine. I'll toss him out myself even if I have to drag him. I stalk his way.

"Who the hell do you think you are?" Prince Rolex shouts as he regains his equilibrium and stands. He gapes as he gets a look at my face—then backpedals. I know what he sees. My father's face. Flashing eyes. Gritted teeth. Clenched fists.

"You shouldn't have touched her, asshole. You crossed a line—"

He sputters, then runs to the right, shoving into people as he slips and slides. I sprint after him—

"Wait!" A woman's voice. "Don't! Please!"

I jerk to a halt as if pulled by a string. That voice came from Princess Bride. My jaw twitches. Control, man, control. Taking deep breaths, I roll my neck as I count to ten, then twenty.

Prince Rolex is an abusive dick who thinks he can get away with hurting women.

Like my father.

The first time I witnessed his rage, I was five. I'd been on a field trip to the zoo and couldn't wait to tell my mom about petting a giraffe. I walked in the kitchen, and my father had her pinned against the wall as he hit her. Later she found me under my bed and told me everything was fine, that she loved him more than anything, that I was her sunshine, that I had to keep smiling—

Nope. Not going to think about it.

I rub my scruff. I'm cool; it's over.

My father's voice snakes in my head. *You're just like me, boy. Rage lives inside you.*

It doesn't! I shove that idea away and walk to the girl, my eyes scanning her body for injuries. I take off my suit jacket and drape it around her shoulders. "You all right?"

She swallows thickly. "Yeah."

Before we can say anything else, an attendant arrives, and I give him the rundown. Then I tell him that they're doing a piss-poor job if they care about consent. The attendant's head bobs as he dashes off to look for Prince Rolex.

I focus back on the girl, pushing my anger away. She's tiny and delicate, maybe five-five in heels, her head barely reaching my pecs.

She weaves on her feet. "I said hello to him once—*once*. Then he tried to dance around me, not *with* me because I wouldn't let him, but it didn't matter; that's all it took for him to, ugh, think I was into him. I tried to report him—I looked for my friend, but . . ." Her voice trails off.

"You don't have to explain. Wasn't your fault. Hopefully he's out of here by now."

Her fists clench. "He got aggressive. Wanna know why?"

I expected more of a damsel in distress, but . . . "Tell me."

She points her index finger as she enunciates her words. "Because God forbid he feel emasculated by a woman's rejection."

"May he rot in pantyhose hell. Bastard."

Her shoulders dip, and she lets out a husky laugh. "Funny. I like you. Oops. I think I called you a pervert earlier. Was that you? Yep, it was. I remember that mask. Sorry. I'd been avoiding him; then I bumped into you and spilled my tequila . . ." Her lush lips form a pout.

I guide her back to the bar. "There's plenty of tequila here. Let me get you one."

She says she's warm and takes off my jacket and hands it back to me with a murmured "Thank you," then eases down on her stool, placing her hands firmly on the bar. "First, water. A full glass every hour is the rule."

"Bad hangovers, huh?"

"Migraines. Big. Huge."

I settle into my seat and order us both waters from the bartender.

"It's going to leave a bruise," I say, my hands flexing as I stare at her shoulder.

She brushes at the fingerprints, then shrugs. "I've seen worse. You, my friend, were awesome. Strong. Fierce. And I'm not saying that because I might be a tiny bit drunk. Thank you so much—you're, like, really muscled and hot. Oops, I didn't mean to say that. By the way, if you saw me crying before, don't tell anyone. I don't cry. I really don't. Yes, my eyes *leaked*, but it was allergies." She glances back at the dance floor and frowns. "Dammit. That's a lie. I did cry. The stupid DJ just had to go and play 'All of Me.'"

"Let me guess. Wedding song you'd picked out for the big day?"

She turns to me, her rosebud mouth parting like petals unfurling. Her cheekbones are high, her raven hair thick and heavy as it falls to the small of her back. There's a perfect widow's peak in the center of her hairline, creating a face that's heart shaped.

"How did you know?"

"You're in a real wedding dress, and your, um, eyes leaked. Something ended your engagement? Today was your wedding date? Am I close?"

"It sucks that I'm that predictable. Yes, today's the day." She weaves a little on her seat, and I slowly ease her back.

"I've got you."

"Thanks." A long exhalation comes from her chest as she toys with a gold locket around her neck. My brow furrows as I gaze at it. The thick chain, the square design, the bird etching on the front. There's something familiar—

"Let's forget about my cheating ex," she declares, stopping my train of thought. "*You* slayed the pantyhose dragon. You're my knight in shining armor." She reads my name tag, then waves her hands around in the air and claps her palms together horizontally. "We need a redo. Take two: when Princess Bride meets Prince Player. A naughty night-time story about a masquerade ball. Ready?"

I laugh. "Sure."

She cups her chin with her hand and smiles. "Hi, handsome. Nice mask. Love the feathers. Suits you. You come here often?"

"My first time, I'm a guest, and my friends chose the mask." I stick my hand out, and her small one takes mine gingerly, a hum going down my spine as our fingers graze. "Nice to meet you. So what do you do, Princess Bride?"

"Um, I wanted this night to be anonymous, so . . ."

A girl after my own heart. "I shouldn't have even asked. We can guess about each other," I offer. "We don't have to confirm if it's true, and it might be fun. Wanna play?"

She turns on her seat to face me, her legs fitting in between my thighs. "Yes, I'm very creative."

And hot.

I graze my eyes over the neckline of her dress, the skin shimmering with some kind of glitter that accentuates the creamy rise of her tits. They're small enough to fit in my hand. Do her nipples match the deep red of her lips?

One step at a time, Tuck.

First, you flirt. Then you fuck.

"Okay, let's warm up by using people here," I say.

"Got it. We're gonna make up stuff about people we think is true. You go first."

I glance around the room, and my gaze lands on Deacon and Snow White as they come back into the club area.

"Not the guy," she says, her gaze following mine. "The girl."

I study Snow White for a few beats. There's a confident air about her, a sense of power. "Hmm, she's an executive who gets her kinks out in the dungeon. She loves the beach, jazz, and pumpkin spice lattes."

She giggles, but come on—what girl doesn't enjoy the beach, jazz, and fancy coffee? Plus I know they left the bar area to visit the dungeon.

"Fine. You try," I say.

She studies Snow White while I drink *her* in. When she bumped into me earlier, I didn't have the chance to appreciate her. She's not the soft-and-sweet pretty I usually go for; she's striking.

My body buzzes, feeling drawn to her.

Perhaps it's the contrast of her hair with the white mask and dress. Maybe it's her fire. Maybe it's the fact that even though I can't see her entire face, it's easy to imagine how beautiful she is.

Or I'm drunk as shit.

Her scent wafts around me, like ripe peaches from the South. I itch to stick my nose in her neck but settle for soaking in the elegant lines of her throat, the shapely shoulders, the lush curve of her waist. I imagine her naked on my bed, her midnight hair spilling on white sheets.

The truth is I haven't had sex since I broke up with a girl a few months ago, and with football starting, I haven't had time to meet anyone. I'm starved for something (or someone) to take my attention away from the block of cement on my chest. Most days I'm able to ignore that pressure, but my birthday just brings it all full circle, a stark reminder of everything wrong in my life.

She taps her chin. "Snow White is a high-class call girl who keeps a burn book of anyone who's ever crossed her. She has revenge plans for every entry, and she's the kind of girl who'll accomplish her goals. She's jaded but wants to fall in love."

"Nice. You win." I toast her, then order us tequila shots. Three each. We slam them back at the same time, then suck the limes.

"All right. My turn to pick someone." Her gaze stops on Jasper. He's sitting by the pool, his feet dangling in the water as one topless Cinderella massages his shoulders while her twin is in the pool giving him a foot rub. "Him. The skeevy guy with the blond hair."

My lips twitch. "Perfect."

"In high school, he was a wrestler, but now he's a shoe salesman. He uses social media to troll for women who love micropenises."

I burst out laughing. Jasper does have a contract with a sneaker company.

Her lips curve up. "Ah, Player, you have a great laugh."

"Really?"

Her voice softens. "Thank you. Again. You're so great."

Unease stirs inside of me. Shit. I'm not. I mean, this started as a bet. I doubt I would have noticed her if she hadn't bumped into me.

My breath hitches when she leans her head on my shoulder, trust in her ocean-blue eyes.

"Okay, now you do him," she murmurs as she crooks her arm inside my elbow. "Wait! Can I touch you? Oh my God, I forgot to ask!"

My lids lower. "Yeah. And I can touch you?"

"Please," she murmurs.

I tear my eyes off her and watch Jasper, chuckling as the woman rubbing his feet tickles him and he cries out like a girl. "He's an athlete, but it's bowling." He hates bowling.

"I don't know. He obviously lives in the gym—"

"I'm not done, smarty."

She makes a flourish with her hands. "By all means, sir, please continue . . ."

"He's the kind of guy who eats food in his bed, like cookies and crackers and popcorn, then sleeps on top of it without a care in the world." He's been staying with me temporarily, and I've seen his eating habits. Food falls out of his mouth when he talks; then there's the trash he leaves everywhere.

She giggles. "You never eat in bed?"

"Food belongs in the kitchen." I flash a smile. "He's also proud of his penis. He's named it."

"What?"

"Cupid. Because every girl who gets the arrow falls in love."

"You win!" she calls out as she laughs, her face upturned to me.

A zing of electricity hits me. I like her lips. Her emotional eyes. My fingers trace the curve of her cheek, grazing down her throat to her chest. I stop at her neckline, caressing the outline. "You're beautiful."

She slides off her seat, settles between my legs, and wraps her arms around my neck. "Thank you, my prince."

"You're welcome, my princess," I say huskily as her breasts press against my chest.

"Are you wicked?" she murmurs as she tugs my hair free from the bun and presses a soft kiss to my jawline.

A deep, primitive sound comes from my throat. "Hmm, very."

"Good." She pulls on my gray necktie, then removes it slowly. She runs the silk through her fingers, brings it to her nose, and then tucks it inside her bodice. "My souvenir."

"If you get to keep one, then I want one."

"I'm your souvenir."

My blood heats at her words, rising higher as she undoes the top button of my shirt, then another. She stops at the third one, spreading the fabric. Heat flashes over me as she kisses the bump where my shoulder was dislocated.

"Now do me." She gazes up at me. "Who am I?"

I blink as my head refocuses off sex and stumbles through the alcohol in my system to recall our previous conversation. "You're smart. Your career is probably something artsy. You're wearing a locket which holds a photo of someone you lost." I pause, remembering her tattoo with the bent wing. I graze my fingers over the yellowing bruise on her arm. *I've seen worse,* she said. "Someone has hurt you before, and if you tell me who, I will make sure he never does again."

The air around us thickens as our eyes hold; then she glances away.

Splaying my fingers on her cheek gently, I tug her jaw back. "Hey. I shouldn't have said the last part. I shouldn't assume."

Her black lashes lower. "Maybe it's because we're strangers that you feel you can say those things. We don't know each other. We can spill secrets, then let it go tomorrow."

"So I was right?" The protective alpha inside me stirs.

"No one hurts me anymore," she murmurs. "I'm different now. Stronger."

"My little brave princess." I ease the veil off her head and arrange her hair around her shoulders and chest, trailing my fingers through the sleek thickness. Her head instinctively leans into my palm when I cup her cheek. She kisses my palm, and scorching lust that's been building since she slid between my legs sizzles like an electrical line dropped in my skull.

My thumb brushes her bottom lip as I picture my cock sliding between those plump petals. "Do me."

Chapter 3

TUCK

Her pale-blue eyes devour me, from my backward hat and heavy scruff to my expensive leather loafers. She takes my hands, traces the calluses, and then drags her index finger from the tip of my middle finger to my palm. She unsnaps the black leather cuff I wear and strokes the ragged scars on the underside of my wrist, lingering for a moment, then dips her head and kisses them.

It's barely even a touch, and I groan.

She looks up. "You work with your hands. Maybe you're a carpenter or own a construction company, a successful one judging by your suit. You don't have a faded line on your ring finger, so you're not married. You're a physical person and not a stranger to fighting." Her eyes trail back up and lock with me. She laces both of our hands together and chews on her bottom lip, and I can't see her true expression, but . . .

"What is it?" I ask softly, sensing her hesitation.

She presses our masks together, nose to nose, and stares at me. "You have the most incredible eyes, green with yellow sparks. Tiger eyes. I see a dark side there."

I huff out an uneasy laugh. "What? No."

Her lips quirk. "We all have darkness. People you see on the street, people you work with, people you love, people you hate. If there's no darkness, then there's no room for light. And when that darkness hits you, and it will, all that matters is that you keep going, one step at a time until you're up and back on your journey." She dips her head, sneaking a glance at me. "Sorry. Tequila makes me chatty."

Before I can reply, Deacon and Snow White show up, and Princess Bride turns to them and hugs Snow White. I huff as I realize they know each other. No wonder she laughed at my description of her.

When a fast song hits the speakers, they turn back to us, take our hands, and tug us out to the dance floor. Jasper and his twins join us. We dance, one song after another. Time blurs as people mill around us. When a slow song comes on, I ease her into my arms. We sway together, our bodies brushing against each other. You'd think we wouldn't make a good fit with the size difference, but we do, her head pressed against my chest as my nose dips to her hair. My hands stroke her back, sliding inside the fabric at her waist to touch the lace of her panties.

This is what I know.

She doesn't know who I am, and she wants me, not the famous footballer.

I lean down to her ear. "Be wicked with me tonight. I'll make you forget the guy who hurt you."

Before she can reply, Jasper pulls me aside, demanding I get cake "because he's a great fucking party planner and it's my tradition," but I barely focus on what he's saying.

I don't want cake anymore. I want her.

But he insists, even telling them it's my birthday, so as a group, we head upstairs to the food area. I grab a slice of chocolate cake off the dessert table, then slide in the booth where they are. My princess hikes up her dress and straddles my lap as she faces me. Her core slides against my groin, and my hands clench around her waist.

Jasper yells out encouragement to her as she flips my cap off and runs her hands through my hair. Giggling, she forks over bites of cake to me, then some for herself. "Happy birthday, my prince," she murmurs in my ear.

As soon as the cake is gone, I ignore everyone as I sweep her up in my arms bridegroom-style. With the others hooting behind us, we venture up to the next level. I ease her down in front of me as we stop at a room with a window where the blinds have been left open. Several people are having sex, a mishmash of arms and legs.

One of the guys, in midthrust, falls off the bed and bangs his head on the wall. Another man bends to help him, loses his balance, and falls on top of him. We step away to laugh.

Holding hands, we take another set of stairs to a quieter level. She picks a room, and I follow her inside. I shut the blinds and lock the door while she roams around.

My gaze lands on a big bed with black satin sheets. There's no theme, thank God, and just like Brogan said, condoms are on the nightstand. There's a small fridge stocked with water and a bathroom off to the right.

"There's a giant purple dildo," she muses as she points to a shelf with an array of toys.

"You won't need it," I rumble as I take her in my arms and press my forehead against hers. "Unless you want me to use it?"

"Maybe I'll use it on you."

"Funny." I card my fingers through her hair. "Do you come here often?"

"My first time."

"But you've had one-night stands?" I mean, I assumed. She's probably in her late twenties, she's bold—

She grips the steel pipe in my pants. "Yes."

"Fuck, that feels good," I groan as she strokes me. Our breaths mingle as she unbuttons my shirt and tugs it out of my slacks, then tosses it over her head.

She buries her nose in my chest. "First, tell me one real thing about you. Or two."

I hold her as we sway to music that isn't playing. "Something real, hmm—well, I do work with my hands. I like to play guitar sometimes. I tried yoga once and nearly broke my neck doing a handstand. And you?"

"Hmm, well, there's no picture in my locket. You guessed right about me being artsy—I am, and let's see, what else . . . oh, I have a thing for ChapStick. I own hundreds in all different flavors."

"Do you have any rules you want me to know?" I gaze at her upturned face.

"No kissing on the lips."

"Why? Your lips are fucking perfect . . ."

I cup her face, studying her features, imprinting the image of her aquamarine eyes, the widow's peak.

She avoids my question. "Anything I should know about you?"

"One night. No names. No strings. And the masks don't come off."

"Deal."

I turn her around and unzip her dress, and it glides down her skin and pools on the floor. A low growl comes from my throat at the white lingerie she wears, a skimpy lace bra and a matching thong. Her hair spills down her back, and I drape it over her shoulder as my lips brush the bruise there. I move down her back, grazing my knuckles over her vivid tattoo. I read the script for it near her nape: *bent but not broken*. Easing down to my haunches, I kiss the two dimples above her ass. I can't kiss her lips, but I'm going to brand myself over every other inch.

Her ass is full and generous, and my hands cup it. My fingers slide up, tracing her spine, going slow to savor her. I ease the straps of her bra off, then unhook it. It falls as I press my nose in her hair. My hands glide down her arms and back up to her shoulders. Jesus. Her skin is addictive. Soft. Hot. Fucking intoxicating.

I drift down to a scar on her side, kissing it, wondering what put it there. I caress the underside of her breasts, my hands drawing lazy circles over her globes, slow and steady, closer and closer, until I reach her nipples. I graze the pebbled peaks, and she cries out, her head falling back to my chest. I rumble in her ear that I'll get to them later as I drift down to her waist and hook my thumbs under the lace of her thong. I drag it over her hips, my hands stroking her thighs and calves as she shifts the panties off her feet.

My fingers slide around her waist to test her core, easing in gently, then sliding back out, groaning at the wetness there. I circle her clit, slow and tortuous. "Princess, you're hot and slick. I'm going to put my mouth there soon and taste you."

She melts against me, her hands sliding into my hair.

"Turn around," I say as I kiss her shoulder, and she faces me, face flushed with desire, lips parted.

My hands curl in anticipation. Petite red nipples and that glorious dark hair.

She. Is. Art.

Serenity hits. Tension loosens in my chest, and anxieties fall away. There's so much shit in my head. She evaporates it into nothing.

No thoughts about the day I killed my father.

No fear about me turning into the monster he was.

No panic that my career is ending.

No loneliness.

I dim the lights, kick off my shoes and socks, and remove my slacks, then my underwear. I palm my cock as a breathless "Damn" comes from her.

"Come to me," I purr.

She bites her plump bottom lip. "I hope you know how to use that thing."

"Hmm, yeah, you'll see. Come at me like you want me."

I catch her in my arms when she jumps, her legs wrapping around my waist as we fall to the bed.

Chapter 4

FRANCESCA

A male hand waves at my face. Donny.

"What's up?" I ask over the buzzing of my tattoo machine. I'm leaning over my client in the chair—not the best time to chat.

"Sorry to interrupt. I need to see you in my office when you're done. It's important."

I stiffen. "All right. This is my last appointment."

In my peripheral, he shoves his hands in his jeans, paces around my station, heaves out an exhale, and then leaves. My lips compress. Donny being out of his office is odd. He owns East Coast Ink & Gallery but prefers to stay upstairs while Harlee, his niece, manages the day-to-day downstairs.

I finish adding the green highlights to the leaves and set down my machine, dabbing at the tiny spots of blood on my client's wrist.

"It's beautiful!" Gianna gushes as she leans forward to take in the ring of daises intertwined with the infinity symbol around her wrist. Dressed in a pink Chanel dress, she's a young twentysomething with a mane of blonde hair she loves to flick over her shoulder with long sharp pink nails. There's a huge rock on her ring finger. A socialite with money, she's our typical client on the Upper East Side.

"I can't wait to show my fiancé!" she says.

I push up a smile even though my head is banging and my throat hurts. A cold hit me a couple of weeks ago and won't go away. I swallow the cough drop in my mouth. "Hey, you never mentioned how you found me."

"Hmm, a friend of mine. She actually bought one of your canvases in the front gallery."

"Ah." I average three to four sales a year from the gallery.

"She's an artist and a collector—paintings, sculptures." Hair flick. "Jewels."

Ah, *lots* of money, then. "Cool. Which one did she buy?"

"It's an abstract of a house."

Ah, the purple Victorian done in acrylics. My locket hangs from a tree in the front yard.

"It's, um, interesting," she says, choosing her words with care.

"You didn't like it."

She waves a hand around. "It's a pretty house, but there was something off about it. It felt dark. I don't know. It made me wonder who lived there."

I did. Until I was kicked out.

"Meh. My art isn't for everyone."

"Well, I adore *you*, darling." She bats her eyes at me. "And my tattoo is marvelous!"

I smile. She came in six months ago and asked for something unique. I worked on some designs for her; then we met at a coffee shop to go over the sketches. Since she had an extended trip to Europe planned, we scheduled today for the tattoo.

She squeals. "Oh my God, I almost forgot! You got married while I was gone and haven't said a word! It's been what, two months since the big day? How's married life? Are you relieved the wedding hoopla is over?"

"Hmm."

She narrows her eyes at me. "Hey, wait a minute. What's going on? Your engagement ring is gone." She glances over her shoulder at the workstation across from mine where Edward sketches, his lean frame bent over his desk. I follow her gaze, taking in his mahogany hair as it glints under the lights, the shimmer of his lip ring. As if he feels my eyes, he glances up at me, swallows thickly, and then turns away.

Every time I come to work, I tell myself this is the day it's not gonna hurt when I see him, but it still cuts.

Especially when I have to see him—with her.

"What the hell is going on?" Gianna hisses as we watch Harlee rush over to Edward as if she has an alarm set for every time I look his way. Harlee slants a smug smile at me as she gives him a hug, her hands lingering on his shoulders like claws.

"They happened," I mutter, and Gianna gasps.

With an hourglass figure and long platinum hair, Harlee's a blonde bombshell in a red dress and Christian Louboutin heels. Of course, she's also younger than me, twenty-two to my thirty. I'm ready for the nursing home next to her.

A recent graduate from business school, she took over as floor manager last year. I noticed her chatting with Edward, flirting, and I assumed it was just her outgoing nature because she was friendly with all the staff. Even me.

She was very friendly in the supply closet. I came in early for my shift and opened the closet, and there she was, on her knees in front of Edward. His eyes were closed, his mouth slack, his jeans at his feet. She hummed like a porn star on his cock as he called out, *Harlee, oh baby, Harlee!*

Unbeknownst to them, I watched them as my head flicked through memories, the times we went barhopping and they'd disappear, the weekends he said she needed help moving into her apartment, then helping her put furniture together.

I remember wanting to yell and pummel them with my fists. I felt as if my chest would explode, but I forced myself to shut down, to pack it all away to sort out later. After all, this wasn't the worst betrayal I'd experienced.

When Harlee turned around, I pointed at the semen on her cheek. *Missed some,* I said, then, *Next time, lock the door.* I flipped around, and Donny stood behind me, his eyes wide as saucers as he took in the scene. I canceled my appointments, left for the day, pawned my big-ass engagement ring, bought paints and canvases, and then went home and let the tears fall.

Gianna takes my hand and gives me a squeeze. "Oh my God, men are so stupid. When did this go down?"

"Three months before the wedding. I caught them in the supply closet."

"Are you okay? I mean, are you being good to yourself?"

My head immediately goes to Prince Player. He was good for me. The first few weeks after we met, I walked around in a bemused haze, my body heavy with awareness. For once, it hadn't pricked to see Edward and Harlee together. At night, I touched myself to the memory of him inside of me, to the feel of his shoulders under my hands. I even found myself searching the faces of men on the street, in restaurants, inside stores.

I wanted to see if a man like him was *real.*

I had to make myself stop. He didn't really exist.

He was a stranger who put a bandage on my pain.

Stuffing it down, I focus on her tattoo. "Here you go." I cover her wrist in petroleum jelly, then wrap it loosely with a clear bandage. "Remove this in twenty-four hours, wash with antimicrobial soap, and pat dry—don't rub. Apply a layer of antibacterial Vaseline, and don't cover it. Do this twice a day for two weeks. I'll give you a handout that explains everything, plus tips for keeping the tattoo from fading."

I pop my gloves off as I stand and roll my neck. It's past seven at night, and I've been bent over for hours.

She hops off the chair and flutters her hands. "Francesca, darling, no way—we have to discuss. You must get revenge or vindication or something. This can't be okay. *You* can't be okay. That fucker." Angry hair flick.

"Yeah."

"I know people who know people who know people if you want him taken out. Or her. Italians don't mess around when it comes to love." She mimics shooting a gun, then stabbing.

I laugh, a rusty sound. "I'm good, thanks."

We both watch as Edward stands from his chair and drapes Harlee's coat around her shoulders. Then he slips on the vintage caramel-colored leather jacket I found for him in a secondhand store in SoHo. They stroll toward the door, and his arm clutches her shoulders, pulling her in as their heads touch. It's the same way he used to hold me.

Harlee stops at the door and glances back at me, her voice sweet as syrup. "Clean up when you're done, Francesca. Have a good evening." Sly, evil smile. "Bye!"

My hands curl. I could take her. Black her eye. Kick a kidney. Show her who's really in charge.

By age five—after a stint in a home with six other kids and alcoholic foster parents—I learned how to defend myself. When you're smaller than your opponent, you have to be fast. You go for the tender bits: the crotch, eyes, and throat. You use your teeth, nails, and knees. You yell in their ear—maybe take a bite of it.

Never let them pin you.

At sixteen, I moved into a group home with fifty other kids. It was a lot like prison; I trusted no one, even the girl I shared a bunk with. My weapon was my ink pen tucked under my pillow. A week after I began living there, an older boy attacked me in the bathroom. He had waited for me, he said, and was going to teach the new girl a lesson about who to give her dues to. Him. He shoved me down on the floor and pinned me with a knife. While we were wrestling, my hands floundered, searching for a weapon. I grasped a piece of broken tile under the sink and jabbed it in his eye, then his neck.

He lived and was sent to juvie.

At the heart of me *is* a fighter—but I'm also pragmatic to the bone. I need this job.

"Holy shit, how can you still work here?" Gianna says after they walk out the door.

I wash my hands in the sink, then pat them dry, thinking about my reply. "Honestly, I was here before either of them, and it's like I'm giving in if I leave. Why should *I* leave? Does that make sense?"

"Girl. I'd be out of here in a heartbeat—but not before I beat his car with a bat."

A long sigh comes from me. "I get that, I do, but this is my life, and there's the gallery for my art. Maybe I'm torturing myself. Maybe I need to see them together over and over so I can move on. I don't know." Plus I have bills to pay. My art-school loan comes to mind. And the warehouse studio I sublet with other artists. And my apartment rent. It's not cheap living in Manhattan, but I've been drawn to this city for as long as I can remember. My hands brush the locket under my shirt, a reminder that someone did care for me. Once. Until she left.

Gianna frowns. "I'm so sorry."

I push up a smile. "Hey, none of that. Don't feel bad for me. I'm fine. Totally."

"All right," she says, then glances up at the wall in front of my station. "Oh. This one wasn't here last time. What's it called?"

The piece in question has a layered gray background with a black door in the center, barely cracked. Two abstract yellow figures are in the room—one on her knees, the other standing with his head thrown back. "I haven't titled it," I say, tearing my gaze away from the canvas. "How do you want to pay?"

She tugs out her American Express. Her tattoo comes to two grand, which includes my time today, the sketches I worked on (which she gets to keep), and the meeting at the coffee shop. Donny keeps 30 percent, and I get 70, a sweet deal I worked out with him once my business blew up and people poured in to see me. At least Edward only gets 20 percent.

She gives me a 50 percent tip, way too much, then signs the receipt. She hugs me, then surprises me when she kisses me on each cheek. Before she flounces out the door, she tells me to keep my chin up and promises to text me for coffee.

With heavy feet, I head upstairs to Donny's office. He's been avoiding my eyes since the closet incident. And the pacing around my station today? Dread curls.

With each step up the stairs, unease rises higher, exactly like the time Mrs. White picked me up from school, took me to get ice cream, and then drove me back to CPS because she was pregnant with twins and didn't need a little kid around anymore. She wasn't the first to decide I wasn't a good fit. Back and forth across the state of New York, I lived in eleven different foster homes before I finally ended up at a group home permanently.

I knock and wait for him to tell me to enter before I open the door. Wearing an old Joshua Tree shirt, he sits behind a big mahogany desk. Around sixty with shoulder-length gray hair, he's a hippie who opened his first location in Boston, gained a reputation for hiring talented artists, blew up on Insta, and then quickly opened two more shops—this one and another in Philadelphia.

"Whiskey?" He nudges his head at the decanter. He's already got one poured for himself.

"Do I need one?" Instead of sitting, I lean against the wall. "I can't remember the last time you called me up here. What's going on?"

He rubs his face and groans out a long breath. "Francesca, shit, there's no good way to say this, but I need to let you go."

My stomach drops. "What? Why?"

"Harlee feels uneasy with you in the shop. The entire situation is uncomfortable for her."

I shake my head, an exhalation of disbelief coming from my lips. "She's uncomfortable? Oh my God, that's ridiculous. She humiliated me; she has Edward. What else does she want?"

"Francesca—"

"Donny. No. Don't do this. I've never said a word to her about what happened. I've been on my best behavior. Professional. This isn't right. It's unfair." I try to hold his gaze, but he refuses to look at me, instead staring at a spot behind my shoulder.

"Regardless, the aura in the shop is tense. The vibe is getting to her—and me. Also, there's the painting above your station. We all know what it is."

My hands clench. The painting was the only voice I had to express my anger. Not for one minute do I think she really cares about the art; no, she probably loves looking at it. This is her wanting me out of the picture because she wants to make sure Edward and I stay apart. I recall her smile earlier, and my anger ratchets up. She's noticed the long glances Edward gives me. She's noticed the way he lingers at my station. Maybe she knows about the texts he sends me, the ones I never reply to.

"I didn't do anything wrong, Donny—you get that, right? Why not Edward? You can't let me go! I'm booked up for months!"

"Harlee wants him, and she's the manager. She's my heir and will run the shops when I retire. I don't have kids or a wife, Francesca. My sister and Harlee are my *family*, and I do what's best for them. Come on; you have to admit this place is toxic for you. You need a new parlor. I'll write a glowing letter of recommendation for you."

I deflate like a popped balloon, fear overtaking the anger. "Donny, please . . ." My voice hitches as I read the firmness on his face.

He clears his throat, then pushes out his words hurriedly. "You're one of the best artists I've had, and I'm truly sorry, really. You're a good human, the clients love you, and I'll miss you. You helped build the reputation of East Coast Ink, and I'm grateful." He takes a breath. "However. Today is your last day. Leave me your key to the shop, send an email to your clients, clean out your station, and take your canvases from the front gallery."

The knife in my heart cuts deeper. They don't even want my art.

It's as if I'm being erased.

Tears prick behind my eyes. "I—I'll need to . . ." My voice trails off, my brain blanking as I think on how to get the majority of my supplies and art back to my apartment.

"No rush on the art." He tries to smile. "I'll have an opening at the Philly parlor in March. If you want the spot, it's yours."

It's currently mid-November. "That's months from now and four hours away. Besides, eventually Harlee will be in charge."

He grimaces. "Right. Well, I'm here for a while. Think on it if you can't find anything else."

Donny's words play back in my head as I leave and take the stairs. *This place isn't my parlor anymore* keeps echoing in my head. It feels surreal, and my chest aches. I've worked here for eight years, and to be let go because my fiancé cheated with the manager—it's almost too much to bear. Normally, I'm a dreamer, an optimist. Even when I struggled through Edward's betrayal, I kept my head up, but this . . .

I clench the handrail when a dizzy spell hits.

I plop down on one of the steps and bend over to clear the black dots dancing in my eyes. Jesus. Have I eaten anything today? I'm running on coffee and cough drops. I pull out a protein bar from my smock, gagging for a second at the smell before shoving it in my mouth. My stomach clenches at the food before eventually settling down. It hasn't been right for a few days. I'm fine. Totally. I rub my forehead with icy hands as I focus on what's next. First, I need to shake this cold, maybe take a few days to sleep off this exhaustion, and then plan for another job.

I find a box in the back and fill it with essentials from my station. I'm walking a couple of blocks to my apartment, and I can't carry everything. When I close the door to East Coast Ink & Gallery, I force myself to not let pity inch inside.

Girls like me don't have time to wallow.

We've been rejected before, and when it happens, we make plans. We move on. We survive.

I look down at the box and see the framed photo of me and Cece and Brogan at a party in Chelsea years ago.

Donny has his family.

And they are mine.

Be tough. Be strong. Take one step, then two—then you're up and back on the journey. That's the motto I live by.

I'll be *fine*.

So why is there a deep churning pit of anxiousness in my gut?

Chapter 5

FRANCESCA

Fatigue ripples over me as I press my back against the wall inside Café Lazzo, my favorite restaurant near my apartment. It's been two weeks since I lost my job. My cold has worsened, and my throat is hoarse. Thanksgiving came and went, a busy time, and I'm hoping that's why I haven't gotten any callbacks from the parlors I checked in with.

I tug my black toboggan down over my forehead, covering my messy bun. I'm sloppy with my glasses, ripped jeans, and faded peacoat. Shivering, I tighten the scarf around my neck. I just want to get my pasta, go home, and starfish on my bed.

"Order up for Francesca!" comes from the server at the takeout stand.

"Here!" I rasp out as I work my way through the throng of people waiting for their own takeout. Sadly, this restaurant doesn't deliver, and their butternut squash soup and crab ravioli have been circling in my head for days. My mouth waters, and I'm almost to the counter—

A man steps in front of me, cutting me off. "Kendra, sweetheart, how are you?"

Kendra, the server who called my name, blushes at the man, then titters that it's good to see him and that yes, she watched his game and is "so devastated" about the loss—and don't worry; her poodle is feeling better after his surgery.

I wave at her. *Look! Me, me!*

He blocks her from my line of vision and leans in over the counter. I take in his clean-shaven, chiseled profile as he lowers his voice. "I'm glad your dog is good. Hey, my friends and I ordered twenty minutes ago. Could you check on it for me? You're looking gorgeous today, by the way."

"I'll check your status." She bats her lashes, then darts to the take-out window.

I tap my three-inch stacked Converse, waiting for him to notice the angry girl next to him, but he's too busy watching the swing in Kendra's hips.

I scan the Pythons sweatshirt he's wearing, and it dawns on me. Of course! It's *him*.

Jesus. Is he everywhere?

Tuck Avery. Professional footballer. Lives in the penthouse of my building. Tawny hair, angular face, big muscles. Arrogant.

I ease the aluminum container of napkins from the bakery case closer to me, then knock it to the floor. A grunt comes from him when it bounces and lands on his foot.

I blink. "Oops."

He bends to pick up the container, then frowns as he rakes his eyes over me. "Did you throw this at me?"

Apparently, I'm not quite a ninja.

Someone behind me, a male, murmurs an affirmative: "Yeah, she did."

My adrenaline spikes, and sweat builds on my face. Part of me wants to play it off as an accident, but . . .

"Um . . . yes?"

"What's wrong with you?" he snaps as he places it back on the bakery case.

My heart thumps like a war drum in my chest as I push out my words in a gravelly voice. "She called my name; then you cut me off before I reached the counter."

Have I mentioned I've passed him in the lobby of our building? He never speaks, just keeps his head down and stalks away. He doesn't want to mingle with the peons who live below him.

"Welcome to New York. Get used to fighting for a spot," he mutters.

"Right, right. I've lived here for years. Not everyone is rude. You think you can do whatever you want because of who you are. Princess." I grunt.

The takeout area goes dead quiet. I hadn't realized we'd drawn attention, and I lick my lips as I look around.

"I could have you arrested," he says. "That"—he points at the napkin dispenser—"was assault."

"Fight, fight, fight! Kick his ass!" a guy calls from behind me.

Tuck sends him a death glare, then leans into my personal space. His scent wafts around me, spice with a hint of peppermint. Like a sexy Christmas. It's a cologne I recognize, something yummy and expensive, but I can't focus as my stomach flip-flops with nausea. It's not my usual "I'm anxious" queasy. It's a new one, and it's decided his cologne is disgusting.

"Phones are recording this," he hisses. "Do you want to be known on Twitter as the girl who attacked me?"

"Are you hurt?"

"I asked *you* a question."

"You aren't hurt."

"Are you a doctor?"

Fuzziness dances in my head as I clench the edge of the counter to stop myself from swaying. A bone-deep exhaustion washes over me. Swallowing, I glance at the server. "Kendra, you said Francesca. I'll take my order now."

She darts her gaze from me to him.

"Kendra?" I ask, my voice rising sharply. "Now."

She fumbles around, then hands over my order.

"Thank you." I leave and make my way through the crowd.

I push open the door and step out to a drizzle on Fifth Avenue. I lean against the brick wall, letting rain fall on my face as I take deep breaths. What is wrong with me? I've never acted so childish—

"I can't believe you" comes a male voice.

Holy cow . . .

He's followed me!

I turn, and there he stands, arms crossed. A streetlamp creates a golden halo around him, and I blink. He really is beautiful. Tall. Chin-length wavy hair. Diamond-cut cheekbones. Perfect full, bitable lips.

As if angels carved him themselves.

Too bad he's a devil.

I hold up my takeout bag. "I have pepper spray."

He points at the passing pedestrians. "I'm not going to hurt you with people around."

"Would you if we were alone?"

"I don't hurt women," he says, lids lowering. "But you do test me."

"Same page," I mutter.

He tucks his hands in black joggers as he shifts from one foot to the next. "I would have been gone in a couple of minutes, you know. Patience is a virtue."

"Should I let Bradley Cooper be rude to me just because he's hot and a superstar? No."

"I'm hot?"

"No," I sputter, then rub my face with my free hand.

"Are you all right? Inside you seemed—"

"I'm *fine.*"

He cocks his head, his expression softening. "You sound terrible."

"I have a cold, so you better stay back."

His gaze goes behind me. "Watch out; you're about to get mowed down by a pack of tourists. They never look where they're going." He takes my arm with a gentleness I didn't expect and eases me out of their trajectory into the mouth of the alley outside the restaurant.

"Oh. Thanks."

We watch them pass by us as the rainfall increases, and I groan as wetness creeps into my shoes.

"Hang on a second." Moving around, he unzips the duffle on his shoulder and pulls out a white umbrella with the Pythons mascot, a coiled black-and-gold snake with its mouth open to strike. "I'm always prepared. My ankle can feel the change in pressure. I fractured it a while back, and it always knows." He pops the umbrella and waves me under it.

My leftover anger deflates like a flat tire as I step beneath the cover.

"Did the napkin thing hurt your ankle?" I mumble.

"Nah. I was messing with you." Our shoulders brush as he turns to face me, and I tense at our proximity, a tingle of something strange dancing down my spine.

Our gazes cling for several heartbeats. There's something about him I can't look away from . . .

"I'm glad you're okay," I admit grudgingly, focusing on his sneakers as I try to suss out why there's a sense of familiarity about him. It's more than just seeing him around Manhattan. I shake my head to clear the fog from it.

"Regrets, huh?" he says.

"I'm not normally a violent person." But my moods have been off the charts lately. I snot cried during a toilet paper commercial yesterday. It had puppies frolicking around in toilet paper; I don't even like dogs.

"I must have really gotten under your skin," he murmurs. "Let's start over, yeah? I'm Tuck. And you are . . ."

I catch my reflection in the puddles, knowing what he sees: a short nondescript girl, my hair tucked up in a hat, old glasses with raindrops on them, and no lipstick.

"Francesca. I told Kendra, like, five minutes ago."

"Missed it. I was distracted by your fiery attitude, but now you won't even look at me."

I move my gaze up, and he's grinning. "Hi there," he says softly.

"Hi."

"Was that so hard?"

"No." I shrug, then say, "I hope no one got us on camera. I don't want to be on Twitter as harming New York's favorite wide receiver."

"Meh. Maybe they did; maybe they didn't. But we've patched things up. Beautiful name, by the way. Are you Italian, Francesca?" He says my name slow, tasting the syllables.

"Maybe," I say, then sigh. "Look. I'm sorry. Really. I thought it would drop on the floor and get Kendra's attention. That's all."

"Truth? I spotted you making a beeline to her, and I was in a hurry. So . . ." He grimaces. "I cut you off on purpose. Now you know."

"Rude jerk."

"Don't hold back."

"I won't."

"I'm friendly with Kendra and knew if I beat you, I might get my food quicker. I'm used to getting what I want when I want it. So you're right. I'm an egotistical asshole."

"I never said egotistical asshole." I smile. It's hard not to. Maybe it's the way his eyes crinkle in the corners when he smiles. Or the line of dimples.

He chuckles, and the sound of it reminds me of—

My thought is lost as the door to Café Lazzo opens and a man ambles out. Wearing a Pythons sweatshirt and joggers, he's tall with frizzy blond hair that falls around his shoulders. "Yo. Kendra said our food will be ready in five. You all right out here?"

"Yeah, we're cool. My attacker adores me," Tuck calls out to his friend.

"I'm adding *narcissist* to your list," I murmur.

"That just hurts, Francesca," he says on a laugh as he glances down at me.

"You should make a list of my flaws."

He searches my face. "Hmm, I'd start with . . . striking."

Oh.

"Nice throw in there. I'm Jasper," says the friend as he walks to us.

"Francesca. I didn't throw it. I eased it to the floor. Were you the guy saying 'Fight, fight, fight'?"

"Guilty." He winks. "I saw the whole thing."

"He lives for drama," Tuck says dryly as he shuts the umbrella as the rain eases up. "So where are you headed, Francesca?"

"Um, actually, I live at Wickham. I've seen you around. In the lobby . . ." I stop at the wary expression growing on his face.

"What a coincidence."

I shrug. "Most of the tenants know you live in the penthouse. You're famous. And the doorman is lovable but a bit of a gossip."

"Really. What's the doorman's name."

What the . . . "You don't believe me?"

"What's his name?"

"Herman," I say, frowning. "He's worked at Wickham for over twenty years. He's married to Catherine, and they have five grandchildren. I live on the twentieth floor with a view of Central Park. Happy now?"

"This little kitten just hissed at you, bro," Jasper says with a smirk as he holds up a fist for me to bump. I ignore him.

A woman breezes out of the restaurant, getting our attention. Even the people on the street do a double take. Tall and willowy with honey-colored hair, she struts to us wearing a baby-blue sweater dress and thigh-high heeled boots. In her midtwenties, she checks me out with arched brows as she sweeps over my attire. She sniffs, her nose wrinkling as if I'm a dead fish. She hands over the bags of food to Jasper, and he takes them with an eye roll.

She places her hand on Tuck's arm possessively and tilts her face up. "You left me alone to get the food, darling," she says.

"I assumed you could handle it, Courtney," he says. "It's already paid for."

Her hands brush at his hair, arranging the strands around his face as if she's done it a million times. "Of course." She glances at me, then back to him. "I just worry about you chasing after a random stranger. You never know what they're after. The city is full of crazy people."

She thinks I'm, what, going to mug him? Rub my stink on him? I'm barely functioning here.

She leans into him. "This girl, who is she? She threw something at you and verbally abused you. She could have *hurt* you—or me. Remember Lollipop? Stalkers can be anyone and anywhere."

I let out a huff. "I'm not a stalker. Hello, I left the restaurant. He followed *me*."

"Courtney—" Tuck starts, but I cut him off as I step back from the couple.

"Trust me," I say with an unladylike grunt. "Your boyfriend is safe from me."

Tuck scowls at me, takes her elbow, and leads her several feet away from us and back toward the restaurant. They lean their heads together, whispering.

"Forget her," Jasper says as he sidles up next to me.

"Who is she?"

"His ex. They've been on and off, and she's trying to hook him again."

"No, I mean where have I seen her?"

He grunts. "She's the Calvin Klein girl."

"Oh." That's it. I've seen her on billboards.

He pauses, peering at me. "Have we met before? It might be Wickham, but I've only lived there a few months."

I shake my head. "You like tattoos? I used to work at East Coast Ink."

He replies that he's never been as I glance over at Tuck and Courtney. She's thrown her arms around his neck, and they're kissing. My gaze is drawn to him, the golden color of his hair, the breadth of his shoulders . . .

He puts a hand on her shoulder, making the arm of his sweatshirt move. A black leather cuff with gold stitching on his wrist catches my eye.

I frown. It reminds me of—

My body stiffens.

Player has a black leather cuff . . .

Nah, nah. No freaking way.

Player had longer hair and heavy scruff!

Player is a construction worker in my head. He works with his hands.

Not Tuck.

Still . . .

That zap of awareness under the umbrella.

His laugh.

His "Sweetheart."

And the cuff. What are the odds that two tall men with the same hair color have the same one?

I look back at Jasper, and my eyes bulge. Blond guy who named his penis Cupid!

Oh my God. I groan. No, no, no.

Player lives in the same building as me!

There are millions of people in this city, and yes, I've looked for him, but never once did I think I'd *find* him! It was a fantasy, something I used to get me through breaking up with Edward.

"What?" Jasper asks. "Your face is red. You okay?"

I manage a "Fine" as my head replays the highlights of our night like a hazy movie reel.

The first time we had sex, it was slow and sweet; the second round followed, rushed and intense as he picked me up in his arms and pressed me against the wall; the third time, his body caged over mine as he took me from behind; the last round, we lay face to face, my leg over his thigh, his hands worshipping every inch of my skin as if dedicating it to his memory. He called me his little brave princess. He said my eyes were unforgettable, that he'd know me by the scent of my skin. By then I could barely recall my own name. All I knew was how it felt to have him inside me, the smell of us together, the sounds we made.

Having sex with a stranger wasn't unusual for me.

In fact, one-night stands were my preference until Edward came along.

I went to Decadence to find someone to make me forget his betrayal.

And Player did. Very, very well.

Even now, my body melts at the way he twisted his hips inside me, at his fingers on my clit, at his devilish stamina—

Dammit. This is so confusing. I was into Player, and Tuck *is* Player.

Tuck is an ass who has a sorta famous girlfriend.

Huh. Maybe that explains the end of the night.

After the last round, he withdrew, a cloud of tension hovering over him. While I stayed in bed, silent and watchful, he dressed as if the hounds of hell were on his heels. He raked his hands through his hair over and over as he stood in front of the door for several seconds, then left without a word.

It hurt. Maybe it shouldn't have. I've slipped away from lovers before, but it felt like another rejection.

"Sorry?" I come back and realize Jasper had been talking.

He grimaces. "You're ignoring me. I asked if you came to this restaurant a lot. Maybe that's why you seem familiar—"

I nod jerkily. "That's it. Totally."

"Wanna walk back together? It'll be nice to have the company, and she gets on my nerves." He glances over at Tuck and Courtney. They've stopped kissing and are talking.

As if he senses my gaze, Tuck turns his head, and his eyes hold mine. His gaze dips to my lips, and my heart jumps in my throat as the electricity sizzles and pops. At least it does for me.

Tuck takes a step in my direction, making me start from my daydreaming.

"Francesca? Hello?" Jasper asks.

"I've got some errands—sorry. Enjoy your dinner; bye," I rush out the words as I turn and take off down the sidewalk in a fast walk.

I get a block away from my apartment when the smell of the crab ravioli assails my senses and makes me gag. I clutch my stomach, make it to an alley, and hurl. My arm brushes my boobs when I wipe my mouth, and I flinch at the flash of pain.

Frustration hits. Ugh. Do I have some awful disease? I've been avoiding a doctor, thinking this cold would resolve on its own, and I need to keep my expenses down until I get a job, but . . .

Fatigue, moodiness, nausea, sore breasts . . .

The flu doesn't last this long, right?

I gasp.

I have an implant for birth control, plus I always use condoms, but I haven't had a period since . . .

No way.

I toss my takeout in the trash and jog all the way to the canopy of my building. My nerves are stretched thin as I picture Tuck and company catching up with me. I'm almost to the door when nausea hits again, and I bend over and hurl into the landscaping. Herman calls out a "Hello," and I toss up a hand and dash for the entrance. I make it to the elevator, step inside, and bang the button for my floor. I've seen Tuck in this elevator once, but I suspect he uses the express one in the garage most of the time. It goes straight up to his place without stopping. Tonight, though, he'll probably come in through the lobby. I stab the button for my floor again.

Mr. Darden, also called "Darden" when I'm not speaking to him directly, steps in with me. Well dressed with gray hair and glasses, he leans on a gold-tipped cane. Cece says its real gold.

I shouldn't be able to afford Wickham, but one of the counselors at the group home said that the owners gave rent breaks to kids who lived in foster care. I filled out the application, wrote an essay, and got in at a discount. It's a tax break for the owners of the building. Darden was born and raised here and was part of the board of directors that made the final decisions on who got in.

Closing my eyes at the motion of the elevator, I lean back against the cold metal and take deep breaths as I force myself not to gag at the metallic scent in the small space. I once read that pregnant women have supersmell. I chew on my lip. No way. Impossible. I am not preggo.

"No hello, Miss Lane?"

I pop one eye open and push up a smile. "Hey, Mr. Darden. Sorry. Good to see you. How are you?"

He grunts. "Forget that. You look homeless in those clothes. No wonder you can't find a job. Kids these days. No work ethic."

I stick my tongue out at him. "It's only been two weeks. I need more time."

"You're a tattoo person." He says it like I'm a serial killer. "Such a waste of a great mind. You should be selling your art. Open your own gallery."

Ah, that's the dream, but it requires money.

"I do sell my art. Don't you own one?" I tap my chin. "Yep, that's right. You requested a honey badger—very odd, and not my usual. I believe it hangs in your guest bathroom. Probably to frighten people away."

"It was a pity purchase." He points his cane at me menacingly. "I'm glad you're out of that parlor. You're too talented for those heathens."

"Don't be such a snob," I say; then another bout of nausea rises as the elevator lurches. I groan, and his scowl deepens.

"What is the matter with you? Are you sick?"

"Nothing. I'm *fine*." If I keep saying it, then it's true. Obviously.

He harrumphs. "I know what *fine* means, Miss Lane. I was married, and it never meant anything good. We've been neighbors for twelve years, and you never say you're *fine*." He grumbles under his breath, and I catch a "Damn that Edward" and "What a bastard."

A ghost of a smile crosses my face. He comes across as grouchy, but he's much more than that.

The elevator stops at our floor, and we step out. My nausea seems to settle as I walk with him to his apartment, trying not to hover when he wobbles a little. My place is next door, although his is three times as big.

"How's the hip doing?" He had replacement surgery several weeks ago.

He grunts as he unlocks his door. "I'm old and wake up every day with a new ailment. *I'm fine.*"

A small laugh comes from me. "Do you need anything? I can bring over some popcorn, and we can watch the nature channel. Your favorite."

"Not tonight."

I search his craggy face, looking for signs of tiredness, but he waves me off and steps inside his apartment. "What are you going to do about a job, Miss Lane?"

Ignoring his question, I smile. "Let's have game night soon. How about Monopoly?"

"Don't distract me, Miss Lane."

"I've said it before, and I'll say it again . . . you're not my mother, Mr. Darden. Good night."

He exhales as he scrutinizes me. "See a doctor. I don't want to catch anything when you come over." With a sharp nod, he closes his door.

I open my door and step inside my small yet elegant three-bedroom apartment. Built in the twenties, most of the original architecture was maintained: arched doorways, thick baseboards, wainscotting, and a stone fireplace—now painted a rich cream. My wing of the building was renovated years ago with beautiful hardwood, marble tile, and an updated kitchen and bathrooms.

I stop in the foyer, kiss my fingers, and press them to my first painting from art school, a brown wren in the snow. I point my finger at her. "I see your judgment, but I'm not pregnant."

I drop my satchel on a bench and go to the den. It's decorated with a modern-style velvet teal couch and two club chairs. Cece made the pillows, and there's a hand-knotted rug that Brogan found. My art, one of my locket paintings, hangs over the mantel. My bedroom is to the left, and their rooms are on the right down the hall.

Home. My first real one.

Across from the den is a balcony that overlooks Central Park, and I open the glass doors and step outside and lean over to see the street. The rain has cleared, and a full moon gazes down at Manhattan. I inhale a deep breath of the city and smile.

I hear laughter, and my heart jumps as Tuck, Jasper, and Courtney walk up the sidewalk. Jasper picks up pebbles and lobs them at Courtney while she yells at him. Tuck walks behind them as he swings his umbrella, lost in thought. Leaning over farther, I recall how he moved me out of the way of the tourists, then shared his umbrella with me . . .

I picture him kissing Courtney and grunt. Player indeed.

As if he feels my gaze, he stops and glances up at the building toward my floor, and I quickly step back.

"Not kicking that hornet's nest," I tell the room as I head to the kitchen and open the pantry. I find a box of Triscuits and munch one slowly, my head churning as I replay my symptoms of sickness one more time.

A long sigh comes from my chest. *I'm fine. Totally.*

Chapter 6

FRANCESCA

It's not every day your friend gazes at a pile of pregnancy-test boxes like they're a stack of Christmas presents.

Cece taps one with a manicured fingernail. Her voice, like her, is airy and sweet. "This one has rapid detection. How preggo are you, honey?"

"*If* I am, I guess ten weeks, and don't 'honey' me. You only do that when you're trying to calm me down. I. Am. Fine."

"You sent the 911 text. You're freaked." She pats my arm. "It's okay. We're here, and we never leave a man down."

I wince at her glamorous makeup, upswept blonde hair, and shimmery evening dress. "I ruined your dinner party. Sorry."

She tsks. "Don't worry about George. His ex-wife saw us together, which is what he wanted. She left him two years ago for her fitness trainer—so cliché. He's one of my favorite clients." She pokes me. "My offer is still open. I can hook you up with a job. Men love petite women. Makes them feel like all alpha."

I met Cece our freshman year in art school. A gorgeous girl from the Gulf Coast of Alabama, she was working part time at the makeup counter at Barneys when a lady pulled her aside and asked if she'd be interested in dating wealthy men. She dropped out of college, makes six figures, and flies between here and LA. Before I landed at East Coast Ink, she got me in at the agency. I went on a few dates; then Donny gave me a callback, and that was it.

"Clients like pregnant women, huh?" Standing up, I mimic a belly over my stomach and puff out my cheeks. I waddle around the room.

"But you say it's just a bug."

I flop back on the couch and throw my head back as I groan. "It totally is. Right? Say you think it is. Please."

She sighs. "Your boobies are sore. That's the first indication—or so I've heard." A gleam grows in her eyes. "Would it be the worst thing in the world? You'd be a good—no, a *great* mom, and I'd be the perfect 'aunt.' Oops, wrong thing to say. Calm down, honey. Don't get all red in the face; it's not good for our 'maybe baby'—"

"Brogan?" I call out. "Cece's annoying me. Are those drinks ready?"

He comes in from the kitchen and leans against the doorjamb and chuckles. With wavy auburn hair, he's tall and muscular with a sleeve of pink and teal roses up his arm. They match the tattoo on my back and the circlet tattoo around Cece's ankle.

He's five years younger than us with cut cheekbones and a square chin that hints at stubbornness. We met Brogan at a party where he attempted to charm us with his British accent—but we knew it was fake. We started a game to pay him five bucks for every person he convinced he was British. By the end of the night, he'd emptied our wallets; then he took us to breakfast.

He gives a martini to Cece, grabs his own off the bar, and then hands me a glass of water. My second. "Drink this, and try to pee again."

"My bladder has drawn up. In fear. I may never pee again. Can you die from that?"

"Doubtful. Worst-case scenario, your bladder will back up to your kidneys and cause them to fail. Could be fatal." He flashes a smile that transforms his handsome face into breathtaking. "That advice comes to you from a man who dropped out of med school. Take it or leave it."

He plops down on the other side of me and throws an arm around me. "I'm feeling bad. I'm the one who got you the guest pass to Decadence."

I lean into him, and he smells like citrus, the one scent that hasn't made me gag today. "But you weren't the one who told me to lock genitals with Tuck Avery."

"Nice image," he says dryly. "Oh, get this—Prince Rolex had his membership revoked at Decadence. Tuck came back a week after you were there and demanded a meeting with the owners and got it. I didn't mention it earlier because of the NDA I signed at work, but now that you know who he is . . ."

"Would he have been kicked out anyway?" I ask.

"Probably not. He's a Wall Street shark and wealthy as shit. Tuck's the one who got him removed permanently."

"Well, well, well, Tuck's good baby-daddy material already," Cece quips, accentuating her southern drawl. She ignores my evil eye and stirs the olive in her martini with elegant swishes. "I'm surprised it took you this long to notice something was up."

"I lost my fiancé and job. And I'm not pregnant. Really. I just know it."

She leans in. "I have this friend—more of a friend of a friend, really. Poor girl didn't know she was pregnant until she started having contractions. Had her baby in an Uber on the Brooklyn Bridge."

"Hope she left a good tip," Brogan says.

"Can you imagine the surprise? She's on her way to a party; then boom, there's a baby coming out of her vagina," Cece adds.

I laugh nervously as we lift our glasses, and we clink them together. "What a wonderful story. Now, moving on; here's to me having a stomach bug—something I thought I'd never say." I finish my water, grab the tests, and take off for my master bath.

They jump up and follow, breathing down my neck.

"I adore baby blankets. Oh, and the cute little onesies," Cece says, then squeals. "Better yet, I could *make* baby clothes, maybe do era themes—polyester shirts from the seventies, acid-washed jeans for the eighties, or those neon colors from the nineties? I could open an Etsy shop! An online store! I'd be the queen of baby clothes! Too much? Hmm, yeah, you're getting red again, and you're right; yeah, no one, and I mean no one, should ever wear neon." She pouts at my glare. "I can't have kids, remember? Big old hysterectomy at twenty. Damn that endometriosis."

"I can't have a baby for you."

She splays her arms out, blocking me from the bathroom door. "Francesca. You're only born with a certain number of eggs, and thousands die each month. Who knows how many you have left? You aren't Fertile Myrtle. This might be your last egg."

"I have plenty of eggs! And I'm not"—I wave my hands around my abdomen—"some kind of chicken."

"Different eggs," she says.

"I know! I was being funny—or trying to." I scrub my face.

Brogan whistles. "It's never good when Fran isn't funny."

"Fran is right here," I mutter. "And I finally need to pee, so move, and let me get to the bathroom."

"You're not twenty anymore," she says. "You've got lines in the corners of your eyes, a few gray hairs—"

"I do not!"

"And, as my dear dead mama used to say, you're no spring chicken—oh look; we're back to chickens." She laughs.

Brogan waves his hands like a marquee. "Picture this: two girls, a guy, and a baby."

Then he plays "Sweet Child O' Mine" on his phone.

"You too?" I ask on a groan.

"I'd be an awesome uncle."

"Guys!" I call. "I'm unemployed with no health insurance; plus there's no father—well, there is, but . . ."

"Consider him a sperm donor. Prime, top-of-the-line swimmers," Brogan says as he toasts me with his martini. "You may have hit the jackpot. Buckets of money."

"No jackpot! No buckets! No swimmers! I am not pregnant!"

"Be the change you want to see in the world," Cece says with the smile of an angel.

"Stop quoting Gandhi all the time. It doesn't apply here!" I push past her and shut the door in their faces.

With shaking hands, I pull up my cropped shirt and rub my hand over my concave stomach. At least that's good—I mean not good that I seem to be losing weight like crazy but good that there's no baby bump. When do baby bumps show up? I have no clue.

I unwrap the first test, read the directions, pee on one stick, and then do two more.

Edward and I talked about kids—well, he did. When his mother brought up grandkids, I just nodded and smiled.

I sit on the closed toilet and rub my forehead.

My own story begins by being left on the steps of a police station in the snow in a small town in Upstate New York. All I had with me was a car seat, a blanket, and a locket engraved on the back with "Francesca."

I picture a woman leaving me.

Did she cry?

Why did she never come back?

Does she ever wonder about me?

The police ran a story about me on TV. They put my story on a billboard. They searched records for babies born as Francesca; they searched for birthing mothers named Francesca—and got nothing that matched.

My parents abandoned me.

With that kind of baggage, am I even mother material?

I shove it aside and stand.

I've barely gotten my joggers up when they spill through the door.

"I'm surprised you didn't insist on watching me pee."

"Didn't want to interrupt the flow," Cece calls as she races to the sink, where I put the tests.

Brogan snatches one first. "Nothing yet—"

"Gross! That has pee on it," I call out.

"I work at Decadence. Pretty sure I've touched pee before." He stares down at the stick as if it's the Holy Grail.

Ignoring them, I grumble as I get to the mirror, brush my hair, and sweep it into a high ponytail. My cheekbones are stark, the hollows beneath clearly defined on my pale face. I take off my glasses and stare into my eyes as a cold sweat breaks out over my skin. Fear curls over me, and I dash out of the bathroom and go back to the den so I can't hear them talking. I flip on the TV, loud, then pop another Triscuit in my mouth. "See. No nausea," I say to myself. "No baby bump. *Not* pregnant."

My phone pings, and I pull it out of my bag. More texts from Edward. My hands curl.

See me.

Talk to me.

Francesca.

Come on.

I'm begging.

Sorry.

Sorry.

Sorry.

The bell from the downstairs front desk rings, and I push the button on the wall. "Yeah?"

Herman's slightly nasally voice comes through the intercom. "Francesca, hi. Edward showed up. You told me to send him away, so I did."

"Thanks for letting me know."

"No problem."

Lost in thought, I don't hear my door opening over the sound of the TV; I don't hear someone walking down the hall, then entering the den. A hand touches my shoulder.

Flinching, I turn as I gasp. "Jesus! Edward! What are you doing here?" I put a hand to my heart. "I hate people sneaking up on me!"

"Sorry." His whiskey-colored eyes hold mine. "I didn't mean to scare you. Your door was cracked, and you were talking to Herman—"

"Is that him?" Herman yells. I still have my finger on the button.

"Yes," I say tersely. "In the flesh."

"I'm so sorry, Francesca. He must have walked in with some residents. Want me to send security up?"

I glance at Edward, taking in the dark circles under his eyes, the way his jeans hang on him. Good.

I sigh. I don't want any drama on my floor. Several of the residents are older.

"Do you plan on murdering me, Edward?"

He shakes his head, then calls out, "I'd never hurt her, Herman. Sorry I gave you the slip."

Oh, but he *did* hurt me, and my face must say that because he drops his gaze.

I exhale. Part of me has wanted to see him again.

Is it because I still care, or is he a habit? I haven't seen him in two weeks, and I wait for the usual bite of pain mixed with longing to hit, and it does, but it's muted, focused on what's happening in my bathroom.

"I'm fine, Herman. Brogan and Cece are with me."

"Good. One more thing," Herman says. "Tuck Avery came by earlier and asked if a Francesca lived here. I said yes but didn't give him your last name or apartment number, but, um . . ."

"Yeah?" I ask.

"He wanted me to describe you, and I'm not good with things like that. I said you were sweet and pretty. Is there an issue with you and Mr. Avery?"

"He didn't believe I lived here. I've been here for years!"

"Well, we do have over three hundred residents." He chuckles, then says, "You sure you're okay with Edward?"

I tell him yes, turn off the intercom, and then lean against the wall as I stare at Edward.

"Hey." He runs a hand through his thick mink hair, tugging on the ends. My heart twinges. It's what he does when he's anxious, and there's a stupid part of me that wants to soothe him.

The same age as me, he's the only man I've ever loved besides my first love. But I don't want to think about Levi now. Not with Edward here. Those memories still hurt too.

"What do you want?" I ask, my throat prickling with emotion.

He lifts his hands. "I don't know, really. I walk past here at least once a week. I can see your apartment from the street, your balcony . . ." He trails off, his teeth toying with his lip ring.

"You won't see me walking past yours."

He sighs. "I know. I—I'm sorry you lost your job. I didn't know. I came in the next day, and your station was empty. Harlee—"

"Don't go there. Don't. I have the job thing under control." Not true, but fuck him.

"Good. I mean, it should have been me that was fired. I have my trust fund to keep me going, and you don't—"

"What else do you need? I'm kinda busy." I dart my eyes to the hall-way that leads to my bedroom, wondering what's keeping my friends. Over the noise of the TV, they probably can't hear me and Edward.

"Remember how we met?"

I shrug. I met him when I was twenty-seven at a bar in Hell's Kitchen where he was singing (badly) in a band and waiting tables. We had mediocre sex in the bathroom, and I forgot about him.

He eases closer to me. "After we hooked up, you wouldn't give me your phone number, so I showed up at East Coast Ink."

"You were determined—points for that. I shouldn't have told you where I worked. It would have saved me years of wasted time."

"I came to see you for a week straight and tried to talk to you—"

"Right, right. We all know this story, Edward. I ignored you until you drew cutesy sketches of us together on dates, one of us at the mov-ies, one of us kissing, blah, blah, blah. I got soft and gave you a shot. We dated, I got you a job, we got engaged, you fucked Harlee, and we ended. That sums it up. What else you got?"

Hurt flashes on his face. "I'm not sure you even wanted to get married—"

"Hold up. This is your excuse for cheating? I wasn't ready? I wore your ring! Leave." I push him toward the hallway to the foyer.

"Let me talk!"

I throw my hands up in the air. "Fine! Let it all out."

His words come in a rush. "After we got engaged, it took three weeks for you to put the ring on and tell people. You didn't like my mother, even though you let her pick out your dress, the cake, the flowers, the venue. She even did our registry—"

"Your mother wanted a society wedding. She paid for it."

"I know."

My anger ratchets up. "You broke my trust and my heart! I don't give it away freely, Edward!"

"I know."

"You can't use me as your scapegoat!"

"I know."

"Stop saying that! You should have told me this before. You were with her for . . . I don't even know how long. Coward." I practically spit the word.

He shuts his eyes, then opens them, wetness in the depths. "I—I wanted to be your everything, but I was terrified you'd hurt me. I was messing around with her, I don't know, to see if, God—I think I wanted you to catch us. I couldn't end us. Because I needed you too much."

Pain knifes me right in the chest.

He *wanted* to hurt me.

What the hell is wrong with him?

Did I even know him at all?

Why do I get fooled by these losers?

His fists clench at his side as he beats them against his leg. "I'm sorry, okay? Sorry, sorry, sorry. So damn sorry . . ."

"Stop, please," I snap.

Tentatively, he lifts his hand to touch my hand, and I pull away.

He rubs his eyes with his palms. "Have you ever wanted something even though you knew it was bad for you? It was like that for me, and I knew in my gut you were going to break me. Someday down the road, you'd wake up and realize that—what the hell?"

Madonna's opening chords to "Papa Don't Preach" blare from my bedroom. Cece sashays into the den slowly, a hairbrush in her hand as she sways her hips and sings the lyrics about a girl who tells her father she's pregnant and wants to keep the baby. In her other hand is one of the pregnancy sticks. She holds it high, dancing to the beat with her eyes closed, a triumphant smile on her face. Brogan pops into the den, gets behind her, and does Madonna's "Vogue" dance, then the Running Man.

My stomach pitches.

I make it to the couch and fall on my ass, gasping as I stare up at the ceiling, my whole world realigning.

I'd convinced myself I wasn't.

Impossible . . .

It can't be.

Stay calm. Breathe in; breathe out.

One step at a time. One step at a time . . .

Brogan rushes over and pulls me into his lap and rocks me as he murmurs in my ear that he's sorry they've been teasing me, that they'll support me no matter what I do, that they're my family forever and ever, that we made a vow to stick together, that he loves me, that she loves me.

"Cece. Stop," Brogan yells.

She opens her eyes and sees me and Brogan, then Edward. An angry squeal comes as she heads his way. "What the hell? No! You aren't allowed here!" She bares her teeth. "If you don't leave this instant, I'm going to stab you in the dick—with these." She holds up the hairbrush and the stick. "Hear me good, Edward. I put up with your whiny ass for years, but I am not a nice person. I will destroy you. I will grind this stick in your balls, then take a picture of you writhing on the floor. I'll add it to my burn book with happiness in my cold, cold, dead heart!"

He backs up. "What the hell . . ."

"Just go, Edward, before she murders you." I push myself to standing.

He turns to me. "Who's pregnant?"

I grab a tissue off the end table and wipe my face. I hadn't realized I was crying. Dammit. "Apparently me."

"Is it mine?"

I flinch at the eagerness in his voice.

Cece pokes the end of the brush into his chest. "No, Einstein! Does she look five months pregnant to you?"

A sharp knock bangs from my door, and we all jerk. What now?

"That's my Chinese delivery," Cece says with a grunt as she takes Edward by the arm and drags him down the hallway to the front door. "Time for you to skedaddle. Don't ever come here again. If I see you, I will break all your fingers—feel me? You'll never draw again."

They disappear into the foyer.

I hear the door opening, a long pause, and then rustling sounds. I picture Cece shoving him out the door. Then comes her sugary voice: "Well, bless, sorry you had to see me throw out the trash! Tuck Avery as I live and breathe, and I thought it was just noodles. What a surprise. Look how handsome you are! The perfect catnip." Five bucks says she has her hand over her heart.

"Um, thanks?" comes his husky voice.

Send him far, far away, I mentally channel.

"I'm Cece," she coos.

"Nice to meet you." There's a low rumble of a laugh, then: "Is Francesca here?"

I groan. Will this night ever end?

She calls back down the hall. "Someone to see you, honey! He's pretty. Can we keep him?"

"Behave, and give me a second," I yell as I dash to the bathroom, straighten my hair, throw cold water on my face, rub on cherry ChapStick, switch to mango and then watermelon, and then dart back to the den.

I can't see her, but Cece is still at the door, yammering about football and the weather.

I twist my hands, trying to rustle up my nerve to face him.

"Are you going to tell him?" Brogan asks.

"What? Why?" I give him a wide-eyed look as I grab the box of Triscuits off the coffee table and eat one furiously. "Plus, it could be a false positive."

"All three tests? Fran—"

I give him a pleading look. "For real. Think about it, Brogan. Would *you* want to know?"

He pauses, then sighs. "You mean if I wasn't into guys and got a random woman pregnant during a one-night stand at a sex club?" His lips purse. "Not really."

"And why is that?"

He frowns.

"Come on," I say. "Be truthful."

"I wouldn't want to know because I don't care about her. It was a one-time thing."

"Exactly."

"I'm also into guys, so this is like comparing apples to oranges—"

"Doesn't matter." I tuck in another cracker and head for the door.

Chapter 7

TUCK

Adrenaline hits as the door opens a few inches. "Francesca. There you are," I murmur to a sliver of her face.

"What do you want?" she asks tartly.

I dip my head and see one dainty foot, the toenails painted black. Of course she'd paint them black. She's no milk-and-honey girl; she's bold and brazen. Mysterious.

"To talk," I say. My smile is all sunshine and charming. Fake.

The crack opens more, and I see the elegant shape of a dark eyebrow, one high cheekbone, a wisp of midnight hair. "Did Herman tell you which apartment I lived in?"

"Nah, Darden lives on your floor, and he knows everyone. He speaks highly of you, by the way. I had to promise him I meant you no harm."

"That traitor." She pokes her head out and yells, "You can shut your door now, Mr. Darden."

I glance over, and his door is indeed partly open.

His rough voice replies, "I was just checking to be sure he found you. Also, I found a job for you since you can't seem to do it yourself.

I expect to see you at breakfast at nine a.m. to discuss. Bring a copy of the *Times* when you come over."

She rolls her eyes. "Fine."

"And tell Cece I know she filched one of my crystal paperweights on game night," he grouses. "And she better stop looking at my Fabergé collection."

Francesca turns to someone over her shoulder—Cece, I assume—muttering words like "Klepto" and "Why do you tease him?" and then "'Papa Don't Preach'? Really?"

Francesca turns back. "She'll bring it over tomorrow, Mr. Darden."

He harrumphs. "I'd like waffles for breakfast. With strawberries. It's not like you have anything else to do since you're jobless."

"You're a belligerent, cantankerous old man," she replies sweetly. "I'll see you tomorrow."

He shuts his door, then opens it again. "There's an all-night clinic down the street, Miss Lane. Get that cold checked."

"Go to bed, Mr. Darden."

"I was in bed!" He slams his door.

"That's an interesting relationship," I murmur.

She shrugs. "We've bonded. Neither of us have blood relatives."

"Really? You know he owns most of this building."

"He also plays a mean game of checkers. If I lose, I cook dinner. If I win, he gets carryout but insists I watch the nature channel. Do you know how long a snail can sleep?"

I arch a brow.

"Three years. Do you know what happens to female ferrets if they don't mate?"

"They get angry?"

"They die. Something about their hormones going crazy. Anyway. I like him."

My eyes skim her face, the stark widow's peak on her forehead. "Fascinating. May I come in?"

She chews on her bottom lip. "Um, we're kinda in the middle of something."

"We?"

"Me and my roomies, Cece and Brogan. You met Cece at the door. Don't trust anything she says."

"Ah. You live with a guy too?"

"Last time I checked, yes." She glares at me. "Problem?"

"Nah. Just trying to keep it all straight. Who was the man who left with his tail between his legs?"

"My ex. His name is Edward. Is this twenty questions?"

Oh, babe, I have a shit ton of questions.

I shift on my feet. "Why is he your ex? What happened?"

"He cheated, Officer. I'm guilty of falling for a dick. Am I under arrest?"

"So rude."

She sticks her wrists out. "Wanna cuff me and take me downtown?"

"No, but will you step out here in the hall so we can talk? Just five minutes?"

"I'm, like, *super* busy. You have no idea. Sorry."

I lean in. "But, Francesca, I want to see you. Your whole person. Without you and Mr. Darden yelling back and forth. Without the toboggan and glasses you had on at Café Lazzo." My voice lowers. "And without the mask, Princess Bride."

Her eyes widen as air escapes her lips. "I, um, didn't think you recognized me."

"And I'd imagined you sweeter. You ran off."

"Too bad you missed me saying goodbye. Get over it."

I wave that off. "I didn't know it was you at first." The alley was dark outside Café Lazzo, but I knew I liked her fire. And when she got under my umbrella, I couldn't stop staring at her blue-green irises, that unmistakable mouth. "It didn't hit me until you were leaving. I came here to confirm . . ."

I've looked for her in other places. Petite girls with a widow's peak and rosebud lips.

No one fit. Until now.

But I don't really know *who* she is.

She opens the door completely, steps out in the hall, and does a twirl with her arms out as she clutches a box of Triscuits in one hand. "Happy?"

"Hmm." I drink her in like a thirsty man. Extravagant black lashes frame steely ocean irises. Her nose is perfectly dainty, and one might assume she is, too, but my gut says she's anything but. Her skin is flawless, even without makeup. Her cropped T-shirt reveals a silver belly button ring that I don't recall.

"Show me your tattoo," I ask.

"As proof?" Her nose wrinkles. "No. You saw my wings already."

I laugh—out of relief or fear, I don't know.

It's really *her*.

"What? Disappointed?"

"No, it's just, after you bumped into me, Jasper bet me I couldn't . . ."

Her brow arches. "Fuck me?"

"No—I mean, yeah, we did fuck, but it's just getting a girl, you know, interested . . ." I halt as her arms cross. "I'm tanking this. It's not how it sounds."

"What did you win?"

I run my gaze over her again. She may not be my type, but she's drop-dead gorgeous with her heart-shaped face and snarky attitude. And her scent. It coils around me, thick and rich.

"A buck."

"You just pick out a girl you aren't attracted to and get her interested just to win a dollar? Douche move. Whatever. You wanted me pretty bad—four times."

"When did you know it was me?" *Or did you always know?*

"It was the cuff that gave it away—while you were kissing your girlfriend."

I wince, not about Courtney but about the scars. She saw them that night. She kissed them. She probably has ideas about them. That I tried to hurt myself—but she'd be wrong.

"Courtney isn't my girlfriend, but we go back."

"I don't really care."

"Not sweet at all. See, I recall a girl who sat in my lap and fed me birthday cake. She said I slayed the pantyhose dragon. She was perfect."

"I was drunk, and perfect girls don't exist."

My eyes linger on her belly ring. There are two stones in the ring, green and yellow. "New?"

She blows out a breath. "I got it the week after we, um, met. Momentary lapse of reason. Pretend it doesn't exist."

"Huh. Is that a story that involves me? Us?"

She groans. "Fine. I might have gotten it to remember your eyes. Emerald green—with those little yellow fireworks."

Satisfaction fills my chest.

"Don't get excited," she says. "I'm over it. You've seen me. Anything else?"

Oh yes, you fascinating creature.

I'm intrigued by you, but I need to know why there are so many coincidences between us.

"Don't you think it's odd, us being at Decadence, living in the same building, then seeing you at Café Lazzo?"

She leans against the wall in the hallway, her aquamarine eyes hardening. "Oh, I get it now. You think I knew who you were at Decadence. That I somehow set you up. But how on earth would I have orchestrated our meeting at Café Lazzo?"

I lift my shoulders. "It's happened before. Women will go through a lot of trouble to run into me. You could have followed me and my friends to the club. Maybe you recognized me there, sought me out, bumped into me—"

"Wow. Stop right there. First, I don't follow men; they follow me. That guy that left a few minutes ago? He's been stalking my balcony, not to mention giving me heart eyes at work when his new girl isn't looking. Second, you had half a mask on your face, your hair was long, and you had a beard. I thought you were a carpenter! Even better, maybe a fireman. Third, I do recall calling you a pervert—"

"Not a perv."

"Fourth, you are so not my type. Like at all. I like artistic men." She smiles tightly. "The way I see it, we never have to see each other again. Just stay out of the lobby and the main elevators. Voilà, your little stalking problem is solved."

"I'll take that under advisement."

"Do that," she says with a huff.

I take a step closer, my voice lowering. "Francesca . . ."

"Stop saying my name like that," she grouses.

"But it's so beautiful. Look, there's a bar I like a couple of blocks away. It's called the Baller, and you need a membership to get in. Lots of privacy. Want to join me? We can discuss how to avoid each other, perhaps?"

"Do you always run this hot and cold? Besides, there's another NFL player on my list to stalk. Tell Jasper I'm coming for him. He's more fun anyway."

A spike of possessiveness rises. "No Jasper for you."

"Scared for him?"

"I just can't see you with a guy who calls his dick Cupid." I press my palm against the wall as I dip down to her. "Tomorrow, then?"

"No."

"The next? Just one drink. We can go to my penthouse. We can sit in front of the fireplace . . . and talk." I trace a finger around the neckline of her shirt.

Her cheeks flush a pretty pink. "Not a good idea."

"Really?"

"Really."

I chuckle. "You need to work on your stalking, sweetheart."

"Was that some kind of test?"

I shrug, not answering. No, not really. It's clear she isn't like Lollipop, or she'd be all over me, but there's still a vulnerable part of me that wonders at the odds of us running into each other again.

Her eyes flash. "Maybe it was just fate that we live at the same place."

"I don't believe in fate. Random events happen, and it means nothing—or it was planned." I tug at her ponytail, and it falls. I card my fingers through her hair, arranging it around her shoulders. "So pretty."

She swallows. "Tuck . . ."

I run my nose up her throat, inhaling. "I want to fuck you again—that's the truth. I want to spread you out and taste that delicious pussy. Again. I want those rosebud lips around my cock. Again." My teeth nip at her lobe, and she gasps as she arches her neck. My lips trace over her cheekbone. I touch the edge of her mouth—

She pulls my face to hers, and our eyes lock as little puffs of air come from her chest.

"Your eyes are dilated." My whole hand covers her cheek as I cup her face.

She leans into my palm—

Ping! The elevator opens, and an older, well-dressed woman steps off and heads our way. She arches her brow at us as she passes.

"Dammit. The widow Carnes," Francesca whispers as she dips below my arm and escapes. "She'll tell the whole book club circle Tuck Avery was at my door by tomorrow." She leans against her door and rubs her forehead.

"I don't care who sees us."

She exhales. "Never mind that. Look. We wanted fun that night. One night, no strings. *You* asked for that."

I pause. I didn't want strings because I never expected Decadence to be the place to meet someone real. "I changed my mind."

"Tuck, I—I don't want . . ." A frown puckers her forehead.

"What?"

"That's just it. I don't know. My life is at a crossroads right now, and dammit, I didn't mean to say that—ugh, but no, I can't have a drink with you or whatever." She rubs her eyes with the heels of her palms. "It's been a really crazy day, okay? I've got things to figure out, and it's not a good time for this, and I kind of need to pee."

She steps inside her apartment.

"Francesca. Wait—"

The door slams in my face.

I stand there, exhilaration rushing through my veins.

Fuck if I don't love a good chase.

Game on, little princess.

I didn't last fourteen years in the NFL without being a competitor. Once I have a goal . . .

I'm already dialing my agent's number as I stalk down the hall.

"Yo, Tuck. It's late. What's going on?" Ben says as he answers.

"There's this girl."

He chuckles. "I thought you'd want to go over the game."

"Later. This girl. Can you look into her?"

"I don't usually do those types of things."

"But you know people who do. The thing is I only date women I know, and I don't know this one. The way we met is sorta weird."

"You could get to know her. That's how normal people do it."

"I'm not normal people. I'm one of your top clients, and I've been burned before, remember?"

He lets out a low whistle. "Damn. Is this about the stripper?"

I exhale. Lollipop, or Mary Fordham, messed me up. She sent threatening letters, stalked me, stalked Courtney, showed up at my mom's living facility. Thank God security didn't allow her inside. The last time was when she showed up with a knife. It was night, and I was coming from dinner with friends when I walked around the corner of Wickham to go inside. She had been waiting on a bench across the street and ran for me. I managed to catch her wrist before she stabbed me. It's not something you forget.

Francesca isn't Lollipop. She's not a stalker.

She lives here. Darden and Herman adore her.

But there's still a tingle of unease . . .

I rub my neck, trying to loosen the muscles there as I circle back to the coincidences that have brought us together. I don't believe there's some magical force in the sky watching us, moving us around like chess pieces to put us in the right place at the right time.

Fate is bullshit. Stars don't align.

I can't believe in it because if it's real, then it means I was meant to be the cause of my father's death, that I was meant to be everything my mother says. Just like him. Like her. My nose flares. Everything I have, I got on my own, not because destiny decreed it.

"Tuck? You there?" Ben asks.

"Yeah." I step into the elevator and tap the pass code to get to the penthouse. "Just some red flags popped up. Do you have someone you can trust to take care of it?"

"We have investigators, sure. What's her name?"

"Francesca Lane at Wickham, apartment 20E. She used to work at a place called East Coast Ink & Gallery. Age is unknown, maybe late twenties. Petite, dark hair, nice ass, big eyes—"

He chuckles. "That's good; we can get the rest. How did you meet?"

"NDA."

A pause. "Okay, I'll get a guy on it and let you know. Back to the Tampa game. Don't beat yourself up about the loss. We can—"

My jaw flexes. "I dropped two passes and fumbled in the end zone. My contract is up at the end of the season, and it's not looking good." I stare down at the last Super Bowl ring on my finger. It's been downhill ever since Ronan left our team.

"Maybe you need a fresh start. Tennessee is looking for a wide receiver—"

"This is home." I lean against the wall in the hallway outside the penthouse. "I can't figure out what's wrong, but we've lost three games in a row . . ." I rub my face.

"Ankle?"

"Scans are fine."

"Your forty-yard-dash time?"

"Four point four was my latest. Good as hell. I'm beating the boys fresh out of the draft."

"Mental?"

"Still in therapy." My coach demanded I attend sessions after I punched a player last season. The doctor's diagnosis? I'm experiencing "open aggression" and anxiety because I feel out of control.

He sighs. "When Ronan was quarterback, you two were on fire. Jasper—"

"Is talented. It's me."

"Don't stress. Come in, and we'll brainstorm—"

My phone beeps, and my body tightens as I see the name on the ID. "Gotta go. Thanks for the help. Get on that investigation. Later, Ben."

I click over to the next call. "Nella? What's wrong?" The director of Greenwood, a state-of-the-art private facility for people with mental illness, Nella chats with me weekly but never at night.

"Tuck. We had a small incident."

"Is she okay?"

"Yes."

"What happened?"

She sighs. "Yesterday she skipped her tennis lessons, which isn't a big deal, but she's supposed to call ahead. Then, this afternoon, she missed her group sessions. We searched the grounds and found her in the fountain. She was naked and dancing to a ballet she'd written."

Mother was never a ballerina, but she could make a person believe she was.

I sigh as I picture the fountain in the manicured gardens, a large statue of an urn pouring out water into a large pool. I imagine her there, blonde hair shining, eyes bright.

Nella continues. "She hit one of the attendings, nothing serious, but I felt this deserved a phone call. She appears to be in a manic phase. I've scheduled her to meet with her doctor tomorrow."

"Where were your people? Why didn't you check in on her when she missed her tennis lesson?"

"Tuck, she has choices, and we're just here to help her make good ones. We aren't an institution—we're a residential facility."

I sigh. "I know. I just don't want anything to happen to her. I saw her a month ago, and she was fine."

But was she? Wasn't she talking faster than usual? Wasn't she jumping from topic to topic? I was just happy she asked to see me. Maybe that feeling felt so good I ignored the euphoric gleam in her eye.

"Your mother is a charismatic woman, manic or not. Sometimes medications stop working, or it's possible she's decided not to take them. She's settled now, so I don't want you to worry."

"All right, let me know how it goes. Has she asked for me?"

"I'm sorry—she hasn't." Her voice softens.

When Mom showed up at my doorstep five years ago, she chose to live at Greenwood, but on her terms. She only sees me when she wants.

My throat tightens as past hurts coil around me.

"Yeah. Okay." I inhale. "Just thought I would check."

I click off with Nella and lean against the wall.

A dad with anger issues and a bipolar mom. It was a spectacular childhood.

I was thirteen the first time she frightened me. Dad was out of town, and she stayed awake for days claiming demons were hiding in the walls. She drew pentagrams to banish them. The housekeeper called Dad, and he came home—and they fought.

Once she picked me up at school in a bathrobe, took me to a bar, and left me in the car for hours. Dad showed up and dragged her out. A half-dressed man followed them and fought with my dad in the parking lot. As our chauffeur drove us home, I watched my father fist his hands over and over, spewing cruel words toward her. *Whore, slut, bitch, psycho.* His fists would hit her later that night as I pounded on the door for him to let me inside their bedroom.

My mom wasn't any of those awful words he called her.

She told fantastical stories.

She called me her sunshine.

She played the cello with such emotion people wept.

She was heartbreakingly beautiful.

My father loved her. And hated her.

She loved him. And hated him.

With those turbulent emotions boiling, they barely noticed me.

I grunt as a pain slices through my chest, lingers for several seconds, and then subsides. My heart pounds, heavy and thick, as if I've finished a ten-mile run. I slide down the wall to the floor and hold my head in my hands.

I've had my heart checked regularly. It's fine.

Is this fear that I'm going to turn into him—or her?

Or is it more self-centered?

My career is dying, and the idea of being useless to my team—I clench my hands at the thought—is like carving my skin off with a dull knife. You know how everyone has one thing, that *one thing* they're great at, that thing that keeps them centered and happy? Maybe it's a spouse, a friend, or a home you love. For me, it's the exhilaration of catching that pigskin and taking it to the end zone. If football is gone, if I lose the *one thing* that's kept me sane for all these years, what will happen to me?

Will I lash out like my dad?

Will mental issues like my mom's rear up?

I bang my head on the wall.

I need sex, a good, hard, rough fucking. It's been months since Decadence, and I—

"Yo. You all right?"

My thoughts cut off as Jasper appears at the door of the penthouse. I glance up, stuffing down the turmoil. I compose my face quickly and rise to my feet. "Yeah. Just thinking."

He nods. "Is this about practice? You seemed off—"

"I wasn't," I say sharply. "I caught your throws, didn't I?"

He holds his hands up. "Cool, cool. So, um, is this about me getting cheese-puff dust on your couch? It might have gotten on one of the loungers too—but it's not bad. I sprayed some cleaner, and it sorta got worse."

My temper stirs as I follow him inside. "You ate puffs on my couch?"

"It was Cherry's fault," he adds. "She jumped in my lap, and I spilled the bag . . ." He trails off as he gives me a sheepish look. "She loves them, Tuck, and it's almost like real cheese."

I pinch my nose. "She has her own treats, special ones I order. Your diet is fucked up. Don't screw with hers."

Wearing his plaid pajama pants, he slaps his bare stomach. "I have needs, Tuck. Sweet and salty needs. Donuts and bacon. Cheese puffs and Snickers."

I take in the mess in the living room: pillows on the floor, sports magazines spread out, soda cans, candy wrappers on the coffee table.

My eyes laser in on the orange-smeared arm of the couch. I'm not OCD, but Jasper could test a monk.

"I'm going to straighten up before bed," he assures me.

"Fine. Where's Courtney?"

"Bed, thank God." He changes his voice to a falsetto and dips his wrist. "I need fresh towels, Jasper; I need sparkling water, Jasper; I need soft toilet paper, Jasper; I want to watch HGTV, Jasper."

A ghost of a smile crosses my face. "You're damn close to her voice."

He groans. "Just curious, how long will she be here?"

"Oh, this is fun. My two houseguests don't like each other."

"She's a spoiled brat and treats me like the help." He raises his arms. "I'm not her maid. I can barely get my own towels."

"She just showed up today, so cut her some slack. She broke up with her boyfriend and has nowhere to go."

"Come on—she's got model friends around town. She comes running to you every time they have a spat. She wants to be your girlfriend."

"Hmm." Courtney and I dated, broke up for a while, and then dated again. Plus, Courtney was with me the night Lollipop brandished a knife. I can't just cut her off because she can be annoying. She's a friend. I don't have many.

"Speaking of roommates, any timeline on your apartment being ready?" He bought three apartments below mine and is having them renovated into one.

"Can't wait for me to leave, huh?"

"You're an annoying fuck."

He bats his lashes. "I know. I'm so great."

"I repeat, you're an annoying fuck."

"I love you, and you love me. We have a bromance. Not sure if bromance is still a thing, but I can make a thing a thing again, am I right? I was reading this article about men's friendships, and we need nicknames—besides you calling me *asshole* and *squatter*. I'm gonna call you Big T. What do you wanna call me? Come on—tell me whatcha got . . ." He rubs his hands together and grins, but there's a serious glint in his eyes.

"Jay Bird because you like to walk around naked after a shower. Put a towel around your junk. This isn't the locker room."

He claps. "All right. Jay Bird and Big T. I like it. We should hug more. It's good for bonding. It might help our game. Cohesive. We move as one, ya know? Yin and yang, peas and carrots. I-throw-the-ball-and-you-sense-it kind of thing? Telepathy football."

I plop down on a stool. "Dude . . ."

"Come on—give me some love, Big T . . ." He hugs me from the back, and I shove him off as I chuckle.

"Jesus, find a girlfriend."

He pouts. "I guess it's not a good idea to tell you that I ordered us matching man bracelets, tungsten and black leather. Very cool and badass. I know you wear one already, so I figured you liked them."

"No." I only wear the cuff to hide the scars on my wrist.

"Maybe Deacon will want one." He sniffs as he wipes a pretend tear.

I throw my hands up and laugh. "Fucking hell. Fine."

He gives me a blinding grin and holds his fist out for me to bump.

Cherry, my toy papillon, comes flying around the corner, her big brown ears waving in the air. I sweep her up in my arms and rub our noses together. "Baby girl, my sweet Cherry, whatcha doing, hmm? Whatcha doing? Don't let the ugly man give you cheese puffs, never, ever, ever." I arch a brow at him. "For real. Don't make my dog a food junkie. It's not good for her belly."

"I guess this means no more Oreos—"

"What the fuck. She can't—!"

"Kidding, Big T. God as my witness, I swear."

My ire settles as I cuddle her in the crook of my arm while Jasper heads to my kitchen and pulls a beer out of the fridge. "Beer?"

I nod. "Hell yeah."

"Ah, guess the meet-cute with your princess didn't pan out?"

I sit down on one of the leather loungers in the den with Cherry. "I'm working on it. Pretty sure her roommate is Snow White. Cece. She has another roommate, too, a guy. His name is—shit, I can't remember."

"I knew Francesca looked familiar." He hands me my bottle, then plops down in the chair next to me. "So let's focus on football. It was a tough loss. You wanna talk about the game?"

My gut clenches. "Not right now."

His fingers drum the arm of his chair as he shoots me a glance. "You know, if you, um, want to talk anything else, you know, besides football, I'm here. It's what bros do: help shoulder the burden and all that shit."

I used to talk to Ronan. But . . .

"Nah, I'm good. Next week we'll play better, yeah?"

He nods and clicks on a game. I lean back and sip on my beer, my head running in circles. I think about Mom in a manic phase, and it stings that those are the moments when she usually needs me the most, but she hasn't called.

The worst thing is part of me still wants to be her "sunshine," to have her approval. I tap my fingers on my leg. I could hop in my car and be at Greenwood in half an hour. Just to check in. I exhale. No. It's late. She doesn't want me there. It's cool. Fine. Whatever.

Later, I head upstairs to my gym on the third floor. It's two thousand square feet of floor-to-ceiling mirrors, mats, a punching bag, three different styles of treadmills, a training bench, dumbbells, barbells, kettlebells, stationary bikes, a rowing machine, and a yoga area that overlooks the lights of Manhattan. It's my temple where I work out my issues.

I blast music on the speakers and pick up one of the jump ropes. Rolling my neck, I inhale a deep breath and start. By the end of my fifth set, my heart thuds, and my body drips in sweat. I shake off the exhaustion and do one more set, just one more until the frustration in my body disappears.

Afterward, I hit the shower and click on the steam feature for my muscles. Hot water sluices down my frame, loosening some of the tension. Pressing my hands against the tile, I shove thoughts in my head away—about football, about my mom, about my career.

Later, I'm in bed, flipping through the channels, when Courtney eases in.

I sit up straighter, trying to not rouse Cherry. "Um, Court . . ."

She walks toward me in a black see-through teddy. My eyebrows raise at the tight silver chains that crisscross around her waist and breasts.

"Does that hurt?"

She shrugs. "Who cares? It's pretty. I picked it up at a shoot last month. Jasper is a total meathead, by the way. You should toss him out."

"Are you sure that isn't cutting off your circulation?"

Her jaw tightens as she waves her hands. "That's what you're going with? This is sexy as hell. I put it on for you."

And this is what I get for returning her kiss outside Café Lazzo. Shit. I scrub my face. My heart wasn't in it, and my head tumbled with why the girl in the toboggan felt familiar.

She stops at my nightstand. "You're tense. Let me make it better."

"We shouldn't have kissed. It was a mistake."

Her lips brush against mine. "I like mistakes. Don't you want to do it again?"

My body tenses, my cock thickening. Yeah, I'm craving to thrust into someone, to push this anxiety away, but it isn't with Courtney. Only one person will satisfy.

"You're lashing out at Mark. He hurt you, and you want revenge." She found texts on his phone from a girl he works with.

"Mark isn't here—you are. Only you're all into chasing some stranger on the street. Jasper told me you thought she was the girl you met at Decadence."

I nod. "It's her, and she isn't really a stranger. That night puts her in a different category."

Her lips tighten. "Something feels off about the whole thing."

I shrug.

"Okay, well, I'm here for you. For anything." Her hands caress my cheek. "We can be here for each other. It doesn't have to be serious."

I toss the covers back and get up to grab her a T-shirt from my chest of drawers.

Everything with Courtney is serious when it comes to me. We broke up twice because I didn't want a white picket fence. She's been in the modeling industry since she was twelve, and when we met, she was ready to give it up and settle down. She wants marriage. Kids.

I don't. Not with the shit way I grew up. Not with my flawed genes. Fear ripples over me, and my stomach pitches at the idea of a family.

I can't be responsible for people who depend on me every day.

"We don't work as a couple—or as friends with benefits. I don't want to hurt you, Court." I toss the shirt at her.

"Prick. Why do you have to be so noble?" she says without heat as she catches it, then glances down at her outfit and pouts. "This piece of torture really does hurt."

"The blood flow has definitely stopped going to your tits."

She sighs. "I should have worn the red teddy. That would have gotten you good."

I huff out a laugh. Doubtful.

"My feelings are hurt, darling."

I roll my eyes. "Fine. I'll make it up to you. We'll go to lunch soon, yes? That Italian place you like?"

"Coletta's, yes!" She throws her arms around my neck and kisses my lips.

"Courtney, no—"

"Um, Big T—" Jasper's voice cuts off as he opens the door. He's stark naked, uncaring. His eyes pop at Courtney, who still hasn't put the shirt on. "Oops. I didn't know you two were getting it on . . ." He trails off. "Jesus, does that hurt, Courtney?"

"Go to hell, Jasper," she snips as she clutches the T-shirt to her chest. "How about you forget you ever saw this fabulous body, okay? And put some clothes on. Your turtle dick is not attractive."

He rears back and looks down at his junk. "What's a turtle dick?"

I groan. "Jesus. We just had this conversation, Jasper. Wrap it up with a towel after you shower!"

"Okay, I'll try, but what's a turtle dick?"

I look at the ceiling, then him. "Do you really not know?"

He shakes his head. "I grew up in a conservative family in Utah and was a virgin till I was twenty-one."

"Boy, does that explain a lot," Courtney mutters. "Immature asshole who doesn't know a thing about women."

"I'm a maniac with the ladies, so shut your face," he tells her, then looks at me. "So, what's a turtle dick? I don't want to have to get my phone out."

I sigh. "It's when your dick retracts. All you have are nuts right now."

"Just two hairy balls," Courtney says with a smirk.

"Because of you," he grouses as he points at Courtney. "Who wants to see chains around boobs, huh? Nobody but freaks."

She glares at him. "Unbelievable! You're the one who goes to a sex club and talks and talks about how awesome it is! You can't find a real woman."

He pumps his hips. "You're itching to take a ride on Cupid."

"Your dick is not the most glorious thing in the world," Courtney snaps. "No one in this room wants to look at it but you."

"Babe, your eyes are glued to my junk. Remove them, please. This is not for you." He cups his groin.

I throw my hands up, then point to the hallway outside. "Please, Jesus, get the fuck out of my room. Both of you. Leave. Now."

Cherry barks her agreement. Poor baby was huddling under the covers at their raised voices.

Courtney sniffs. "Night, Tuck. Fuck off, Jasper."

Jasper smirks as she walks past him with her nose in the air.

Finally the door closes, and I plop back on my bed and beg for sleep.

Chapter 8

FRANCESCA

"Are you feeling better, Francesca?" Herman asks as he opens the door for me a few days later. "I saw you throw up in the petunias a while back. There's a nasty bug going around."

Ha. "I'm fine. Thanks for asking. How's Catherine?"

We stand near the entrance as he tells me about his wife's root canal, then shows me a pic of his youngest grandson's first birthday. My chest tightens at the image of a little toddler with cake smeared on his face.

"Are you going for a walk?" he says as I inch closer to the sidewalk.

I nod. "See you soon."

He nods. "All right. Sorry again about Edward getting past me. Don't tell the manager, yeah?"

Edward hasn't even crossed my mind. He came to apologize, maybe absolve himself, and then found out I was pregnant. Priceless. "I doubt he'll be back, Herman."

I wave goodbye as I stick my hands in my black leather moto jacket and step out into the early December air. I walk down Fifth Avenue, then turn on East Seventy-Third Street and go inside Lottie's Coffee and Book Shoppe. I'm yearning for a steaming cup of coffee, and the nutty, caramelized smell nearly makes me break my vow to ease off the caffeine for the pregnancy. With a sigh, I order a dragon-fruit-and-mango tea. It's been the only thing that settles my stomach. I buy a book, then head back out.

I'm halfway back to Wickham when a man walks briskly past, then stops and glances at me.

His voice is deep and husky. "Francesca?"

My lips part in surprise until I find my voice. "Hey."

"Hey," he says, walking to me. Wearing a black wool coat, a thick scarf, and a Nike wool cap over his head, he's not easily recognizable, but it doesn't stop the women from giving him second and third looks.

"How are you?" he asks, and I can't help but stare at his lips, the deep V at the top, the plump bottom one. Wicked lips. The way he used them on my neck, my breasts, the curve of my waist . . .

I shake myself inwardly.

Must stay away from the hot baller.

"Good." Pregnant. I start walking again, and his steps adjust with mine.

"You headed home, I guess?" he asks.

"Yes."

"Mind if I walk with you?"

"You already are."

"My sweet princess is long gone." He chuckles, then sobers. "I'm glad I saw you. You've been on my mind."

"Oh?"

"Yeah."

I don't know who stops walking first, me or him, but we do. We end up near the overhang of a store, and our eyes cling. Without dropping my gaze, he takes his hat off and pushes tawny hair away from his forehead, the ends brushing against his diamond-cut jawline. A small smile curls his lips. "I had a dream where you worked at Café Lazzo. You tossed spaghetti in my face when I asked for my order. Then everyone turned into breadsticks. Even you."

A small laugh wants to erupt, and I bite my lips to hold it in. "You must have gone to bed hungry."

"I had another one. Horrible." He pulls his gloves off and tucks them in his pocket. "There was this virus that hit the world, and everyone turned into clowns. Little kids in bright clothes and makeup were running around everywhere trying to kill people. Women—did you know women clowns are called clownettes?"

I blink. "No."

"Now you do. Anyway, these clown women were chasing me. They had crazy hats and big floppy shoes." He shudders. "I'd just outrun them when I bumped into you as you ran from a ferret turned clown. We ran to Wickham, jumped on the elevator, and hid on the roof of my penthouse. Then, Jasper showed up as a pirate clown. He had a hook on his arm and said he wanted to slice us up and eat us. You grabbed a chain saw—from where, I don't know—and tossed it at him. It hit him right in the forehead, and he fell off the building. Then I woke up."

I shake my head as a laugh comes from me. "What do you think it means?"

He smiles, slow and sexy, and a shiver dances down my spine. "To make sure you have a chain saw when the clown apocalypse hits."

"I read Stephen King's *It*, and that was it for me and clowns. They're awful," I say.

"Same! Jesus. Clowns are fucking scary."

We laugh at the same time, and I start, my laugh ebbing as I realize that he's really funny. A silence settles between us as our gazes bounce off each other—and dammit, why can't I look away? I dip my head, swallowing. "Ah, we should go."

"Ah, right." We take off again, our steps in sync. "Walking clears my head, you know, especially when it's cold. It needs clearing a lot these days." He grimaces. "You a football fan?"

"No." I've watched a few games with Brogan, but that's it.

"I can teach you, little princess. First, I'm a wide receiver. My job is to catch the ball, then outmaneuver the opposing team and get yardage. Jasper is the quarterback. He's the one throwing the ball."

I roll my eyes. "You and Cupid are in the NFL. I'm still wrapping my head around it." I glance at the white scars on his knuckles.

His eyes follow mine. "Ah, those came from glass. Plus the ones on my wrist."

"How?"

A frown flits over his face. "I pushed my hands through a window. Someone was inside a car . . ." His voice trails off. "It's not important."

I nod, pushing away my curiosity. He doesn't want to talk about it, and really, the less I know about him, the better.

"Wait a sec, will you, Francesca?"

I'm not sure what he means, but I stop near a streetlamp.

He gives me a quick nod, then walks over to a man, maybe in his sixties, sitting on the concrete near an antique store. With his legs crossed, he wears a torn T-shirt, ragged jeans, and tennis shoes. Next to him is a cat and a cardboard box stuffed with junk, although I'm sure it's not junk to him. Tuck bends down and talks to him longer than I expected, at least ten minutes, yet I don't have the urge to leave. Tuck pets the cat, then takes off his coat and scarf and hands them over to him. They clasp hands; then Tuck walks back to me.

"Sorry I took so long. Ready?"

"That was nice. Most people just keep walking." Me. I do. It's as if you don't see the homeless after a while. It's a terrible thought, and I cringe. "Do you hand out coats frequently?"

When he doesn't answer, I glance over at him, then gasp. "Oh my God, you do! What . . . do you just walk around at night and give out winter apparel?"

He shrugs. "There's over fifty thousand homeless in Manhattan. If you count the entire state, it's up to eighty. Some go to shelters—some don't. The ones on the street, sometimes all they want is to talk to

85

someone and make a connection. Giving him my coat isn't much, but to him it is." He pauses, wincing. "The tricky part is I feel good afterwards. Is that bad, that I do it for me too?"

"Not at all."

He nods. "My therapist told me to help others last year. I started with giving more money to charities, but it was meaningless to write a check. So I started this." He huffs out a small laugh. "Wow. I've never told anyone this."

I mimic zipping my lips. "I'm surprised the media didn't pick it up."

"Most of the homeless don't know who I am."

A couple walks toward us holding hands, and we sidestep them to give them more room.

He glances over at me. "So do you ever think about that night?"

I don't have to ask which night. "No, never." Big. Fat. Lie.

"Yeah, me neither. It really sucked. Worst ever."

"Totally, right?"

"Totally." He smirks.

We walk up to the entrance, and Herman opens the door for us, a smile on his face. "Two of my favorites. How was the walk?"

"Great," we both say at the same time, then glance at each other.

We head to the elevators and step inside. He's on one side, and I move to the other as he types in his password for the penthouse. Several other residents get in, and we end up at the back together. Our hands brush as we face straight ahead.

"Would you like to come up?" he murmurs under his breath. "I'll be good."

I side-eye him. "No."

"I never dreamed I'd see you again. Life is crazy, hmm?" He laughs, and Widow Carnes glances over at us. Her real name is Iris Carnes, but since the day she moved in and put her sights on Darden, we've referred to her as Widow Carnes. (She does have three dead husbands already.)

In her late sixties, she has bobbed dark hair and beady eyes—which are currently staring a hole through me.

"Hmm. You mentioned you're at a crossroads. Is that about your ex?" he asks.

"No. I'm way past him. Something else."

"Ah, I see. Personal troubles. Jobless."

"I got a job. I'm an art procurer." Darden arranged it yesterday when he emailed everyone in his contacts who bought art. His words to me were *Get clients. Throw my name around. Tell them you've purchased all my art for the past few years.*

"You like art?" I ask.

"I do." His gaze lingers on my face. "A lot."

The elevator stops to let residents off, leaving us alone. He faces me as I do the same. His eyes brush over my locket.

"What?" I whisper. "It's a locket. I wore it at the club."

Green eyes blaze with heat as they rise to meet mine. "I know. You wouldn't take it off. I fucked you while it bounced on your tits."

Red colors my face.

I recall us in that bed.

The fire between us.

The delicious harmony.

I turn back to face the door.

"Sorry I brought it up," he whispers. "It was an awful night, hmm?"

"Terrible."

"Are you walking tomorrow? Same time?" he asks.

I pause, my head racing as the elevator stops on my floor.

He grabs my hand. "Francesca?"

I pull my hand from his grip, but before I walk away, I murmur, "Bring a coat."

❖ ❖ ❖

Dr. Lovell, my gynecologist, sits across from me and Brogan in her office. Tall and lean, she has short white hair, wire glasses, and a kind face.

Cece wanted to be here today, but she's in LA. She came to my first appointment last week to confirm the pregnancy. During that visit, Dr. Lovell did blood work, examined me, and used a fetal Doppler to find the heartbeat.

It sounded like horses racing—and made everything terrifyingly real.

Because she knew my pregnancy was unplanned, Dr. Lovell went over different options in a factual, nonjudgmental way. She told me to take some time and think.

Brogan and Cece kept quiet in the apartment after that. There were no more songs, jokes, or discussions of baby clothes.

I went for walks, rode the subway, went to MoMA. I even borrowed Cece's Range Rover and drove out to the shore. All of it was me turning everything over in my head.

What to do, what to do . . .

Choose door one or door two.

Keep my life the way it is or change it irrevocably.

I got pregnant while using the implant and condoms—impossible odds. You'd think I'd be cynical about the idea of fate considering the childhood I had, but I believe there's good in everything. A grain of worthiness. Purpose.

Without my journey, I never would have moved to a city I adore.

I might never have met Darden, Brogan, and Cece.

I must believe in fate, or I'm just a kid someone abandoned.

What if my story was leading me here?

What if *this* baby was meant to be?

People have left me my whole life. Foster families. My first love. Edward.

Could I let this baby go?

Clarity arrived on the way back from Central Park a few days ago.

Perhaps I knew the moment Cece jumped out singing Madonna because before the fear of the unknown kicked in, part of my heart filled with *hope*.

My own little family. With Cece and Brogan and Darden.

She—for some reason it feels like a girl—will be mine to love forever.

I'm brought back to the present as Dr. Lovell glances at my chart on her laptop. "Just to recap, you're in the first trimester. You know the date of conception, but we also add two weeks from the date of your last period, so technically you're fourteen weeks. We don't have medical history for the father, but your blood work is great with no underlying conditions. You have some weight-loss issues, but your baby measures normally." She hands over the ultrasound picture we took earlier. It's just blobs of black and white, but I clench it tight.

Brogan gives me a high five. "That's what I'm talking about. My girl is primed to push out a bowling ball in June!"

Dr. Lovell laughs. "Your baby is soft and flexible. It *will* fit through your birth canal."

"Med school dropout here," he says. "I get it, but I like the bowling-ball analogy. Makes Fran sound like a badass."

I roll my eyes.

"What about her nausea?" he asks a bit later. "She's a vomit machine."

"Thanks," I say dryly.

"We'll keep a check on it. How are your moods?" Dr. Lovell asks.

"Not fit for humanity," I say with a grimace. "Everything makes me cry, even episodes of *Gilmore Girls* I've seen a hundred times."

Brogan smirks. "When she tries to stop crying, it only makes her cry *more* because she's pissed."

"The nausea, the moods—it's all to be expected," she says. "For the nausea, focus on staying hydrated, and eat several smaller meals. Also, take naps to help with the mood swings." She gives me a pamphlet with a list of healthy foods plus other information.

"Do ten Triscuits count as a meal?" I ask.

"No."

My hands brush over my belly. "She's going to be okay, right? Even though I've been living on cough drops, crackers, and coffee before I knew?"

She pats my hand. "Your appetite should increase now that your virus has passed. You've been sick. Don't feel guilty, Francesca."

My eyes catch on a framed diagram on her wall, a female abdomen with a full-term baby inside it. "Speaking of pushing out a baby . . . will my vagina be the same, you know, afterwards?"

She sets aside her laptop and chuckles. "I'll give you some info about pelvic-floor exercises."

My eyes flare. "So what I'm hearing is it won't be the same?"

She pushes up her glasses. "Our bodies are meant to change and adapt during birth. All women are different."

"Still not what I wanted to hear," I grumble. "Doesn't it just pop right back into place?"

She holds up her hands to form a circle. "This is about ten centimeters dilated, which is what you need for the baby."

A clammy feeling rushes over me. "Uh . . . what?"

"I'll make sure they stitch up your happy place so it's not floppy," Brogan says as he pats my hand.

I tense. "Promise you won't look, Brogan! You'll have to stay at my head, okay?"

"Maybe just a peek. I want to see a live birth. Whose better than yours?"

"Never," I mutter.

He ruffles my hair, and I lean into him.

After getting more pamphlets and prenatal vitamins, we leave and head outside to a brisk December wind. I tug my peacoat closer around me and inhale the air. It feels like snow, and I sigh. Winter in Manhattan is my favorite: the Christmas decorations on the lamp-posts, the elaborate shop displays, the people milling around with smiles.

My mind invariably turns to Tuck the closer we get to Wickham. We've taken three walks, counting the first one. We haven't talked about anything personal. I do, however, know that his jersey number is eighty-one, he's been playing since he was ten, and when he was in college, he sometimes played quarterback. I know you can score different ways on the field: touchdown, extra point, two-point conversion, field goal, and safety.

I kept information about myself brief: I grew up all over New York, I don't have siblings, I love Manhattan.

On the last walk, we stopped at a food truck and got hot choc-olates, then wandered through a Christmas tree farm illuminated by crisscrossing strings of fairy lights. As "Jingle Bells" played over the loudspeaker, he asked me to have dinner with him.

I wanted to say yes. That really stupid, gooey part of me. I watched the man hand out a coat a night. But I also knew from the tabloids that he was a party boy who dated supermodels.

I haven't been able to resist the walks with him, but anything else . . .

I told him no.

I glance over at Brogan. "About Tuck. If I tell him, is he going to be angry I didn't terminate? No way does he want a kid with the girl from the sex club. Right?"

"Sure, his feelings *are* relevant, but it's your body. You don't want time or money from him . . ." He gives my hand a squeeze. "Look, you don't have to tell him. You've got a new job, and I've saved up a shit ton of money—"

"Hang on. You said you were going back to med school. You need to use your money for that."

He keeps his face straight ahead so I can't read it. "Meh, whatever. I changed my mind."

No, he didn't. I've seen him buried in his old textbooks when he gets off work. He's prepping. His first year of med school, he dropped out to take care of his sick sister. After she got better, he got a job at Decadence to pay her medical bills and put school on hold. That was three years ago.

"You're going back," I say. "You've always dreamed of being a surgeon, and you will be one."

"I'm gonna help with whatever Baby Ivy needs. Get over it."

I huff. "That's your last name. And you're trying to change the topic."

He steers me inside my favorite pastry shop. "Let's see if they have any of those peanut butter balls I like. They aren't on your food list, though."

"Just cruel. If you're getting them, I'm eating one."

We walk past a pastry case, and my stomach rumbles. "Brogan. Oh my God, look at those lemon bars—"

I glance up for Brogan and see Tuck at the checkout counter several feet away, the rest of my words dying on my lips. He's buying chickpea vegan cookies. And Courtney is next to him.

I tug Brogan behind a display of Christmas cookies. It's been over a week since our last walk—when I still didn't know what I was going to do. Annoyance stirs. Part of me is pissed he hasn't tried harder to see me. The other side is upset that Courtney is with him. Then I'm ticked because I'm upset. I have no right to him. We aren't dating. We took some walks. Big whoop.

"Are we going to hide behind these cookies for a while?" Brogan murmurs.

"We aren't hiding," I say. "We're avoiding. How bad do you need a peanut butter ball?"

"Peanut butter is a wonder food. It boosts your immune system—"

"There's chocolate chips and old peanuts at home. Let's run out the door in three, two, one—"

I grab his hand, and we dash for the exit.

"Life sure does want you to see him," he murmurs.

I grimace. Fate is a tenacious bitch.

And sometimes when she doesn't get what she wants, she tries again and again.

Chapter 9

TUCK

"Tuck, hey, you got a second?" Coach Hardy calls from his office as I walk out of the locker room. Barry Williams, the offensive coach, is with him. Shit.

I keep my face bland and my body loose even though my back aches from a hit I took at practice. "Sure."

I take a seat on the leather couch in his office and stretch out my legs.

Williams sits in a club chair, not meeting my gaze, while Hardy sits on his desk, eagle eyes fixed on me. I stiffen. Lately his attention feels keener, sharper, when he looks at me.

"You're having trouble on the field" is how he starts. "You're missing cues. Hell, son, you look like a fucking amateur out there."

I exhale. "We're working on the plays, making them sharper." I look at Williams, hoping he'll jump in and take up for me, but he's silent.

Hardy scoffs as he rubs his jaw. "Hmm, yeah, so why did we get beat by the worst team in the league this week? You seem . . . preoccupied lately. I need your focus on the goddamn game."

My hands clench, and I release them slowly. "It is, sir."

It fucking isn't.

I'm thinking about my mom.

About how my body won't do the things it used to do.

"I'm taking heat for keeping you on the field, but I can't do that anymore. The owner is breathing down my neck . . ." He pauses as he holds my eyes. "Just wanted you to know that we've decided that River Tate will start against Kansas City. Look, you're smart—you know this is the right thing for the team."

It feels as if he's slapped me. Sure, I've envisioned this very thing, but I never thought it would happen so soon. Being a starter is prestige; it's confidence that the franchise believes in you. Panic makes my heart flutter, and I breathe in and out slowly. My words come out low and rough. "He's not seen the experience I have."

"We've got faith in him."

Another slap. Harder. But no faith in me? My jaw flexes. "Is this permanent?"

Hardy gets off his desk and opens his door. "It's a one-game-at-a-time thing. Show me you want to be the number one receiver on the team, and we'll reassess."

Fear ripples over me as I leave in a daze. If they're benching me, then what will they do when my contract comes up at the end of the season? Is this the beginning of the end?

A few minutes later, Jasper and I head out of the stadium.

"What did Hardy want?" he asks.

"Tate is starting against Kansas City," I say tightly as I open the trunk of my Ferrari. I throw my duffel in.

He starts at my words, his mouth gaping. "Tuck . . . shit . . ."

"I don't want to discuss it," I say.

He gets in the passenger side. "Okay, but are you all right?"

No. I'm bitter. I want to pummel something with my fists. I need to pound the shit out of everything in my workout room.

I grumble out an unintelligible response as we squeal out of the garage.

Jasper flips on the radio, and two familiar voices fill the car.

"And they aren't scoring any points. That's where it starts, and that's where the problem is," says Dog's voice from the *Dog and Jerry Show*, a sports-radio talk show.

I huff. A few years ago, I was their shiny star with a standing weekly interview on Tuesday afternoons. I'd talk about our game and news around the league, but this year I haven't felt like talking to them—and they haven't called. My hands clench the steering wheel.

"Amen. Our Pythons offense is the worst in a fifteen-year history, and it's not the QB's fault, folks. Jasper Janich can't throw the ball *and* catch it too," Jerry says on a chuckle.

"These guys are hilarious," Jasper says.

"Really? You like them now? A couple of years ago you called my lawyer to see if you could sue them for saying that you ran like that kid who wore a scoliosis brace in third grade."

He bristles. "Meh, they like me now."

Dog is back. "Janich is a stud quarterback, but he's running for his life, and the ole veteran, Tuck Avery, is stinking up the joint this year."

Bitterness eats at me. Where's the love for a player who's spent the past fourteen years bringing championships to our city? The speedometer hits eighty as I pass a BMW on the expressway.

"Yep, he's gone from being ole reliable on third down to just being old," Jerry says.

They both laugh as I hit ninety and pass a sedan.

"He's fumbled more than he's caught passes," Jerry adds.

I grit my teeth. Not true. I speed around a truck, hitting triple digits.

Jasper puts his hands on the dashboard, then his seat belt, checking it. "Dude. You've got special cargo here. Take it easy."

Dog chuckles. "Tuck's so old he farts dust."

Jasper gives me an uneasy look. "That one was kind of funny?"

"Yeah, sure," I mutter as I downshift and accelerate around a tractor trailer.

Jasper crosses himself. "Baby Jesus, save us."

Blue lights glitter behind me. Cursing, I ease off the accelerator. Gravel sprays when I pull off to the side of the road.

"Shit, shit, shit, fuck, damn, sorry I cussed, Jesus," Jasper says as I jerk to a stop.

I lean my head back against the headrest and close my eyes. Breathe. Breathe.

A cold sweat breaks out over my skin—not about the cop but at the helpless feeling inside me.

I can't *make* myself be a better football player. I can't fix this. The team is going to dump me. My team is going to leave me behind. Even Jasper.

The trooper taps on my window, and I roll it down. Jerry and the Dog are still making jokes as Jasper turns the radio off.

The cop, a tall dude around my age, leans down. A disbelieving scoff comes from him. "*The* Tuck Avery. This is crazy. I was listening to the show when you passed me."

I snap off my sunglasses and force a smile. "Love that show."

"You enjoy them talking shit about you?" He hooks his thumbs in his belt.

My knuckles turn white on the steering wheel. "It's all for attention."

He nods. "Have you been drinking, Mr. Avery?"

I snort. Fuck this guy. I don't drink and drive. "Have you?"

The trooper narrows his eyes. "Do we have a problem here, Mr. Avery?"

Jasper leans over. "Him? Hell nah. He's cool, right? You're cool, right, Big T?"

The trooper shifts around, and Jasper gulps when he sees his firearm.

"I watched the Houston game," the cop says. "You really sucked. I'm guessing it still stings a bit."

I grunt.

"Anyway, I'm supposed to ask you why I pulled you over, but we both know why I stopped you, right?"

"I was speeding, Officer. No excuse," I snap.

"You passed several cars. You endangered the lives of others." He peers in to see who is sitting next to me. "Is that Jasper Janich?"

Jasper swallows. "How are you today, Officer? We are, like, super sorry. I'm an upright citizen, and so is Tuck. I come from Utah. We never speed."

The trooper nods, then pats the Ferrari. "My boys will never believe I pulled you two over."

Digging deep, I wrangle my anger. It's not at him anyway. I force a smile. "Let's prove it with a selfie. Bet they'd believe it then, am I right?"

He looks down at his ticket pad, then looks back at us. He closes it, puts it into his belt, and then points to the area in front of the Ferrari. "Can we do it from there? That way we will get your car and my squad car in the picture."

"Of course," I say as I get out of the car.

We take a couple of shots. I take one of him pretending to catch a pass from Jasper and another where he pretends to handcuff me. Finally, he records a video of Jasper and me saying Merry Christmas to his two boys.

He tells us that he didn't notice us speeding, really, and it was just a safety stop. "But between us, slow the fuck down."

We get back in the car and sit in silence.

Jasper clears his throat. "Big T, I gotta say, you scared this kid. I've never been pulled over before."

A rough laugh comes from me. "Live a little longer. This is my third time this year."

"Did you get tickets?"

"Nah. I just smile, and it all goes away. I need some air." I get out of the car, slam the door, and walk off into a field. My head churns with what the future holds for me.

What is there after football?

What the fuck is there?

I hadn't realized he'd followed me, but Jasper appears and steps with me as I walk.

"Where are we going?"

"Nowhere. No destination. No goal. No plan. No fucking idea," I say as I tuck my hands in my joggers.

"I see."

I scoff.

He huffs. "Don't dismiss me because I'm young. You're going through some shit."

"What do you know about it?"

"You're having your worst year in football. It's getting close to Christmas, and it's a tough time for you."

I cut my eyes at him. "What are you talking about?"

"Last year, you got in a mood over the holidays. You stalked around all pissy and shit. You didn't put up a tree or come to my Christmas party."

"Sorry."

He kicks at the gravel. "I'm going home next week. I've got four sisters and all these aunts and uncles coming. They think I'm the shit, you know. They've got a big party planned. Lots of homemade pies and cookies. I was wondering, um, do you have plans over the holidays?"

My face feels hot, and I look up at the gray winter sky. No, I don't. I have distant relatives, but when they see me, they ask for money, and I usually give it. I went to Virginia last year, and when a cousin asked me to invest in his political campaign, I agreed, then left as soon as dessert was cleared. "Sure, I have plans. I'll go to Virginia. I have family there." My gut twists at the lie.

"And your mom?"

"She's going on a trip to Vermont with some of the residents at Greenwood."

Jasper fidgets. "Ah, I see. Well, I'm your Robin, Batman. I'm your bestie. Yeah, I know Ronan was your number one, and he was your age and wise and all that, but I'm the one now. I'd love for you to come to Utah and meet my family. My sisters will piss their pants, but you can't touch them, feel me? They're off limits, bro."

Jesus. He's feeling sorry for me.

"I'll pass, but I appreciate the offer."

"You can tell me stuff," he adds. "Make some peace with what's bugging you. How do I say this—what's the word . . . you're like, at critical mass. You're at the zero hour, and you can go either way: figure it out or blow the fuck up." He mimics an explosion with his hands.

My lips twitch. "Blowing up sounds ominous."

"Then don't."

Oh, if only it were that easy. He's right about one thing. I'm at a turning point. Then I recall Francesca's "crossroads." A long sigh comes from me as I tuck my hands in my joggers. We have that in common. Does she have holiday plans? I enjoyed our walks; then she stopped showing up. She said she didn't want to have dinner with me. I shake my head. It's not often I get turned down cold.

"Talk to me, Big T."

I kick at a piece of gravel as I face him.

No one can understand abuse unless they've lived it.

The constant fear.

The absence of security.

The crawling sense that you're not enough and never will be.

He grew up in Utah with a good family. What will he think of mine?

"My mom and I—shit, she had a manic episode and didn't even call me. The director had to fill me in. I don't know; she's been back for five years, and I just thought that things would be better between us, but they aren't. Toss in football, and my head is spinning."

He looks out over the field.

"She's still upset about your dad, yeah?"

I rub the scars on my wrist. "Yeah."

"You've never told me what happened."

My throat tightens. "I can't . . ."

"Put it out in the universe. Let the words out. Release your truth."

A long exhale leaves my chest. "You wanna know why she hates me?"

"Yeah. 'Cause I gotta tell you—you're a good fucking person. I can't understand a mother not wanting to see a man like you."

His words hit me in the chest, the truth in them, and I stare down at the ground, not wanting him to see the anguish on my face. "When I was little, she called me her sunshine. She marveled over how much I looked like my dad. She'd kiss me and say, 'You're gonna break hearts just like he does mine.'" I pause. "It was hard, being the person between them, but I did my best. I hated him but loved her energy, you know, the excitement. She'd write a play in one night. She'd design me an elaborate tree house and have someone build it. She'd put on her mink coat and go out and buy three cars at once. When I was in high school, she got obsessed with art. Over Christmas, we went to Paris, Rome, Milan—and hit every museum. We barely slept. I wanted to call my dad, but he knew—*he knew* she was in a phase and just let me deal with it." A scoff comes from me. "She made me love art."

I sigh. "It all went south when I came home for my twenty-fifth birthday. I was a superstar in the NFL; nothing could bring me down, but when I walked in that house . . ." I pause, keeping my voice calm, factual. "Mom was in one of her phases. She'd invited half the town, decorated the whole place. I brought my girlfriend and Ronan. An hour before guests were supposed to arrive, she got agitated. Nothing was right: the caterers, the decor, her dress, me. She said my dad invited his mistress. I don't know if that is true. My dad . . . he and I . . . we weren't close, but I wouldn't be surprised."

Jasper nods.

I clear my throat. "Anyway, she spent fifty grand on the party and called it off. Ronan and I tried to talk her down, but nothing would convince her. She accused Dad of cheating. He accused her of being a psycho and fucking any man she could find. She hit him; he punched her—then me and Ronan pulled him off. My girlfriend called the police, and my mom freaked. They were high society, and she didn't want anyone to know how fucked up we were. She tore her clothes, went after Ronan, then me. My dad stormed out of the house . . ." I stop, sucking in air. "He backed out of our driveway, revved the engine, then drove into a giant tree in our front yard."

I stare down at my hands, frowning at the scars. "The car door was stuck—and the other doors locked. I tried to go in through his window with a rock, then put my hands in to touch him. He was dead." I shake off the memory of my father's busted face, the blood from his chest. "My mom was screaming that it was my birthday, that it was my fault, that I shouldn't have been born. It was a mess. I had to manage the funeral and took a few weeks off." A huff comes from me. "My girlfriend tried to sell the story to the media, and I had to pay her off and get an NDA."

Jasper's eyes are wide. "Jesus, I'm sorry."

I nod. "Yeah. When I came back to New York, Mom sold the house, bought a million-dollar RV—one of those motor homes—and drove out west to meet a man she met online. She married him, some sleazy movie guy, then got divorced. She bought a house on the beach in Carmel, then sold it and moved to Nantucket with another man. She met another guy and moved to Boston. It just went round and round—a different guy, a different place. Some of them used her for her money. Maybe some loved her. Five years ago she got arrested for attacking a woman who was with her ex. She needed help and came to me. I paid off the woman, got the charges dismissed, and got her into Greenwood. It's not a mandatory place. It's not like an institution, so don't think I locked my mom away. I offered help, and she took it. She wanted to get herself straightened out. It felt like a restart for both of us, her coming to me, then getting treatment, but . . ."

"I'm sorry. What can I do?"

"Nothing." I face him. "My own mother despises me, and there's nothing anyone can do about that." I exhale. "Let's go home."

Chapter 10

FRANCESCA

Hey is the text I get from a number I don't recognize.

I pause under the canopy of Lottie's Bookstore and Coffee Shoppe. I only give my cell out to priority clients and friends.

Who is this? I send.

It's me. What are you doing right now?

I text out a reply. I'm super busy rewatching SpongeBob SquarePants, the Band Geek episode. You got my drugs? Me and my frat bros are waiting. Bring the good stuff this time.

Is this the episode where Squidward tries to impress his fancy cousin?

Okay, they know their *SpongeBob*. Wrong number, weirdo.

I throw my phone inside my leather satchel and walk inside and take my favorite table. The scent of coffee washes over me, and I inhale deeply.

When the waitress comes, I settle for a cup of apple cider. I study my appearance in the window, and excitement tingles over me. Today's meeting is with Mr. Jones, my first art client.

I fix the layered bangs I impulsively decided to cut last night, then apply more red lipstick. My cream silk blouse features a keyhole front, a vintage Versace piece from a secondhand shop. My black pencil skirt has a high waist and a gold belt. My leather ankle booties are scuffed but sturdy. My hair is up in a loose chignon, and my eyes are heavy with smoky eye shadow and black eyeliner.

I adjust in my seat. At fifteen weeks pregnant, I still have no noticeable bump, and all my clothes fit. My nausea has eased, my energy has spiked, but the moodiness still lingers. I guess it will until the end.

"Hello, Francesca. It's good to see you."

That voice. Soft and uncertain.

My heart stutters, and it takes several beats for me to move my eyes from the window to the man. I swallow thickly at his swept-back dirty-blond hair, the sapphire-blue eyes that always showed every emotion he felt.

"Levi?"

He tucks a hand inside a pair of stylish skinny jeans. A tentative smile curls his lips. "In the flesh. How long has it been?"

My cup rattles as I place it back on the saucer. "Um, years."

"Yeah. Too long." His shoulders do that hitching thing, where one rises fast and quick on one side, his nervous tell.

I clasp my hands in my lap and focus on appearing cool. "What are you doing in town?"

"I moved back last year. My dad passed away, and Mom wasn't in the best of health, so it seemed like the right thing to do." Before I can protest, he takes a seat across from me, then signals the waitress.

"I'm sorry about your dad." I tap my fingers on the lace tablecloth as realization dawns. "You don't seem surprised to see me. You're Mr. Jones?"

A slow blush creeps up his face. "Mr. Darden and I met a few years ago at an art gala in France. He sent me the email. I'm assuming he didn't realize our history."

He doesn't. "Well, let's hope the rest of my exes didn't get the email."

"I was shocked to see your name there." He winces. "Not because you wouldn't be a great art dealer; I was just surprised to see it in black and white. I couldn't pass up the chance to see you. I thought if you knew it was me, you wouldn't meet with me. Forgive me."

As always, he's apologetic and sweet. On the surface. Perhaps it goes deeper. I don't know.

Our eyes cling for long moments until the connection is broken by the waitress. He orders an espresso, then turns back to me. "I should have just called the number Mr. Darden sent and asked if it was okay to see you."

I prefer to be prepared when seeing the man who broke my heart, yes. "I don't like surprises, Levi. Besides, I thought you said it all in Rhode Island years ago."

He rakes a hand through his hair, then hitches his shoulders. "We're both living in the same city. We used to be friends, Francesca. Good ones." He dips his head, a soft chuckle coming from him. "I still laugh about the time we got married with a bubble ring—then it wouldn't come off your finger. No one would help you, and I gave in and stuck your hand in a bucket of ice."

"Hmm."

He smiles. "Then there was the time you were convinced a rat was in your room. You made me take part of a wall in the attic down to the studs. All we found were mouse bones."

A small twitch comes from my lips. "Those were some freaky bones. So tiny."

"You made me bury them far from the house."

I sigh, pushing those memories away. I focus on the ugly parts. "How's Maribelle?" I saw on Insta where they'd moved to Europe after college. In the early years of our breakup—if you can call it that—I used to keep up with him on my socials.

"She's married to a vineyard owner. Happily."

His espresso arrives, and he takes a sip. His lashes lower. "We broke up years ago. She wasn't you. No one really was. You were the perfect muse, Francesca."

I stiffen. "You can't say things like that."

"Even when it's true?" A wistful smile flashes over his face. "First love. My muse. It's hard to forget, Francesca."

I stare into his soulful eyes. I chew on my lip, my gaze brushing over his shoulders, the blue sweater he's wearing under a leather jacket. I used to lean on those shoulders as we stared up at the sky from my window in the attic. I stare at his hands, the fingers that used to trace the outline of my skin from head to toe as he memorized me.

"I'm sorry," he murmurs. "For all of it."

Emotion pricks at me, threatening to spill over. I swallow, my throat tight. I didn't mean to fall for my foster brother all those years ago, but I did.

Artistic and dreamy, Levi was the son of the affluent family I lived with for three years. My social worker promised they lived in a doll-house, and I didn't believe it until she drove up the driveway to their restored lavender-and-baby-blue Victorian. Three stories high with tall windows, wraparound porches, and a square tower that rose out of the center of the structure—nothing about it was subtle. I wanted to live there forever.

They gave me a room in the attic, a fancy canopied bed, designer clothes, and sketching pads and pencils. They enrolled me in private school, and I managed to make friends. I even liked his dad, one of the few males I trusted. His mother was kind, his little sister a joy, and, well, Levi—I think my young heart fell for him instantly. I'd never met anyone who loved art as much as I did.

I let my guard down and slept without worry.

The sun rose in his eyes.

The stars twinkled for him.

Oh, it was a foolish kind of love, but I believed he felt it too.

It all came to a halt when Levi's mother caught us having sex in the boathouse the summer before his senior year in college. He was twenty, and I was sixteen and enthralled with making love with him. We'd been doing it since I was fifteen, him sneaking in my room or vice versa.

I remember scrambling to cover myself with his shirt as his mother said horrible things—that I wasn't good enough, that he was toying with me, that he had a girlfriend at college. Maribelle.

He didn't stop her when she packed my bags and called CPS. I stared at the dollhouse as the social worker drove me away, weeping the entire way to the group home.

Everything I'd known for three years was ripped away. The best home I ever had.

"Francesca?"

I glance up.

"I didn't come to ambush you." His fingers draw patterns on the tablecloth. "I've kept up with you. I saw your engagement announcement, but I don't see a ring." His gaze lands on my left hand. "But then some people don't wear them."

"We broke up."

He tries to take my hand, but I ease it away. "Don't."

His head dips as a long exhale comes from his chest. "The day you came to see me in Providence, I should have followed you when you left. I was in shock. I didn't expect to see you, and I flaked."

Oh yes. That.

My lips curl. "You should have seen your face when I walked in your apartment with my ragged jeans and pink hair."

"Francesca—"

"And Maribelle? She literally called me an urchin. Who talks like that?"

"Uptight girls from Connecticut."

I glance away from him. Eighteen and fresh out of the group home, I'd tracked him down, caught a Greyhound, and shown up unannounced. Once I saw her with him, it was finally finished. It was a relief to let him go. I could stop dreaming. I could stop loving. I moved on, went to art school, got my apartment, and buried my heart deep, sleeping my way through a long string of Levi types. Edward fit that bill.

Clarity hits. Is that why I never completely committed to my relationship with him? I huff under my breath. Edward is a bastard for cheating, but he was right about him not being what I wanted. I must have been insane. Or lonely.

He takes my hand. This time I don't pull away, part of me curious if there's any feeling left. "My parents insisted I keep my distance. I was too old for you, but you were so beautiful that I—"

"Francesca?" comes another man's voice, one who's just stepped into the store and walked to our table. I tear my eyes off Levi. Tuck's wearing black joggers and a tight long-sleeved workout shirt, and his hair is tousled from the wind outside and hangs around his stark cheekbones.

A small laugh comes from me, and when I speak, my voice is teasing. "Hey. I was here first. Did you follow me this time?"

His green eyes skate over my face, taking in my features one by one, lingering on my mouth. His gaze narrows in on my hand in Levi's. He smiles. "Or did you know I like this bookstore? They have great protein shakes. I get two a week."

"I've been coming here long before you showed up. My tea, remember?"

"Sweetheart, I found this place when I first moved here fourteen years ago. Stop stalking me." He smiles, slow and easy, then leans down with a palm on the table. His massive body fills up the space as his fingers toy with my locket. "I figured out where I've seen this."

"Where?"

Ignoring that, he touches my cheek. "You look fucking magnificent, Princess. It's been a while, and I've missed you."

A blush crawls up my cheeks. I've missed our walks. The random chitchat. The brush of his shoulder against mine.

Before I can rear back, he brushes his lips over my cheek, then purrs in my ear, "Just when you think I'll zig, I zag."

I sputter and pull my hand from Levi's.

"Who's your friend?" Tuck says.

"Levi, an old friend of Francesca's," he says tightly. "And you're Tuck Avery, right? Player for the Pythons?"

"Hmm," Tuck murmurs as he grabs a chair from a table nearby and sits down at the end. "Mind if I join you?"

"By all means," I say dryly.

Levi stiffens. "Actually, we were in the middle—"

"Lori, I'll have a green smoothie," Tuck calls out to the waitress who's at the counter. He gives her a blinding smile, and she titters and gives him a thumbs-up.

"Apparently, you know every waitress's name in Manhattan," I say.

He smiles. "I'm a charmer."

But underneath, darkness simmers. I sense it on the verge of spilling over. I like that about him. The shadows.

"Now, what were you saying?" Tuck murmurs as he places his elbows on the table. "Oh, yeah, you and the princess know each other . . ."

"Princess?" Levi asks.

I take a sip of my cider, ignoring Tuck and Levi's question.

Tuck nods knowingly. "Yeah, man. Pet names usually follow after sex."

My mouth parts as the waitress sets down his green smoothie.

"Tuck—" I snap, but he cuts me off.

"Yes, sweetheart?"

"Can we talk later?" I hiss. "Please."

He takes a sip of his drink. "Sure. In a few."

I grit my teeth, and he smiles back.

"Ah, so you two are . . . ?" Levi asks, his voice trailing off.

"Yes," Tuck says. "Very much."

I groan. "It—"

"It's complicated," Tuck interrupts, giving Levi a steely look. "But it's going places." He slides his eyes to me. "Did I tell you that Herman wants in on the coat thing?"

I blink, readjusting my train of thought. "Oh?"

"He's putting boxes in the lobby for donations. It's going to be a thing. Here's my idea: I want to start a nonprofit that sets up stations all over the city. We can purchase coats from stores; take donations from businesses, from athletes I know; put up billboards. Of course, it's just on the ground level, but by next year it could really be special. What do you think?"

"You're going to fund it?"

"Yep." He leans closer to me. "It could be a nationwide thing. What do you think?"

My lips twitch. "Imagine the endorphins your brain will release. Can we discuss it later?" I really need to settle this Levi thing, and Tuck doesn't have the right to sit down and act like we're together.

He nods. "The nonprofit could do more than just coats. We could set up centers in major cities for free counseling and shelter." He slaps the table and checks out Levi. "Sorry to monopolize her. Who are you again?"

"An old friend," Levi snaps. "You've interrupted—"

"Ah, an ex, I presume." Tuck twists his lips. "Don't feel special. She has several. I really think you should go. Like now."

I gape at him. What is wrong with him? Is he . . . jealous?

Levi exhales. "I see. This isn't the best moment for a conversation, Francesca." He rises from his seat and places a twenty on the table. "It was great seeing you. You're even more beautiful than I remember." His blue eyes burn as they drift over me.

111

"Get moving," Tuck says as he waves his hands at him.

"I have an opening at the Reinhart Gallery in February," he continues, ignoring Tuck. "It's an exhibition for several artists, and I'd love for you to come and see what I've been working on. It's invitation only, a gala. Perhaps you can do some shopping for your clients."

"Sure," I say uncertainly.

He nods, then walks out the door.

"I don't like him," Tuck says as he takes a sip of his drink. "Super douchey."

My temper stirs. "I'm happy about your nonprofit idea, but you shouldn't have been so rude." I put down money on the table for my cider.

"Where are you going?" Tuck asks as I grab my leather satchel.

"Not your business. I'm not your property, nor do we have anything that's 'complicated.'"

"Is it weird that I sort of wish you were stalking me? Yeah, I guess it is."

I huff. "What's wrong with you today?"

"I saw you from the street," he mutters. "Not on purpose. I was just walking by to get my shake."

"I'm sorry you had to witness me with another man."

Before he can follow, I flip around and head up the stairs to the books. He's still on my heels as I pass other patrons milling around the shelves. "That guy was your ex? Was he an important one?"

"Ha, you seem to already know about my exes, and don't give me grief—I've read about yours. I can't even count that high."

"So you looked me up?" I hear the smile in his voice.

Of course I did. He grew up super rich. His parents owned most of Virginia. Old money.

I hit the third level of the store. Shelves of books create dark shadows as I walk faster. It's quiet, with most of the customers downstairs. Our only company is a few cobwebs and old books.

"Slow down. Pretty sure you'll hurt yourself in those shoes."

I face him. "What was that down there?"

He leans down to me, his nose to mine. He smells like sexy Christmas again, peppermint and spice, only this time it doesn't make me queasy. It makes my insides quake.

"I want you. You want me. What else is there? I've missed you."

I shake my head at him, floundering for words.

"It's like this. I was just walking past and saw you in the window. You had this, I don't know, sad expression on your face when he sat down. I watched for a while, debating; then I decided you needed rescuing."

"I see." I march down one of the aisles, heaving a breath when I realize it doesn't connect and I've hit a dead end. There's a large window, and I glance out at the traffic on the street. With only five days left until Christmas, the shoppers are everywhere.

"Do you wanna talk about it?" he asks.

I turn, and he's leaning against a shelf, a somber expression on his face.

It's a surprise, that somberness, as if he cares, and I swallow. I pick up a book and hold it. "Do you like sappy stories about young girls who get their hearts broken?"

Anger flashes in his eyes. "He hurt you."

"It was a long time ago."

"Hearts don't forget."

"You don't even know what happened or who he is."

"I know enough."

I set that comment aside for a moment. "You've had your heart broken?"

He comes closer. "I tend to keep it locked away." He touches a strand of my hair, curling it around his finger. "Women leave me eventually. Can't say I blame them."

"Why?"

"I don't want marriage and kids, and I'm up front. I just want to play football until I'm done."

"And after?"

"I like the nonprofit idea. It's a way to give back. Plus, I have a yacht. I take it out every February after football is over. Ever been to the Amalfi Coast?"

"I've never left the States." I've vacationed with Cece and Brogan in California, but my heart is always in New York.

"Wanna go?"

I scoff. "I'll start packing today. How many bathing suits should I bring?"

He laughs, then stops, his lids lowering. "You'd look great in a bikini, a black one. I'd show you every island in the Mediterranean. We'll go to Sorrento, see the cliffs, the fishing villages. We'll go to dinner at a place with a view of the water and coastline. You'll never want to leave."

A wan smile crosses my face. "No family for you, huh?"

He glances away. "It's complicated, but since I was twentysomething, I knew it wasn't part of my goals."

"You're honest about what you want. Most men aren't."

"Are you honest?" His finger traces my neck, and my breath quickens.

I moisten my lips as my nerves jump. "Not all the time. I have secrets."

"Little Miss Dark."

Our eyes hold, and electricity zaps down my spine.

He is everything I shouldn't want, but . . .

I close the distance between us. My hands move up his chest and curl around his neck. My fingers tangle in his hair. "Here's a secret for you."

"Yeah?"

"I knew you came to this place. I've seen you here several times. You bumped into me once. You were wearing preppy shorts, a blue collared shirt, and boat shoes. I bet you were on the way to your yacht for the summer. There was a movie star with you or some pop singer. She couldn't stop giggling when I dropped my muffin. I found you—and her—annoying. Don't get excited about it. I never followed you here."

"If there was a way to go back in time, I'd dump her and take you with me." His fingers trace down my spine, then cup my ass. I brush my hips against the tent in his joggers, and he shudders. "Finally. Baby. Been wanting you to touch me."

Memories assail my senses: how he needed me that night at Decadence, the loss of control when we fucked, how he let it all out, his shouts, the wild look in his eyes. He was a storm of insatiable need. And I felt our communion, reveled in it.

We had *something* that I'd never experienced.

As he kisses my neck, a battle is in my head as I war with what I *should* do.

"You undo me, Princess . . ."

My body gives in, and I press a kiss against his neck, my body melting. I whisper in his ear. "I've seen you in Café Lazzo. Always with beautiful women."

His lips brush my cheek, then trail down my neck. "I don't recall their names. All I want is you, Francesca." A hand tugs my blouse out of my skirt; then his fingers graze the lace of my bra. "Jesus," he rasps as I arch into his hands. "Your tits are perfect."

And bigger.

His hands cup my jaw tenderly. "Let me kiss you."

My hands slip under his workout shirt as we lock gazes. My no-kissing rule is to protect myself from getting attached to the men I have sex with. The number of men I've kissed on the lips can be counted on one hand. "No."

His lashes flutter. "Yes."

"No."

"Yes," he murmurs as his lips kiss my collarbone.

I gasp as heat pools deep inside me, my core tightening and fluttering. He pulls my skirt up to my waist as I inch up his shirt, then tug it over his head.

My breath hitches. I'd forgotten what a work of art his body is—hard, chiseled muscles; the beautiful color of his skin; the pink nipples; the delicious V that dips down to his waistband. I lick his nipple, and he shivers.

"Princess, if you do that, we're gonna fuck right here." He pulls me up and sets me on the window ledge. His fingers dance over my panties, tracing down the center of my core.

"I haven't been able to get you out of my head," he murmurs, his gaze hooded. "You don't show up for walks."

My head falls back against the glass as his finger moves the fabric of my underwear and dips inside me. He comes back out to circle my clit.

"I want to know why we met. Why you drive me crazy . . ." He slips another finger inside me, and I groan. "Yeah, that. I love the sounds you make, sweetheart. Let me tell you some secrets. I went to Notre Dame. My parents were a piece of work, and I couldn't wait to get away from them. I majored in history, then got drafted to the Pythons."

My hand reaches under the elastic of his pants. I take his cock and caress it with my palm, pumping him to the rhythm of his fingers. "I can find that out on the internet."

"I have superugly feet. Downright scary." He presses a kiss to the cream lace of my bra. His teeth bite one nipple, then the other. Shocks ricochet over my skin.

I gasp. "I've seen your feet. That's an accurate assessment."

He pulls down the cups of my bra, pushes my breasts together, and rubs his scruff over them.

"Cece gave me your cell," he mumbles, the reverberation of his voice against my skin delicious. "I saw her in the lobby today. She said, 'The best way to find yourself is to lose yourself.' Is that odd behavior?"

My fingers tangle in his hair, and my voice is breathless. "Normal. So that was you earlier? Texting me?"

He grins against my skin as he glances up, and the genuineness of it takes my breath. I've only seen his real smile a few times. "Yep. And you can't be mad at me. She offered it."

"I'm going to kill her slowly." I run my fingers over the sharp angles of his jawline. "Maybe you're the real stalker . . ."

My words trail off as his finger slides back inside of me. He pumps slow and steady, his thumb circling my nub. I bite my lip to hold in my groan.

"Does that feel good?"

I nod.

"You wanna come?"

"Yes."

He strokes, exploring the dips and valleys as my breath quickens.

"So responsive . . ." His eyes glitter down at me. "So wet."

He sucks a nipple into his mouth. My hips thrust to meet him, aching to reach the pinnacle, to grab hold of ultimate pleasure.

"Have you been finger banged in public?"

When I nod, his eyes burn with jealousy. That glint only sends me a little further under his spell.

"I want to see you in my bed. I want to fuck you. I want you to suck me off." His voice rumbles against my skin, and goose bumps dance over me.

My fingers dig into his arms as he draws circles on my clit, getting closer and closer, and when he finally hits one place, I stiffen. My breath hitches as I come, my core grasping around him. It feels so good, so perfect.

He kisses my cheek. "I want to see your face over candlelight. I want to take you to dinner."

Oh. I suck in a breath and drop my gaze from his.

He tugs my face and holds my eyes. "If I can't kiss you, you're going to look at me when I fuck you."

I shiver as his fingers delve back inside me.

"We might get caught," I manage to say.

"Isn't that part of the fun?"

I hear the clink of glasses downstairs, the low murmur of patrons on the floor below us. "Yes."

I ease my hands back inside his joggers. He's long and thick, a slight curve near the tip that I recall always hit the perfect spot when he was inside me. I stroke his mushroom-shaped tip to his root, my fingers brushing over his balls. I find the precum and caress his knob, touching the underside of his tip. His chest expands, his pupils dilating as he moves his hips in sync.

"Talk to me," he demands. "Secrets."

"I went to the New York School of the Arts. I woke up wet this morning thinking about you. I woke up wet for weeks after the club. You were the best fuck. I looked for you. I stopped at construction sites. I peered into shop windows."

He bites his bottom lip, his teeth tugging hard. "Go on."

"Your dick tastes like salt and sea. I could swallow you in one gulp."

His lashes flutter. "Let's forget this place. Come home with me." His throat bobs. "Now."

"I wish you could rip my clothes off. I wish you could get on your knees and lick me where I want."

Sweat mists his face as he leans into me. "My place . . ."

I trace the plump outline of his lips. "Here."

He groans as he tugs my hair and places his lips on my skin. "You're killing me, Princess." With a skill that suggests he's done this a million times, he eases me down, drags my underwear down my legs, and then hoists me back up in his arms and sets me on the ledge. My heart flutters as wetness drips down my legs.

I hear the crinkle of a wrapper; then I watch as he slides the condom on. My arms wrap around his neck as he picks me back up. "Look at me."

I do, and he thrusts inside of me. My body welcomes his thick girth like a lost lover, warm and willing.

His hands cup my ass as he swivels his hips and sets a slow, methodical pace.

I moan from deep in my throat, trying to suppress the guttural sound. I've been with lots of men, but he's a master at fucking.

My back pushes against the cold glass of the window, and I wonder if anyone on the street sees us. If someone comes around the corner, they'll see me with my shirt and skirt in disarray, my legs tangled around his, the pump of his naked ass. I don't care right now if they do—my brain is lost, my body is lost, all is lost. Just this. Just this. And it's so damn good.

We fuck quietly, gasps held back as his forearms strain and pop.

We fuck slow, savoring the glide of his cock.

We fuck.

And fuck.

And fuck.

Hard. Slow. Hard. Slow.

It's as if we're working out our aggression, our crazy need, while inside I know this can't mean anything. He doesn't want kids; he's not a commitment guy. I'm his, right now, and that's okay, but men like him . . . a month from now, it'll be someone new for him. He has a yacht. He dates models, movie stars, and singers. I'm just . . . me. Whatever. Who cares right now?

He says my name, and our breaths mingle, our lips a hair's breadth apart as we stare each other down.

He moves my knees up as his hands hold my legs. He dips his head to my neck as tingles of heat boil in my spine. He fucks me with purpose, a hot, desperate look on his face. I feel the burn in my spine.

It's coming fast, too fast, when I want to savor it. My nails dig into his skin as I inhale his scent, tasting the spice, his pheromone that drives me crazy.

I lock eyes with him as I circle myself.

He murmurs my name . . .

It's the trigger I need.

Little quakes of pleasure multiply and build until they spring free. I spasm, my walls squeezing him.

He's talking, saying something, his body hardening, his hands bruising my hips. His body jolts, and he stiffens as he goes over the edge, his breath coming in short bursts of air. His chest leans into me for several moments; then his hands card through my hair with a gentleness I didn't expect.

Moments later, he tips my face up to his and gazes at my lips. He kisses his finger, then touches it to my mouth. "You. Are. Fucking. Hot."

My legs are weak as he stands back and slowly untangles us. I ease shaky legs to the floor.

He removes the condom and ties it off while I grab my panties and tuck my shirt back in my skirt. I toss him his shirt, and he slips it on, then adjusts his joggers.

"Want to grab some lunch?" he says, watching me as I reapply my lipstick.

Do I want lunch?

What else do you say after fucking in a public place?

"I have to go."

"Where? I'll come with. I'm free most of the day." He uses the window reflection to brush his hair back off his face. It's sexy as hell, and when he turns to look at me, a long exhale comes from my chest. Unease crawls over me, this urge to tell him that I can't see him because I'm having his baby and he doesn't want one.

My hands fist. I want to have lunch with him, to get to know him better . . .

"I, um, have another client this afternoon." Truth.

He frowns as he searches my face, then sticks his hands in his joggers and fidgets. "I got the email from Darden. Congrats on the position. You've got a powerful man backing you. Impressive. He must care a lot about you."

"It's not like that, you know. We're only friends. We just click."

A half smile crosses his face. "I wasn't implying anything."

Good. I nod.

"If you come to my place, I'll show you my art." He bats his lashes at me, and I can't help the smile it brings to my face.

I take my satchel off the windowsill. "That sounds fun, but some other time."

He narrows his gaze as he puts his hands on his hips. "You're brushing me off. Unbelievable."

I sigh. "We both got what we wanted. Don't make this awkward—"

"I'm not awkward. In fact, I'm pretty fucking confident that was the best fuck you've had since Decadence," he growls.

"Tuck. This—"

His jaw twitches. "Yeah, whatever, this was great. Awesome, really. Thanks for the hookup."

I walk toward him and stop at his side as the chemistry we share tugs at me.

I have a plan. Save money, have a baby, keep living my life. Without Tuck knowing.

I swallow. I should be dashing out of here as if the hounds of hell are at my feet—so what's keeping me from walking away?

"I had you looked into," he mutters, his gaze on the window. "I want to be honest. It's what I would have done to anyone based on how we met. I've had women I've dated who've tried to sell stories of me."

I gasp. "You investigated me?"

He shakes his head. "Just listen. The worst was a stripper, Lollipop."

Frowning, I nod. "I recall the cops came and arrested someone who attacked you."

He sighs. "Yeah. Maybe I was nice to her—I don't know—but she got fixated on me. She sent emails, letters, even posted images of me going into places on her socials. Me in the supermarket, at dinner, at the stadium. She tried to get into my mom's facility. It went on for months. Then she tried to stab me." He rubs his jaw. "You'd think I could have handled the stress, but it hurt my trust in people. It made me think maybe I was naive when it comes to judging others. It's funny because the homeless people, they don't care who I am. They're some of the kindest people I've ever met." He exhales. "So, anyway, that's why I had you investigated."

"Your experience must have been horrible." I swallow, my head tumbling. My hands clench. "So what did you discover about me?"

"I know about Brogan—and that he works at Decadence."

I inhale sharply. Tuck met with the owners of Decadence and got Prince Rolex kicked out . . .

My words come in a rush. "Brogan had nothing to do with us. He only got me and Cece a guest pass. He never knows who's coming in until that night, when he's given an envelope of names and guests. Don't you dare get him fired."

He turns to me. "I know he doesn't know who's coming in. I checked. When you've been through what I have, you check and recheck."

Fear ripples over me. I have some secrets I don't want him to know. "What else did you find out?"

He glances away. "Cece is an escort."

"Ah, you got the whole story, huh? What will you do with this information?"

"Nothing, Francesca. I'm sorry I had to do it. I'm sorry I needed it to make myself feel better." His face softens. "You were abandoned as a baby."

Unbidden, tears pool in my eyes.

"I know you were sent back to a group home at sixteen because of Levi. He should have been prosecuted, but his family brushed your relationship with him under the rug, and CPS let them. You were attacked by another resident at the home; it's how you got the scar on your hip. You were arrested for weed at twenty, but it was dismissed. You dated various men, briefly, then ended up in a relationship with Edward, a trust fund idiot with zero ambition. You worked at East Coast Ink & Gallery but got fired because the manager wanted to humiliate you a little more. You came to Decadence on your wedding day—which just happened to be my birthday. It was a coincidence."

My chest rises. "You had no right! Was all of that necessary?"

"Put yourself in my shoes, Francesca." He cups my cheeks, his thumb wiping at a tear that escaped. "This is me apologizing. I'm sorry I had to do that."

"How long have you known all that?"

He pauses. "A couple of weeks."

"On our walks?"

He shakes his head. "No."

"So you were risking it then, huh?"

"Because I wanted to be around you. Don't be angry. When you're who I am, it's not unreasonable to look into people." His voice lowers as he touches my shoulder, a soft caress. "Let's put this behind us. Tell me I'm not the only one who wants this . . ."

My throat tightens as I ease away from him. It's less about the invasion of privacy and more about my personal secrets. I have to keep us shallow. It's the only way.

"Francesca—"

"I'll see you around," I manage to say, then push past him, down the stairs, and out the door.

Chapter 11

Francesca

"You're starting to annoy me," I grouse to Cece as we walk down Fifth Avenue on our way back to Wickham.

"Only now? I thought it was when I dragged you into Pottery Barn." She sighs dramatically. "I loved the ducky bedding. Gray and yellow. So soothing. And gender neutral since you don't want to find out the sex. I could make something if you want. Sewing—and sex—are my superpowers."

"Uh-huh." We spent an hour there, and all I wanted to do was take a nap on one of the beds.

"Back to food. No raw fish or undercooked meat. No unwashed produce. No unpasteurized cheese, milk, or fruit juice. We don't want any gross bacteria to hurt baby Cecelia."

I grunt. "First Brogan and now you. I'm aware of the food list! I had sushi one time, and you freaked out, but it *was* cooked. Even Brogan said it was okay."

She ignores me. "Raw eggs and hollandaise sauce are also off the list. Homemade cake icing, ice cream, and mayo."

"No issue there." I swallow down the urge to gag. "Mayo is gross."

"No coffee. You snuck some this morning."

"I had three sips! Three!" I throw my head back and shake my fist at the sky. "Maybe that's why I feel violent! I need caffeine! It's not fair!"

"No alcohol, no processed food . . . hmm, so that means no fries, chips, bacon—"

"You're vicious! Give me bacon! Come on!"

"For Cecelia—whose middle name can be Ivy—no bacon."

"Mmm, fries from McDonald's would be so good. With bacon."

She takes my arm as we walk up to the entrance of our building. "Let's get you upstairs."

"I'm not a baby deer. I can walk by myself." I untangle myself from her. "I need some space. Please. I'm cranky and kind of horny. It's a weird combo."

"But—"

"No more monitoring my coffee in the morning." I stomp ahead of her in my three-inch stacked black Converse. "While you were in LA, I had fries. Herman had them delivered; bless his soul."

"Get your pregnant ass inside, missy."

"You're pregnant?" Herman bellows, and I turn to see he'd followed us to open the door. Wearing a scarf with Santa faces on it and a red bow tie, he gives me a wide smile.

"Er, um, well . . ." My eyes dart around the entrance to see if anyone else heard. I sigh. He'll notice my growing belly soon in the coming months. "Yeah?"

"Congratulations!" He gives me a hug. "How are you feeling? If you need anything, just ring me, yeah? Or ask for Tony. He's my nephew who works security. Hard worker. He'll dash out if I'm not here and get you anything you're craving. Christmas is just a few days away, so if you feel weak and need someone to do your last-minute shopping, the girl at the front desk is looking for extra work—"

"Herman . . ." I glance around again, nodding and smiling at passing residents. One of them is Widow Carnes. Shit, shit. I adjust my black moto jacket over my harem pants and stand taller. She's like the mean teacher you had in school, the one who carried a ruler around and slapped your palm if you misbehaved.

"How are you, dear?" she asks, pausing as Herman opens the door for her.

"Oh, just wonderful." I give her my biggest smile. "You?"

"Just wonderful." She narrows her gaze. "Tell Mr. Darden I said hello." She snubs Cece, their usual.

"Have a nice day," I call as she walks away. I exhale slowly. I imagined that look she gave my stomach. Right?

I mean, sure, people *might* know if they see me later in my pregnancy, but winter and cold weather are great for hiding with baggy sweatshirts and coats. Frustration hits as I chew my lower lip. I've managed to not run into Tuck for the last few days. My only outings have been a doctor's appointment, a client meeting, and today.

Football season wraps up at the end of January, which means he'll be on his yacht in February and gone for months. His summer camp—I googled it—starts at the end of July. By then, I'll have a two-month-old. I groan inwardly. He's going to see me. Eventually. Should I move from Wickham? Never. It's my home. And Mr. Darden is here. He's elderly. He needs me. Okay, fine. I'll become a hermit. I'll take side exits. I'll avoid the lobby and elevator. I'll say it's not my baby. I'm babysitting. I adopted.

Oh my God. I'm officially insane.

How will this ever work?

Just tell him, a small voice says.

March right up to his place, knock on the door, and say the words.

My heart squeezes in my chest, and my mouth dries. What if he rejects me? What if he rejects our child? My hands settle on my stomach. I'm supposed to protect her from people who don't want her in the world. I've tasted the sharp sting of people not wanting me. I've lived with it for thirty years. I don't want it for my child.

Herman breaks into my thoughts. "You think you might need a crib? My daughter might have one—"

"I'm buying it," Cece says tartly. "All white. Sleigh-style. It's being delivered soon."

Oh. I didn't know. It's the one I liked from the catalog, and I smile at her, then glance back at Herman. I give him a wink. "Hey, let's keep this pregnancy on the down low. It's a secret, okay?"

He stands straighter. "Right. Best to see if it sticks. My wife was the same."

"Well, it's more than that," I say, floundering.

Cece takes over as she hooks our arms together and gives him her kindest smile. "Herman, it's like this: I may look angelic, but I will stab you in the nuts if you spill the news—or bring her fries."

He blanches as I nod and whisper, "We call her the Angel of Nut Stabbing."

"Oh." He swallows. "You always look so nice, Cece."

She puts a hand over her heart. "Why, thank you—but don't trust me, yeah?"

The desk attendant, a pretty girl in her early twenties, calls my name, and we leave a frowning Herman and head that way.

"You have a package, Miss Lane," she says excitedly from behind the desk. She darts to the back and returns with a small box wrapped in brown paper. "It came last week, but somehow it got put in the wrong place. Apologies."

"Okay." I'm not expecting anything. Edward hasn't left flowers or notes lately. I feel certain he said everything he wanted that night in my apartment.

She blushes. "It's from Mr. Avery."

"Oh." I frown. I assumed he was done with me, but if this came last week . . .

"He's, like, the hottest guy in the building," she adds. "You're such a lucky girl."

"Hmm." I sign the receipt.

She leans in, her voice lowering. "I like you better than Courtney Neil—you know, the supermodel. She's been coming in and out of his place. I think she lives there—"

"Hey," Cece says sharply, cutting her off. "We don't need a play-by-play. We already know how virile he is. He's got big-dick energy. Just ask Francesca—"

"Cece," I warn.

She scowls and mutters under her breath as I lead her away from the desk to the sitting area of the lobby. We plop down in a pair of club chairs near the windows. I set the package on a side table and focus on her. My moods come from pregnancy hormones, but she's been extra snippy today.

She throws her hands up as she crosses her legs. "Ugh. She's just so perky and pretty and . . ."

"Young?"

She adjusts her green Stella McCartney minidress. "Yes, it's true; women in their twenties annoy me, all dewy complexions and innocence. Disgusting." A long exhale comes from her.

"What's really wrong?"

She pauses for a moment, wariness on her face. She then leans in and squeezes my hand. "Okay, you know how I've been planning to retire from being a companion? I'm getting older, and men want the young girls. Plus, design is something I've always wanted to try."

I nod.

"I've decided I'm moving to California—with Lewis."

My head races. "Wait. What? You're *leaving* New York?"

She chews on her lip. "Not right away. I'll stay until the baby is born in June, then fly back and forth, maybe once a month? Auntie Cece, remember?"

I shake my head. "When did all this happen?"

"Life changes when you least expect it—you know that." She stares at her hands. "Lewis asked me to marry him a few months ago, but I didn't mention it because you'd gone through the Edward thing, then lost your job—then the baby news came along. Plus, I was still deciding if I'd accept his offer . . ." She pauses. "This last time I saw him in LA, I said yes. You'll adore him, Fran."

I process through my muddled brain. Lewis, right. Geeky Silicon Valley tech-business owner. Billionaire.

"He wants to get married next fall. He loves me or thinks he does. Dumb, right? Anyway, he bought me a house in Palo Alto a while back, remember? I've barely been there, but he gave it to me to use whenever I want. It's so pretty, Fran: lakes and gardens and gorgeous furniture."

Nausea bubbles in my stomach. She never told me. She never asked me for advice. What is happening to us?

"Oh, Fran, honey, your face is doing that red thing. I'm sorry to throw this at you right now. I really thought I'd end up staying here with you, but this feels right. The good news is that since I told Lewis yes, I've let my clients go. You're my focus right now."

She continues, "And, if you want, we could all make a new start in California. You can get settled in my house and figure out what you want to do. Maybe find a cool place in LA to work. Brogan can go back to med school. Lewis is totally on board with whatever makes me happy, Fran, and me happy is knowing you are okay." She tightens her clasp on my hands. "I know how you feel about being left behind, but I'm not really leaving; I'm just moving. We can text and talk all the time."

Help from Lewis? I don't want his help. I don't freaking know him. And he's taking my friend away.

"Are you okay?"

I pull away from her. "No, Cece, I'm not. You didn't even tell me. I'm your best friend. You're . . ." Abandoning me. "My family. I'm having a baby! I thought you'd be here!"

"I'm sorry." Her lip wobbles. "Truly. I didn't want to upset you, honey."

I rub my forehead, willing the stupid tears away.

It's just . . .

She's the friend who knows all your dirty secrets and doesn't bat a lash. She's the life of the party who makes sure you get home, then tucks you in. She's the girl who makes you giggle even when it feels like the end of the world. My head plays snapshots of us bingeing *Gilmore Girls* in our pj's, the game nights with Mr. Darden where she steals something just to make him come looking for her. I've seen her fall apart—and held her—when she lost her parents, when a client got handsy and smacked her around.

She's one half of my ride or die.

I wrestle with my emotions, part of me wanting to be happy for her. But the other side is terrified of losing her. "Do you love him?"

She smiles slowly, the sincere one. "Oh, honey, I don't have a heart, but he makes it beat. I like him a whole, whole lot."

My throat tightens. What can I say to *that*?

I push down my anxiety. "If you stick me in some god-awful fluffy southern bridesmaid dress, I will stab *you* in the eye. I do not do bows on my ass."

She throws her arms around me. "Honey, your dress will be couture and make you look fabulous. Now open that gift before I have a hissy fit wondering what it is."

"Fine." I tear the brown paper, open the box, and gasp at the gold necklace. The chain shimmers in the sunlight from the windows, highlighting the two-inch teardrop emerald in the center. On either side are two slightly smaller topaz jewels. My fingers rub the stone in the middle. It's his eyes: green with yellow sparks. "Tuck," I whisper.

"So pretty, and oh my God; nothing says 'I want to fuck you' like shiny jewels." She claps her hands. "Just looking at them makes me hot."

"It matches his eyes." I ease the necklace back inside the velvet box and pick up the handwritten note.

For the beautiful girl I met by chance . . .
Merry Christmas
Tuck

I picture him writing the words. It's sweet. So very sweet. I'm chewing on my lips as a woman waltzes into the lobby.

Courtney. My eyes narrow, forgetting the necklace. She stops for a moment, tightens her lips when she sees us, and then puts her nose in the air. As she disappears around the corner to the elevators, I stuff the necklace in my satchel and motion for Cece to follow me.

"What's going on?" she asks as she stands.

"Remember when we crashed Daniel Radcliffe's party in the West Village?" I say as we fast walk to the elevators.

"I do love me some Harry Potter, and he was so sweet. Adored his wife. You made out with one of them, right?"

"Um, that was you, with her, while he watched."

"Huh. Fun party," she says. "Okay, so we're following the supermodel. No matter what happens, I'm your human shield. Like Captain America, only better. My life before yours—oops, I meant your life before mine. Believe me; I will take that bitch to the ground and stomp on her with my Jimmy Choos."

"Never doubted you."

We ease inside the elevator like two church mice. Several residents are there, and as we go up, they get off on their floors. Courtney has already punched in the code for the penthouse and scrolls on her phone.

We reach the penthouse level, and she looks up, eyes flaring. "Hey, what's going on? You need a pass code for this level."

"But, darling, you already punched it in." Cece wiggles her fingers at her as we dart into the hallway.

"And why are we doing this exactly?" She crooks her arm in mine.

"Um . . ." My heart jumps in my chest, not because we pulled one over on Courtney, although that was deliciously fun, but because . . .

Dammit. Because I want to see him.

I stop for half a second to fluff my bangs and check my lipstick. I'm about to knock when a shirtless Jasper flings open the penthouse door. "Dude. I thought you were my bracelet delivery, but hey, I fucking love company! Come on in!"

Rather bemused, we follow him inside and enter a three-storied marbled foyer. The walls are stark white with a modern-looking chandelier hanging from the ceiling.

He chuckles. "In person, Snow White and Princess Bride together. I love it. Welcome to my temporary home. I'm in the process of getting a kick-ass place below this. It's gonna be awesome when it's done. Big T is going to miss me; he just doesn't know it."

Cece gives him a smooch on the cheek. "Congrats, Prince Cupid. How is Prince of Princes? I hope he misses me."

"Deacon? I can text him if you want." He pulls his phone out and wiggles it.

She puts her hand over her chest. "Sadly, I'm taken, but give him a kiss for me."

"He enjoyed his evening with you," Jasper says.

"Did you have sex with Deacon?" I whisper out of the side of my mouth.

"I'm wonderful without sex, honey. He'll never forget me," she hisses back.

Jasper clears his throat and smiles. "So what's up? You ladies just out strolling and popped by?"

"Yes. Is Tuck around?" I ask.

"They snuck up on the elevator," Courtney grouses as she marches in the foyer, her four-inch heels clicking against the marble. She hangs a short pink fur coat on a hook and tosses her handbag on an ottoman.

"We missed our floor and kept going," I say.

"You did it on purpose," she snaps.

"Get over yourself, Courtney. These girls are always welcome." He turns to me. "Big T is out, sorry, but stay. I got a new margarita machine I'm playing with. It's my present to myself, and it's fabulous. How about a drink? I've got strawberry, pineapple, or regular?"

Cece waltzes past Courtney. "How kind of you! You pick my flavor, Jasper. Extra tequila, please."

"Francesca? You want one?" he asks as we follow him deeper inside the penthouse to an open plan with a den and kitchen. I take in the white leather furniture and heavy glass tables, the floor-to-ceiling windows that show Central Park and Manhattan. A white fur rug is in front of a split fireplace that opens to a room lined with bookshelves.

My eyes widen at the metal-fenced staircase that leads to the upper levels. Jeez. I mean, yeah, it takes up three stories and some of the rooftop, but it's a freaking mansion in the sky. My apartment would fit in the den-and-kitchen area alone.

"Strawberry, please," I murmur faintly as my anxiousness ramps up.

He's rich. He has power. He had me investigated. He has freaking lawyers.

"Francesca, are you *sure* you want alcohol today?" Cece says as she elbows me and nudges her head at the margarita machine.

"Oh, right. Nothing for me, then. I'm going to a gallery later," I tell Jasper as he moves around the kitchen, gathering supplies.

"Big T mentioned that Darden hooked you up."

I nod, then explain how I meet with clients, get an understanding of what they want, and then shop for them at various places.

He motions us to take a seat. We ease down on high-back caramel-colored leather stools around a granite island. He tells us about the machine, how it holds three pitchers at a time with different blending and shaving settings. He talks fervently about how the machine makes mojitos, piña coladas, daiquiris, and mudslides. I hide my smile at the mess he's making as he digs out strawberries, pineapples, and limes from the fridge. Juice drips down his hands as he gathers them together and puts them in the pitcher along with tequila and other liquors. He explains the deal he got on the machine—a thousand dollars—about the game they won last week, about his new car he ordered (an Aston Martin). He stops to take a breath. "I feel like I'm doing all the chitchat, sorry. What's up with you guys?"

Before we can reply, Courtney plops down on a kitchen stool next to me. "I'd like a margarita too."

"Say *pretty please*," he says.

She flicks a strand of honey-colored hair. "*Pretty please* may I have a regular margarita."

"Fine." His arm muscles flex as he pours ice in the machine, his gaze on her. "Did you find a place to stay? There's a hotel a block away. I'll pay if you'll go. Pretty please."

"I'm leaving tomorrow to see my parents in Florida for Christmas, but I'll be back to harass you." She smirks. "Did *you* find a place?"

His brown eyes glitter. "I *live* here. I was invited. You just showed up with a bag and some fake tears."

He turns the mixer on, the sound of ice drowning out whatever Courtney's reply is.

"I'd like mine with salt on the rim," she says when he sets her drink in front of her.

"Try sugar," he mutters. "It might make you nicer. Better yet, eat a chocolate bar for me, huh?"

"Go to hell, quarterback." She glares at him. "And put on a shirt. No one wants to see your six-pack."

"I do," Cece says.

"Same," I add.

"Thanks, guys, and Courtney, get it right. It's an eight-pack." He slaps his abdomen, then shimmies his hips.

Biting my lips to not laugh, I watch the back-and-forth between them with bated breath.

He gives Cece a strawberry margarita, then me a sparkling water. "Ladies. Enjoy." He does a bow with a hand flourish.

I look around, and a gasp comes from me. In the hallway is . . . "Oh my God. Is that a . . ."

"Yes, it is. Come on; I'll show you," he murmurs. "I need a break from a certain someone anyway." He leads me to the hallway and out of hearing range.

"Jackson Pollock?" I breathe as I take in the large painting.

"Yep." He chuckles as he sips from his margarita. "It gives me a headache, but people freak over it."

Illuminated by museum-style lights, the canvas glows with muted blues and greens that slather the surface. "This is embarrassing, but tingles just went down my spine. I've seen them before at museums, but wow, to think Pollock painted this, and it's here."

"Looks like a kid did it to me. I can whip one out for you and sign Pollock's name to it, if you want?"

I grimace. "We can't be friends anymore. Bye. It was nice knowing you."

I pretend to leave, then come back and gaze up at the work. "Sorry. I can't walk away from Jackson Pollock."

He laughs. "You came back for me, darling."

"Sure. You're like a baby dolphin at feeding time. Adorable." I pinch his cheeks, and he practically swoons at the attention.

He grins, then points at the painting. "Tuck's mom gave this to him for his twenty-fifth birthday. He stares at it a lot. Gets all moody and stuff. Tuck likes to talk about Pollock. Apparently, he had mental issues and was an alcoholic. He died in his forties driving drunk. He hit a tree near his house." He stops, frowning. "Whoa. Tuck's father died in a similar accident." He winces. "I shouldn't talk about him

135

when he isn't here, but he's my best friend, even if he doesn't know it. I worry . . ." He stops.

"About?"

A pained expression crosses his face, and he shakes his head. "My guy . . . he needs something good in his life right now. Jesus, let's change the topic. I'm gossiping like the old ladies at my church back in Utah."

"I didn't mean to pry."

"It doesn't take much for me to talk. You talk now."

As we look at Tuck's art, I tell him about some of my favorite pieces I've seen in New York. I ramble about Titian's *Venus and the Lute Player*, his sensuous, naked women. I thought he might like that, but when his eyes glaze over, I switch. "Then, there's Monet and his *Bridge over a Pond of Water Lilies*. The peace, the pastel colors, the soft brushstrokes—"

He holds up a hand. "Enough with the TED Talk. I heard *naked*, then started thinking about sex. *Brushstrokes* is the same."

"I used to tell Brogan about art so he could go to sleep. Cece enjoys it. She loves art."

"Ah, yeah, Brogan. Big T found out he's your roomie. I thought he'd be weird about it, but . . ."

I stiffen. "There was no plan to meet Tuck."

"I believe you, but I don't want anyone to hurt him, ya know?" He exhales. "He likes you."

"Does he?"

He gets a text on his phone and pulls it out. "Whoop! Someone is bringing up my bracelets! Keep looking around; I think there's a Georgia Somebody Famous drawing down the hall."

He disappears, and I keep walking until I find a Georgia O'Keeffe drawing. When my bladder chimes, I keep walking, hoping to find a restroom. I'm about to try a door when Courtney steps out of one, a handful of lacy fabric in her hand.

"Hi," I say, startling her. I study the garments in her hand. "La Perla? I recognize that blue bra. I have a taste for expensive lingerie."

She glances down at the clothing, her face reddening. "You caught me. I was picking up my things from Tuck's room."

I have a hard time believing her, especially after the bookstore, but he is a man, and she's beautiful. "Oh."

She shrugs a delicate shoulder. "Don't look surprised. Tuck is open with me. I'm aware of your history. He told me how you spilled tequila on him, then Jasper made a bet to seduce you."

I wave my hand. "There's a debate on who seduced whom."

Her lips tighten. "Fine, whatever, I see your appeal—you have that whole mysterious, artistic vibe, but Tuck and I go way back. What you have with him is a night at a disturbing place."

Her words bring a swell of bitterness I didn't expect. She's been living here for weeks, seeing Tuck, eating with him, talking to him.

Swallowing thickly, I remind myself of who he is.

A playboy. With a yacht.

I'm not going to get in a pissing match over Tuck with a supermodel.

I nod. "We've had sex since the club, no bet involved." I point at her lingerie. "I wore those exact panties, but in a thong. Where's the restroom?"

I'm. So. Mature.

She stammers as I walk away, find the restroom, do my business, and then exit back to the den. Cece sits on a stool, laughing at Jasper as he pours more margarita into her glass. She sees me and pauses. "Honey? You all right?"

"Nope. Are you ready to go?" I grab my satchel.

"No way! I thought maybe you two would stay for dinner," Jasper says. "I can't cook, but we can order out." He's holding a box but sets it down. "It's my last night in town. I'm off for Christmas."

"I'm back!" Tuck's voice calls from the foyer. He stalks into the den wearing jeans and a long-sleeved green cashmere sweater that clings to his arms.

His eyes widen when he sees me, his gaze lingering. "Francesca."

137

To my frustration, my blood heats.

"Big T!" Jasper heads his way, his hands spread wide as he engulfs him in a hug. He lets him go and grabs the box. "Check it! Our bracelets came in! And we have company!"

"Cool," he murmurs, then looks around the kitchen. "You guys tried out the machine. I missed it." He looks back at me, his gaze quizzical.

"Hi," I say. "Sorry to come uninvited. We hitched a ride up with Courtney."

"They're leaving," Jasper says with a pout.

As if there's no one else in the room, Tuck walks straight to me. "Stay awhile."

A frantic feeling swirls in my veins.

As if he reads my mind, he steps forward and touches my bangs, a rueful look on his face. "I miss the widow's peak."

Some of the tension I brought into the room from my interaction with Courtney eases. "I miss your scruff," I admit grudgingly.

"You came to see me." There's satisfaction in his tone as his hand wraps around my shoulder for a brief moment, then brushes down my arm.

Courtney chooses that moment to come back into the room. She sees Tuck and dashes to him and throws her arms around him.

He untangles her and sets her to the side. "Hey. We have guests."

"They snuck up," she replies, cutting her eyes at me.

I get right to the point. "Courtney says she's having sex with you."

A dead silence fills the room. I hear Jasper grunt from the kitchen. Carrying a pitcher of margarita, he slams it down on the counter and walks toward us.

Courtney gapes at me, eyes blinking. "I can't believe you said that!"

"She says and does inappropriate things all the time," Cece murmurs as she slides in next to me. "You should have seen her at Daniel Radcliffe's party. She made out with his wife."

"Shield up, Captain America," I mutter under my breath.

"It's not true," Tuck says as his jaw twitches. "Courtney, why would you say that?"

She sputters. "I—I don't know. I was worried—"

Jasper takes Courtney by the elbow and spins her to face him. "What kind of trick are you trying to pull, Courtney?"

"I didn't mean it!"

"She did," I say sweetly. "She showed me her lingerie as she was leaving his room."

"It was my room," Courtney says. "It was a joke. I was just kidding!"

Jasper's nose flares as he glares at her. "You're an insecure, stupid little girl. Grow up, okay? Grow the fuck up. Or you might lose Tuck and me! Just because he's seeing someone else doesn't mean you're not important! Do you know Tuck? Huh? Do you? He's a friend for life. Till the end. He went through some shit with you, and that's the only reason you're here right now. This is too much, just too much. I'm so pissed at you! His room? You haven't been in his room. Lingerie, my ass! Go to your room, get online, and find an apartment!"

She runs from the room, tears spilling down her face.

"She's moving out, Tuck. I'm going to find her an apartment myself. One far, far away from Wickham!" He storms off to the back.

Cece whistles. "We *must* do this again. With music next time."

"We have to go," I say. "I'm working tonight."

"I'll show you out," Tuck says as we head to the foyer. He opens the door, and once Cece is out in the hall, he takes my hand and pulls me aside.

His fingers lace with mine, his hand warm and protective. "I'm sorry about her. She was with me the night Lollipop showed up, and I've given her too much leeway." He pauses. "She's attempted to get in my bed, but she's been turned away."

"Ah."

One arm curls around my waist as his fingers card through my hair. "I've missed you."

"Yeah?"

"You got the necklace? I heard there was a delay in delivery from the front desk." His hand tightens around my waist. "Look up, beautiful."

I gaze up at him—and get lost a little in his stormy eyes. I press my face into his neck. Jesus. I'm a sap. I can't resist this. Someone make me stop!

"What are you doing after the gallery?"

I shrug.

"Come up when you're done. I'll text you the code."

Visions of us in bed dance through my mind. I swallow, searching for strength. "Back to the necklace. Thank you. It's beautiful, but I can't—"

I'd been reaching inside my satchel, but he takes my hand. "Don't," he says sharply. "The necklace was meant for you. It's a Christmas gift."

"I can't keep something that . . ."

"Reminds you of me?"

"No. I . . ." I stop, feeling uncentered by his annoyance. Focus, Francesca. "Keeping it makes things complicated."

"We are complicated." He frowns. "Look, you know what I'm about. We've discussed it. The last thing I want to do is hurt you."

Men *do* hurt me. The ones I care about.

My lashes flutter. I care? "No one sets out to hurt someone in the beginning."

He drops his hands from me, a cool look on his face. "Text me when you want to see what this is. See you around."

Then he gives me a little shove over the threshold and shuts the door in my face.

"He literally pushed me out." I look over at Cece. "What just happened?"

Cece taps her foot in the hall, then exhales noisily. "Good gracious, you tried to give the necklace back! Yes, I was eavesdropping, you stupid hussy. You don't return a Christmas gift. It's clear the man is waiting for you to make the next move, and you, honey, don't have a clue. You know what you are?"

"A hussy? Oh, look at the time. I need to rush." I pick my steps up.

"You're nuttier than a squirrel at a peanut festival. I know because we have a *national* peanut festival in my hometown. The squirrels race here and there with their tails swishing, not knowing if they're gonna poop or sneak a peanut."

"Forget squirrels. You gave him my cell number. I'm still pissed about that."

"You can't make up your mind."

I change the topic. "Aren't squirrels rodents? Gross."

She shrugs. "Squirrel scat is the size of a grain of rice. True fact. Mr. Darden made me watch the nature channel after I stole his pen."

I snort. "Is there a Ferris wheel at your festival? Cotton candy? Oh, those funnel cake things?"

Cece swishes down the hall like a beauty queen, the strap of her black Chanel purse draped over her shoulder. "It's quite the shindig, so no making fun of it, yeah? I won Miss National Peanut my senior year in high school. I was so pretty everyone hated me to bits." She smiles. "I loved it! The attention. The boys. The crowns and sashes." A sigh comes from her. "My dress, oh my dress; it was divine—all white with a sweetheart neckline and jewels. You know how good I look in white. Gah, I'm going to be a beautiful bride."

"Like an angel."

She waves her hands. "You're distracting me."

"You distract yourself. Squirrel."

She huffs. "Forget me; let's circle back to Tuck. You're holding maybe ten grand in jewels and tried to give it back!" She pauses, her voice lowering. "Besides, if you're not gonna wear it, you could always pawn them and use it for baby Cecelia."

"Back to this peanut festival. When is it?"

"You're trying to change the topic."

"I bet you were gorgeous in that dress . . ." I eye her.

"The festival is in October. See, all the other girls wore these fall colors, but I wanted to stand out. Mama raised me right. 'Forget learning to cook and shoot guns,' she told me. 'Dress how you want, be yourself, and when he's mean, kick him in the balls and move on.'"

"I'm sad we missed the festival. Let's go next year, take the baby, and show those Alabama girls how New York does it. You wear something white. I'll wear black with lots of makeup. Baby Cecelia will be in couture. Yes?"

"I'm getting married in the fall."

Right. My stomach lurches. "Maybe you can get married at the peanut festival."

She studies me. "Once you make up your mind, that's it, isn't it?"

"What do you mean?"

"When Edward cheated, you refused to see him. He was a dick and deserved to never have you, but some girls would have listened to him, maybe tried to work it out. You slept with Tuck, and that was it. No more is allowed. You're stubborn."

"Edward and I were over the moment I opened the supply-closet door."

"Okay, that was a bad example. What I mean is you make up your mind and don't budge. All I'm saying is maybe you should tell Tuck about the pregnancy."

Unease tingles over me. Maybe, just maybe, part of me has thought about telling him; then I remember how sure he was in the bookstore. "Why would I? His goal is to retire and hang out on his yacht with beautiful women. He's a *player*, Cece. He doesn't want kids, and I appreciated his honesty. Toss in the fact that I got pregnant on two forms of birth control the night we met—well, he's going to think I trapped him."

"Fine. I'm just worried about when I'm in California and you're here. Who will you have to turn to babysit in a pinch? To grab some diapers at the store?"

I try to picture Tuck in CVS buying baby stuff and can't.

"I'll have Darden and Brogan."

She snorts. "Darden and diapers? Please. And Brogan needs to go back to med school. How's your money situation? I keep offering you help, but you won't take it."

Because it's her retirement, and even though she's going to marry Lewis, I don't want her going into a relationship without an escape route. He bought her a house, yes, but her name isn't on that deed. What if it doesn't work out for them?

I've looked over my savings, and I have enough to cover my part of the rent and school loans until May or June, but after that . . .

Anxiousness rises, and I shove it down.

It *will* work out.

I can make my own way. I've been doing it for years.

We walk to the elevator and get in. I punch our floor. "Tuck isn't interested in long term, and babies are forever. He doesn't *want* to know."

"You can't be sure."

I stiffen, frustration rising as I face her in the elevator. "Cece. Think about it. He's famous. Everyone knows him. He's on television. What if he completely rejects her as a person? What if he never wants to see her—and she knows? How do I explain that to her?" Tears pool in my eyes. "I know what that's like, okay. I don't want it for her."

A sigh comes from her. "But, honey, *you've* always wondered about your parents. Maybe it's better to know something and be sad than know nothing at all."

"I turned out okay," I say faintly as I finger the locket around my neck. Someday I'll put the baby's picture in it. I'll have her name engraved below mine on the back. When she asks about her father, I'll . . .

I don't know what I'll do.

My stomach flutters again, and I gasp. The first time I thought it was a fluke, but . . .

I grab Cece's hand and put it on my belly. "She's moving! Isn't it too early?" I fumble with my phone and look up when a baby kicks, excitement rising as I read. "It can happen!"

Cece squeals and bends down to my stomach. "Hi, sweetie pie. This is your auntie Cece. Someday I'll buy you a debutante dress. White. You'll shine, baby girl."

We didn't notice the doors opening on our floor. Both of us are smiling down at my belly as Cece coos. It's the throat clearing of Widow Carnes that makes my eyes fly up.

Darden also waits for the elevator. He weaves on his feet, then straightens and points his cane at me. "Miss Lane! You're pregnant?" I've never seen him gasp like a fish, mouth opening and closing, but it's happening.

Widow Carnes lets out a grunt. "I knew I overheard Herman say something!"

"She is," Cece says sweetly, and I groan.

"Thanks, Cece. Really. Now the entire building will know!" I call out.

Widow Carnes blinks innocently. "But why do you mind, dear? People are more modern these days. No one cares."

"I care," I mutter.

Darden glares at Widow Carnes. "This doesn't leave the four of us."

"Of course, Felix." She bats her lashes at him. "I hope this means you'll be coming to our next book club in the lobby, yes? We can sit together."

"What's the book again?" he practically spits.

"*The Notebook*. History and a little romance. You'll love it." She titters.

"Heavy on romance," I correct. "He'll hate it."

He looks at the ceiling, then tersely agrees. She smiles at him, gets on the elevator, and leaves.

"You never let me call you Felix," I mutter to Darden, hoping to distract him from the pregnant girl in the hall.

He turns to me, clearly not going wherever he had planned. I swallow, feeling like a teenager in front of her dad. *Yes, I had sex. Yes, I'm pregnant.*

"Well, Miss Lane, this certainly explains a few things. Who's the father? I'd like a word with him. Now!"

My stomach flutters again, and I gasp. "Oh! She moved again. Probably because you yelled, Mr. Darden."

He blinks at me, dumbfounded. "What?"

"The baby. It moves inside the uterus, and you can feel it." He never had any of his own, so I feel the need to explain.

"I know that," he snarls.

"Do you want to touch my stomach? It could stop any minute, so you better hurry."

He shakes his head fervently, but at least I've distracted him. Score.

I kiss him on the cheek, then run for my apartment, leaving Cece behind. She calls out for me to wait, but I'm gone, leaving her to deal with Mr. Darden—which might not be the best idea, considering how she's blurting things out left and right, but I'll take my chances. I need to get myself together before I talk to him.

I open the door and flip the lock. Miss National Peanut can dig out her own keys.

I dash for my room, remember I want food, run back out to the kitchen and snag Brogan's chips, and then make it back to my room and lock my door before she's even made it to the den. With a satisfied exhale, I plop on my bed.

She knocks. "Why are you running from the kitchen?"

"I'm sick of the food police," I call out. "I could legit starve."

"Jesus. The salt-and-pepper chips again?"

"It's been a tough day!" Crumbs fall out of my mouth. "You didn't help matters!"

She is quiet on the other end, then says, "I'm sorry I'm leaving, Fran. It's going to break my heart to not see you every day. You're true blue, my little boo bunny."

"Not today," I grouse.

I hear her sigh. "Sorry I announced your pregnancy to the widow and Darden. You can escape this, you know—get away from Tuck and not worry. Move with me to Palo Alto. Beautiful weather, warm salt air, walks on the beach. Wouldn't baby Cecelia look divine in a white bathing suit?"

I munch on a chip and lie back on the bed. "I hate sunshine and beaches. This is home."

"I love you," she says in her sweet voice.

My heart cracks. "I'm going to get ready for the gallery now, so . . ."

"Have fun, and score some deals." I hear her footsteps walking away, and tears threaten. Her walking away feels like a metaphor for when she really leaves.

Before I can think too hard about it, I send a text to Tuck. Thank you for the necklace. I love it. I chew on my lips and fire off another one. I saw your Pollock. It's amazing.

I toss the phone down and let out a squeal. I said I was going to keep our relationship light, but I'm slipping into the unknown.

I blow out to the ceiling, then starfish on my bed and then cover my face.

I tap my fingers, waiting for a reply that never comes.

After quickly showering and changing into an ankle-length strapless black maxi dress and three-inch crystal stilettos, I am about to head out to the den when my phone pings from where I left it on the bed.

I jump on my comforter and grab it. I want it to be Tuck.

You missed seeing my girl when you were here. This is my Cherry. Attached is a pic of a small brown dog on a bed. Tuck holds her, a wry grin on his face when he took the selfie.

I dart to the bathroom, take the moth I'd seen earlier on the windowsill, and send him a pic of it on my shoulder. **Meet Moth. He doesn't eat, poop, or bark.**

He sends me a pic of him without his shirt while lying on his bed, so I send him one of me in my dress. He replies with one of his feet, and I laugh, then threaten to block him if he sends more feet pics.

You shoved me out your door, I send him later as Herman gets a cab for me.

I was pissed.

And now?

I'm glad you have the necklace. When you wear it, think about us.

Us?

I put my phone away and watch the passing lights of Manhattan.

Chapter 12

FRANCESCA

I've browsed the gallery for about two hours, taking photos and notes for my client. I'm considering a blue-and-orange abstract landscape when my cell pings with a voice mail. I pull my phone out of my clutch. Donny. Scanning it, I notice a few texts from Brogan but put those on hold. Why is Donny calling me?

My head circles back to the last time I saw him in his office. Yes, we've spoken on the phone once to clarify some details, but that's been the extent of it. A long exhale comes from me. Leaving East Coast Ink & Gallery feels like a million years ago, but it still stings. It's not so much about Edward's betrayal but that Donny severed our longtime connection.

I looked up to him. Admired him. Worked with him for years.

And then rejection.

I play his message. "Francesca, um, hi. I put your paintings in the storage facility upstairs like you asked the last time we spoke. Brogan came to the shop to pick them up today." He pauses. "I'd actually forgotten about them, and when I went to look, they were gone. Harlee said someone bought them a couple of weeks after you left, and she forgot to tell me. Call me back."

The voice mail ends, and my anger stirs. My commission is 80 percent of the price of the paintings, and with four of them, that's a large sum of money. She didn't tell him because she didn't care. Maybe she was truly miffed about the painting of her and Edward in the closet.

I sigh as I scan Brogan's texts, and it's him repeating what Donny said. He'd told me earlier this week that he and some friends were borrowing someone's van to pick up my paintings and then put them in a warehouse co-op I share with other artists. I send him a text and tell him that I didn't know they'd sold and I'm sorry that he and his buddies went to so much trouble for me. He replies back that it's cool and that he'll see me later. I put my phone away. The truth is I shouldn't have waited this long to get them, but Donny said he'd make sure they were safe.

Ducking into a quiet hallway, I call Donny, and he answers on the first ring.

"They all sold?" I ask. "And she didn't think to call me or let you know?"

He sighs heavily. "She said she meant to, but you know how busy she is . . ."

"Uh-huh. Sure." I can see her now, prancing around in her dress and heels.

"I heard you got a job," Donny murmurs. "I'm glad."

"Brogan told you?"

"Yes. With glee. Your clients miss you. We get at least one a week who walks in and asks for you." I hear the clink of ice and picture him in his office with a whiskey.

"I'm loving my new career." It's not like owning a gallery, but it's close, considering I get to visit them and spend other people's money.

He clears his throat. "So I hear congratulations are in order."

I stiffen. "Oh? For what?"

There's a pause. "Um, well, Edward said you were pregnant. I hope it's happy news?"

My hands clench. Good grief! How many people in Manhattan know my personal business? At this rate, the entire world will know.

"Also, Edward doesn't work here anymore. He quit. Long story. I won't bore you."

I don't care. "Let's talk about the paintings," I snap. "There were four left after the dollhouse painting sold. One of a little girl in the back seat of a car, one of a boathouse, one of a girl on a Greyhound bus, and the one of Harlee and Edward. I want receipts."

"I remember them."

"Who bought them?"

"I don't know. They paid in cash, and there's no signature on the receipt."

Cash is odd. My head circles to Darden. He cares about me, knew I'd lost my job, and thought he'd help by purchasing the paintings. Or perhaps Cece. It sounds like something she'd do in secret, like she bought the baby bed. Obviously, it's not Brogan. He went to pick them up today.

I tap my fingers against my leg. "Did Harlee tell you anything about the buyer?"

"She doesn't recall. She does have memory issues."

"She's a liar."

Donny exhales.

I lean against a wall, stumped. I can't see Darden going inside the parlor. He'd rather die. But he has people who handle his affairs. Perhaps they bought them.

I smirk. Cece could have popped in to buy them, but Harlee knows her. Besides, where did she put them?

"You know my address. Send the commission check there." I click off, then turn and bump into a hard chest. His drink spills on my skirt, and I rear back.

"Edward!" I say when I look up.

He gives space even as his hands try to steady me. "Sorry there, Francesca. I didn't know it was you. Is your dress ruined?"

"No, I whipped around. It was my fault. It's not terrible. At least I'm wearing black." I grimace.

He smiles tentatively. "I wondered if we'd run into each other soon. We used to go to all openings, remember?"

I stiffen. I don't need reminders of our time together. "I'm here for work. I have a new job. Why are you here?"

"Ah, well, my date wanted to come . . ."

"Edward!" comes a female voice, and I steel myself to face Harlee, only it isn't. It's a cute girl in a black minidress that highlights her tiny waist. She's coming from the restroom area and slides in next to Edward and wraps an arm around his waist, a smile on her lips. Younger than me, maybe twenty or so, she has an oval face and short blonde hair cut in a pixie style.

He gives me a lopsided smile. "Surprise. I ended it with Harlee."

Wow. So that's why he quit.

"This is Vivien," he tells me, then gazes adoringly down at the girl. "We met when she came in for a tattoo."

"Karma at its best," I murmur under my breath. My lips twitch as I picture Harlee broken up with jealousy over the pretty blonde as she sat in Edward's tattoo chair.

"What?" Edward asks.

"Nothing," I say as his date pumps my hand, and we chitchat about the gallery. It's the oddest thing. I feel nothing. Oh, I'll never forget his betrayal—he's a dick—but at least there's no ache in my heart. Life has given me other things to focus on, and he seems so small.

I'm looking for a way to excuse myself when I hear a shrill, excited voice.

"Darling! I didn't know you'd be here!" comes from Gianna. Wearing a pink sheath and a diamond choker around her throat, she strides toward me with confidence. She flicks a strand of blonde hair over her shoulder.

I glance at Edward and his date. "Excuse me." I rush to her, and we hug.

"God, finally, a fun person in a gallery. I hate these things . . ." She dips her wrist, giving me an eyeful of the rock on her finger. "How are you?" She sees Edward, and her eyes narrow as she swishes me away. "Your ex is here—oh my God. And he's with a silly-looking girl. What is she, fifteen? Are you in despair?"

I laugh. "Not at all."

She takes me in from head to toe. "Look at you! You're positively glowing! What kind of foundation are you using? God, I adore your dress. I almost didn't recognize you. And you have bangs now, but I saw your face and knew it was you. Those eyes are unmistakable . . ."

"Thank you."

She flashes a smile. "Is there a man in your life? Who is he? *Where* is he? I want to meet him."

"There might be a man . . ." Maybe.

"Is he hot? Tell me he's better than that awful Edward!"

Tuck is a thousand times the man Edward is.

He's honest and up front. Authentic.

"I don't give away details," I say.

"You're a secretive one." She looks at my locket, her eyes widening. "Oh, your necklace looks fabulous with your dress. I noticed you wore it at the shop. Do you always wear it?"

My fingers brush over it. "I guess. It's not your typical heart or oval locket."

"Hmm. So why are you here? Tell me all the things."

I tell her about my new job and the client I'm here for, a Wall Street couple who don't have time to shop for their new apartment. She tells me about her fiancé, who's currently out of town, and how she's looking forward to her wedding next year. She hooks her arm through mine as we walk through one of the hallways in the gallery.

She grabs a glass of champagne, and I pick up a club soda with lime from one of the bars.

"I'm actually here with my sister. She needed a plus-one, so I came along." She leans her head down conspiratorially. "You must meet her. She's not nearly as fun as me, but try to like her. There she is!"

She pulls me toward a petite woman in a floor-length red flared dress. It's the kind of dress that makes you gasp when you see it—over the top for a gallery, yet she wears it like a princess. Her hair is brown and cascades down her back. Something about her is familiar, making me rack my brain, but I can't put my finger on it.

"Valentina, this is the tattoo artist I was telling you about," Gianna says as she introduces us.

Valentina's flawless face is expressionless as she looks me up and down. Her eyes are the same color as Gianna's, blue, and her face is similar to her sister's, rather square with high cheekbones, but that's where the resemblance ends. She looks around my age.

"I've heard about you."

"Good, I hope?" I ask with my brow raised.

She shrugs, then points to the piece she was looking at before we arrived, a bronze of two little girls on a bench. "You're a tattoo artist. What do you think of this?"

"I'm an *artist*," I say smoothly. "Not just tattoos."

"Of course," Valentina replies with narrowed eyes as she waves her hand at the statue. "Your thoughts?"

Gianna huffs at her sister. "Can we at least chitchat before you ask for her opinion?"

"Oh, it's cool. I love to talk about art." I study it. About the size of a watermelon, it reminds me of something you'd put in a garden, perhaps at a school or library at the entrance—only it would be a shame to leave it outside. I tell her this, then: "You can see the work the artist put into it, how the older girl's leg is crossed, the stitching on her socks, the bow of her tennis shoes, the ruffles of her dress, how they lean toward each other, the small bird on the bench. One of the girls is taller, so older, and I'd guess they're sisters."

I back up and eye the two ladies, and it dawns on me. I recall Gianna's comment at the parlor about her sister being an artist. "It's yours," I say, pointing at Valentina. "I see the resemblance of the little girls. The smaller one is Gianna, and you're the older one holding her hand. Yes?"

She nods.

"Amazing," I say. "Making a bronze is an intricate process. It's beautiful."

Gianna claps. "Isn't Francesca awesome?"

Valentina crooks her arm with Gianna's as she nods. "Thank you. I made it as a memorial for our parents. They passed away last year. It's not for sale, of course. A friend owns the gallery; otherwise it wouldn't be here."

She glances at my locket, a gleam I can't decipher in her eyes. "That's a pretty piece. There's a bird engraved on the front?"

"A wren, yes." A wren symbolizes peace and rebirth. I've done my research on my locket. "I believe it belonged to my mother or was in her family. I've had it cleaned a few times, although it rarely tarnishes."

"Interesting. Have you had it appraised?" Valentina asks. "It looks expensive."

"It's nineteen karat gold, the chain and locket." I had its value checked at three different jewelers, and they all said it was worth several thousand. I'm lucky I never lost it or had it stolen.

Gianna takes a sip of her champagne. "You *believe* it belonged to your mother. There must be a story there."

I shift around, fidgeting. A story? Ha. It's the only link to my mother. I picture her placing it in my car seat.

"As a baby, I was left at a police station. All I had was this locket. My name is engraved on the back," I say lightly with a slight smirk, not wanting pity or even for this discussion to continue. "Have you seen the marble sculptures upstairs? They're beautiful."

Valentina ignores my cue. "The locket must be very important to you. Gianna and I grew up in a large Italian family. I can't imagine how hard it was not to have family."

"I have family now," I say coolly. "Besides, it's all about how you define yourself, yes? To not let the past rule your future? Life picked my path, and I'm just a traveler."

"How poetic," Valentina murmurs, but I'm not sure I hear sincerity.

"Maybe I should put that on a tattoo . . ." I smile back with the same level of earnestness she showed. I didn't live in seven different foster homes without becoming a tough girl. I know how to punch back with a socialite and her artist sister. Tit for tat. Show them you're made of sterner stuff.

Because I am. The fact that I'm in a dress doesn't make me sweet.

I glance away from them, pretending interest in another piece. When I was little, I used to tell myself that my parents would find me, that I was a princess sent from the fairies to live among the humans until it was safe to retrieve me. Another was that I was kidnapped and my parents would pay the ransom and get me.

Pipe dreams. Parents who leave their kids in the snow don't come back.

"Francesca?" Gianna says. "We must do coffee soon. Text me."

Ah, a cue to leave.

I nod at them, but inwardly my heart twists. It's been a strange, tumultuous day. Cece is leaving, I got a necklace from a man who wants to get to know me, too many people know I'm pregnant, a random stranger bought my paintings, I saw Edward, and now these two.

"It was nice to meet you," Valentina says, her tone flat as she stares at my locket.

I murmur the appropriate niceties and head for the exit on the bottom level. As I walk down the steps, I glance back up, and they're still at the bronze with their heads together as they whisper.

I try to suss out the root of what's pricking at me and come up with one thing. Talking to the Russo sisters brought back memories of my past, of how it felt to be truly alone. They had each other and parents; I had a locket.

Guilt flares to the surface. Even with the childhood I had, I'm still planning on not telling Tuck about his baby.

Cece's words circle in my head. *Maybe it's better to know and be sad than know nothing at all.*

My child won't be lonely with me—I know this—but a father figure means something. I place my hand over my stomach. She kicked today, and maybe that's part of my turmoil. She's real. She'll be in this world soon. Is it fair to deprive her of her father?

Maybe I should tell him.

Family is the compass that guides us, a light that leads us, the most important aspect of a child's life. It is unconditional and loves you no matter your shortcomings. It brings hope, courage, and protection, a port in the storm of life, all things I hungered, prayed, wept, begged, and trembled for as a child.

I wanted anyone, someone, to just pick *me*.

I want him to pick our child. Would he?

Tears threaten, and my breath quickens as I picture disbelief, then anger on his face.

Shouldn't I at least give him a chance? Give our child an opportunity to have a father in her life—if he wants?

A clammy feeling hits me as that awful fear of rejection hits. It's a cloak around me, a cloud that never disappears, no matter how tough I may act. Taking a deep breath, I fist my hands and try to squash it, to gather the strength I need to tell him. I should, right?

The sisters send a wave, and I blink, coming back to the present.

I don't reciprocate their goodbye. I step outside to the cold December air.

There's another pair of eyes on me as I exit—and a camera—but I'm too lost in thought to notice. I catch a cab and pull out my phone.

Text me the code, I send to Tuck.

His reply is immediate with the numbers, then, I'm waiting for you, princess.

Impulsively, I ask the cabbie to stop at a late-night market. I tell him to wait and walk briskly through the stalls, find what I want, purchase it, and then get back in.

When Tuck opens the door, he's wearing gym shorts and no shirt.

We stare at each other.

"This. I want this," I hear myself say. I'm not thinking rationally.

Maybe.

I don't know.

But I want to know who he is and what this harmony we share is about. I want him to want our child.

I run into his arms, and he picks me up.

Chapter 13

TUCK

Jasper gives me a fist bump as he takes his chair. He'd been up at the bar getting us another beer. "We pulled it out at the last minute, yo! You think it was the bracelets?"

"Absolutely!" I laugh.

He salutes me. "You kicked ass, Big T!"

Yeah, I guess I did. Tate, my replacement, limped off the field with a twisted ankle, went to the locker room for scans, and never came back. I played my ass off with no mistakes. I fidget in my seat, trying to relieve the pain in my hips from a fall I took.

I take a sip of my beer. Yeah, the win was good, but this season is the first time the Pythons haven't made the playoffs.

The waitress sets down my grilled chicken and veggies, then gives Jasper his chicken and Cheetos. I shake my head at him as we sit inside the Baller.

Shawna, a brunette with big tits, sits across from me. She keeps giving me the "Do you wanna get lucky?" smile. A friend who hangs around with Courtney, she homed in on us when we sat down.

I'm midbite when she slides her bare foot up my calf. I set down my fork and raise an eyebrow as she takes a long sip from her red wine.

"I've been missing you," she says. "You used to come in every weekend."

"He's pining after someone," Jasper tells her with relish. "You should focus on me. He's not interested."

I haven't seen Francesca since she left the penthouse the day after the gallery. We spent the night together, then woke up and went for a walk. She insisted I get a tree for my place, so I bought a nine-foot evergreen; then we ran into boutiques for ornaments. After the tree was delivered, we decorated, had dinner delivered, and then fucked for hours under the twinkling lights. She gave me a compass keychain as a gift, something she bought secretly while we shopped together. *Something to guide you home,* she said, her eyes glittering, an earnest look on her face.

The next day, she, Cece, Brogan, and Darden celebrated their Christmas in his apartment while I spent it in the penthouse, just me and Cherry. I told her I was seeing family in Virginia for a few days. Embarrassment and pride kept me from admitting that I was alone.

Refocusing, I think about the compass. I am lost. I have no direction. How does she *know* me?

I exhale.

Yet I'm not surprised at our connection. Is it the great sex?

After Christmas, they flew to LA to meet Lewis and see Cece's house. I pull my phone out and scan through the texts we shared as Shawna renews her efforts on my other leg.

I smile at one I sent her. It's raining here today.

She sent me a photo of her and Brogan in a lush garden outside Cece's house. The sun was shining, her hair was in a ponytail, and she looked young and beautiful.

Later, I sent her a pic of my scruff I'd let grow out. She sent me a pic of her unshaven legs.

The next day, I asked her if she'd had the lemon bars at the bakery around the block, and she said she loved them with ten heart emoji.

I walked down to the bakery and had some overnighted to Cece's address.

One morning, she sent me a pic of a charcoal sketch of a woman wearing her emerald-and-topaz necklace. I saved it to my phone and added it as her contact photo. I like her art. She's talented without being obvious or pretentious about it. She's so real. Genuine.

On New Year's Eve, I sent teal and pink roses (for her tattoo) and several bottles of Dom to her at Cece's. She sent me a pic of her smelling them.

We passed each other in the sky when she returned to New York on New Year's Day while I was flying to Vegas for the game.

My lips twitch. I'm back now, and we *could* have seen each other. We do live in the same building, but I'm giving her leeway and letting her come to me. Whatever we have, it feels easily breakable.

Shawna's foot sneaks close to my crotch, and I'm in the middle of moving it when a woman's voice reaches my ears.

Wearing a halter-style black leather dress, it's a raven-haired beauty with ruby lips and leopard-print heels. She sways through the throng, and males eye her as she comes toward us. She wears a smile, and her eyes shine, aquamarine and outlined with black. Her straight hair spills around her face. "Hi. I didn't know you came here."

My gaze eats up the creamy shoulders, the hollows of her elegant throat, my necklace around her neck.

"Uh . . . ," I start.

She leans over. "Just when you think I'll zig, I zag."

A rumble of laughter comes from me. "How did you get inside?" Then it dawns on me. "Have you been here before?"

"Once."

"Were you here with an athlete?" Ire threatens to rise.

Not answering, she grabs a chair from another table and places it at the end of ours and sits. She waves at the waitress, who hurries over, and orders a club soda with lime.

"Mind if I join you?" she says.

I roll my eyes.

Jasper chuckles as he licks cheese puffs off his fingers. "Finally. Where have you been hiding out, Princess?"

I grunt. "Only I call her that."

He snorts.

"Who the heck are you?" Shawna asks her, a sour look on her face.

"I'm his princess. Who are you?"

Shawna blinks. "Um, a *friend*."

"Oh, I get it." Francesca swivels her head back to me, then takes a look around the bar. "I imagine there's quite a few *friends* in here. Should I be worried, boo?"

I laugh. Shawna and I have a brief history, but . . .

"Nope," I murmur.

Jasper leans over to Shawna. "Told ya. Pining."

"We're having sex," Francesca tells her. "It's complicated, but . . ." She kisses her fingers. "Hot."

Shawna frowns.

Francesca waves her hands at her. "Leave. Go. Find another man. This one is mine."

Shawna jerks up, her chair scraping the floor. "You could have said something, Tuck."

"Sorry . . ." I laugh, still watching Francesca as she shoos at Shawna. I never expected her to draw a line in the sand because a woman was flirting with me.

After Shawna leaves, Jasper talks about the game, shows her our bracelets—she's already seen mine, but he doesn't mind—asks about her holiday, and then eventually gets up to grab more beer.

"I need to go to the ladies' room." Her lids lower. "Want to come with?"

"Hell yeah. You aren't going anywhere alone here." I drain my beer, throw a wad of money on the table, and take her hand as I stand. "Follow me."

We pass several tables of players, and they murmur hellos. I barely notice. I've missed her, and she's here. She came to me.

I stop at the restroom, and she tells me that she doesn't really need to go, but *do the stalls lock?*

My cock thickens. I tug her farther down the hall, open a door, and usher her inside, then lock the door.

"A private room. Cool." She takes in the couch, the cowhide rug on the floor. Two televisions play football games. One shows hockey.

"Do wicked things happen here?" she asks.

My arms cross over my suit. "You have to be a member of the Baller or know someone. So who have you been here with?"

"You're jealous, boo. Tsk, tsk."

"Yes," I grind out. "Immensely."

She closes the distance between us and laces her fingers around my neck. "I like you all growly that I was here with an athlete, but I only fall for artists." Her lips trace up my throat as her fingers rub the scruff on my jawline. "This is so sexy."

"Who was it?"

"Brogan. He dated a basketball player."

"Did you see me?"

A small smirk crosses her face. "Yes. Not on purpose, of course. I just happened to be here. You had two girls draped over you."

"Why didn't I see you?"

She presses her nose to my chest and inhales. "Sadly, I'm too short."

I chuckle, my fingers sliding through her hair as I hold her scalp.

"Hey, I'm glad you came to find me. I fucking missed you."

"I missed you."

Over the texts, we somehow grew closer? I don't know, but I know what I need from her right now. I gaze at her rosebud lips. She's never let me kiss her on the mouth, and I need it.

"Kiss me. For real," I murmur as I touch her lips. "Show me you missed me."

Her eyes hold mine, uncertainty in their depths. "Tuck . . ."

"Hmm?"

Her eyes fill with water, and I tug her closer, pressing her face into my shoulder. "Hey, don't do that. I can't have you crying over it."

She pulls back, her eyes searching my face. "No, it's not that; it's just . . . there's something I should tell you."

"What?" I cup her face gently. "You have a phobia of kissing?"

"No. I want to kiss you."

Our gazes lock for several moments. She bites her bottom lip, a vulnerable expression on her face, maybe a touch of fear.

"Hey, baby, come on—don't. It's nothing, okay. Forget it—"

Before I can finish, her rosebud mouth presses against mine. She caresses me with tentative brushes, back and forth. I sigh as she deepens the touch, her lips nibbling on my bottom one. A guttural sound erupts from my throat when her fingers feather through my hair.

"Baby . . ." My fingers tighten around her as fire dances down my spine. Her breasts press into my chest as I lift and carry her to the couch. "Don't stop, beautiful; don't be afraid. This is good, so fucking good," I manage to say as our lips lock again.

Our breath mingles, her lips parting as her tongue slides against mine. Gone are the hesitant touches as our mouths grow bolder, taking more, giving more. I take control of us, pressing deeper. I want to touch every part of her: her teeth, her tongue, the roof of her mouth.

"I want you," I rumble.

"Same," she murmurs as her hand reaches between us and palms my cock through my slacks. I arch into her hands.

"Why did you stop?" I breathe as she pulls back. Her lips are red and swollen, and I brush my fingers over them.

"To do this." She jerks my suit jacket off, then undoes the buttons on my shirt. Her lips press against my chest and trail down to my stomach. Her fingers undo my pants, tug down the zipper, and then pull out my thick, hard length.

She gazes up at me. "May I?"

I caress her face. "Don't make me come. That's for your pussy."

Her lashes flutter as she starts at my root and licks up my shaft. Her palms cup my balls, her nails tracing the skin as she takes me in her mouth.

Her tongue flutters around my head, and I lean back and groan. She plays over me, then sinks down. She's ravenous as she sucks, and when her throat swallows around me, I call out her name. She inhales me, making a meal of me. My cock throbs, and bolts of heat radiate up my spine as I pull her off.

"Panties. Off. Now." I fumble with the condom in my wallet and slide it on.

She slips her lace panties off, tucks them in a pocket in her dress, and then straddles me while bunching up her dress. My breath hitches as she takes me in her hand and sinks down. I hold her hips as she inches down, little gasps coming from her as I push up, teasingly, delving deeper. I pump on the way home and shudder. Our fit is exquisite. She's the ultimate fuck, her pussy tight and wet.

She unties her halter dress and shoves it down. Her bra is black and see through. Her hair cascades down her back, and when the strands brush my fingers at her hips, I grasp them and slide them through my hands. "You're the most gorgeous fuck I've ever had," I gasp as she rotates in my lap.

Her peach scent mingles with the smell of sex as I tweak her clit. My tongue flicks over her breasts, sucking on the soft skin. She cups her breasts, and I bite my lip. She's fuller, plumper, and when I suck her erect nipple in my mouth, she jolts as her channel flutters my cock.

"Baby. Yeah. Yeah. *Yeah.*" I pump inside her, my hands bruising her hips.

I fuck her hard.

Again and again and again.

We're loud, our breaths gasping.

"Touch me," she calls, and I find where our bodies meet. Wetness drips from my hands as I explore her, the outline of her pussy, her stiff nub.

She arches her back and shouts, her breath ragged as tremors shimmy over her body.

"You undo me." I thrust inside her velvet channel.

There's a knock at the door and someone saying my name.

"Come," she whispers, and I stare into her eyes and explode inside her.

I'm trying to catch my breath as she rises up and slips her panties back on.

I haul myself up, tie off the condom, and throw it in the trash. I zip up, fix my shirt, and then grab my jacket and slip it on.

"Someone is at the door."

I grasp her nape and pull her to me and kiss her hard. "I really don't care. Do not run off." I walked into the bar with tension in my chest, but now it's gone. Vanished. She's the magic that keeps it away.

I lace our fingers together and open the door. Jasper is there, his eyes widening as he takes in her just-fucked look. "Oh, um, Big T, I didn't think, um—well, I'm heading out and wanted you to know."

"All right. You got a ride?" I tug Francesca along, hooking her hand in my arm.

He follows on our heels. "Yeah."

"Who?"

He doesn't say anything as we reach our table, and his face has reddened. "Um, I'm taking a cab to Courtney's. She needs help moving the furniture around."

She moved out right after Christmas. "That's really nice of you," I say dryly.

"What?" Jasper asks. "I'm a nice guy. It's what I'm known for."

Francesca chimes in. "You two seem to have a little, um, opposites-attract thing going on—"

"No, we don't!" He scoffs. "She's a total bitch. And I'm a meathead. Not a match. Pfft. Fuck that."

She shrugs. "Maybe you can help her be kinder, hmm?"

"Um, yeah, totally," he says as he fumbles around to get money out of his wallet. He puts it on the table. "You don't mind if I help her, right?"

I grunt. "Please, so *help* her."

"All right, I'll see y'all later." And then he's out the door.

I toss an arm around Francesca as we watch him go. "He's totally fucking her. He thinks I don't know—maybe he's worried I wouldn't approve—but it's been going on since the night he went off on her."

I tell the valet to bring my car around.

"Back to Wickham?" she asks.

"Not yet. I want to show you something, sort of a surprise."

Her eyes light up. "Fun! Can we stop at McDonald's and get some fries?"

I laugh. "McDonald's seems like a great first date. Thank God they don't have that clown up anymore."

The valet brings around my Ferrari. We pull out on the highway. I find the nearest McDonald's on the map and head that way. When we pull up to the drive-through, she asks the teller to add chopped bacon to her fries. I didn't know that was an option, and she says that if you ask, you shall receive.

I shift gears as I hit FDR Drive, then head south, leaving Upper Manhattan.

"Where are we going?"

"SoHo, about thirty minutes away." My body tingles with anticipation.

"You know this isn't our first date." She's got a mulish look on her face.

"Oh?" I grin. "Are we counting Decadence?"

"Hypothetically, that night was like ten dates in one."

I speed through a yellow light. "Most people call themselves couples after five."

"Did you just make that up?"

"Maybe," I say on a laugh.

"Anyway, we *could* say we met via a blind date. It was an awful date because I called you a pervert. Our second date was when you rescued me from a real pervert and we did shots. On the third date, we played a game and went dancing. By the fourth we celebrated your birthday, then watched live porn. On the fifth, we fucked like bunnies on crack." She stuffs a wad of fries in her mouth and chews. "Five dates in one. Works for me."

"We took walks, there was the bookstore, the night at my penthouse, then the Christmas shopping."

"Hypothetically, we're going steady," she announces.

"Should I buy you diamonds?"

"No more jewelry."

"So since we've been on these hypothetical dates, I have questions." I glance over, lingering on her face before turning back to the road. "If we were dating, and I wanted to cook you dinner, what would be your favorite?"

"Avocados, ice cream, and bacon. Kidding. Um, I guess pasta. Any kind of sauce will do, red or white—with lots of garlic. What would be yours?"

"If football training wasn't involved, a big chocolate cake."

"What about the meal?"

"Filet. Baked potato with tons of butter and sour cream. And bacon."

She laughs. "Okay, new one. Tell me your favorite female actress."

"Hmm, I sense danger in this question."

"Who is it?"

I sigh. "Fine. Betty White."

She scoffs. "You picked her because she's passed away."

"Because I knew you'd ask some silly question like, Would I dump her for you?"

She smirks. "Something like that, yeah."

"I don't even want to know which male movie star you lust after."

She smiles.

"Okay, I do. Who is it?"

"No one, really. He's barely even handsome."

"Who. Is. It?"

She bats her lashes. "I'm not telling. It doesn't matter."

"Who is it?" I mutter.

She laughs. "Boo, you're so jealous! Okay, it's Jensen Ackles."

"Who the fuck is that?"

She gasps. "You've never watched *Supernatural*? Oh my God, there's fifteen seasons."

I shake my head. "Would you dump me for him?"

She taps her chin. "First, you need to watch the show. I'll sit with you. His character, Dean Winchester, fights demons and ghosts and vampires. He's cool and loyal—and sexy, of course."

I grunt.

"He's a bad boy, sort of reckless, but he'll do anything for his brother, including going to hell for him. His best friend is an angel, he knows his way around a knife, and he drives a kick-ass 1967 Chevrolet Impala. Nah, I'd keep you around if I met him, but come on; you must watch it! He kinda reminds me of you. Tough on the outside, kind underneath." She sighs. "Okay, my turn. If you had one wish, what would it be?"

I had been watching her and pull my eyes back to the road. "I'd be an ass if I didn't say world peace."

"Forget world peace. What would you choose?"

I sigh. "World peace. I insist. Or a cure for all disease."

"Nothing for yourself?"

I speed past an SUV. "Hmm, I really can't decide. You tell me your wish."

She gazes out her window, her voice soft. "I'd want to know who my parents are. Not that I can go back and change anything—my life turned out being the one meant for me—but to know what happened. Maybe I'd have closure."

"Do you think they might still be out there?"

She chews her bottom lip. "I have this gut feeling my mom couldn't take care of me. It's funny, but when I was in the group home, I had dreams about her. She always looks like me and lives in Manhattan." She smirks at me. "Okay, your wish. What would it be?"

"My wish is that you're amazed by what I'm going to show you."

Her eyes narrow as she studies my profile. "You must have another one besides that?"

My hands tighten on the wheel. Yeah, I have a wish—that my parents had been different—but I can't say that. We're having fun, and it would bring the mood down.

"Fine," she says as she studies my face. "New question. Hypothetically, if we made it to, let's say, fifty dates, would you agree to get a tattoo of my face somewhere on your body?"

"I hate needles. A lot. Almost as much as clowns. It's called try-panophobia. I passed out once as a kid when I got a shot, and it messed me up. Even giving blood for my checkups makes me freak. I have to psych myself up and meditate. It's not a fun experience. Needles suck."

Her mouth parts. "Seriously? Oh my God, I would do it for you!"

"You love tattoos—and needles! Little, tiny, vicious ones that dig into your skin—ugh, it makes me want to hurl to even think about it."

She crosses her arms. "Fifty dates! I've never had fifty dates. That's it. We're over. I'm breaking up with you."

"Are you going to give back my class ring?"

"Pawn it, of course."

I clutch my heart. "You've killed me. I'll never date again."

"You will. She'll be twenty and tall."

I chuckle.

She scoffs. "I'll start dating an artist."

"Then I'll run into you at Café Lazzo and beat him up."

"And I'll have a girl fight with your model."

"Then we'll go back to my penthouse."

"And I'll still be angry because you didn't get a tattoo for me and go straight to my apartment."

"That wasn't the direction I was going in." I'm still chuckling as I park on the street. Around midnight, the neighborhood is quiet, lit with ornate iron lampposts. Just a few streets over are high-end hotels, galleries, and restaurants.

"I love SoHo," she says, then sighs. "It's pretty."

I tell her that I own rental property here and in Tribeca. I don't mention the real estate I have in the Hamptons, Boston, and Virginia. I lead her down the corner and turn down West Broadway until we reach a cobblestone side street. We walk to a large yellow building with an old royal-blue double door.

I unlock it and show her inside. Even without lights, the white-and-black diamond-tiled floor glows. "The first floor used to be a boutique, and there's a loft upstairs. There's another entrance to the loft that bypasses the downstairs, but I wanted you to see the full effect of the door. I'm partial to it."

"You wanted to impress me." Her gaze drapes over me. "You don't need real estate. You had me at the scruff."

I laugh as we take the side stairs and enter the loft. I turn on the lights, and she looks around, surprise on her face as she takes in the various styles of art, the wooden beams on the ceiling. She sees the clothes I was folding on the couch, the ragged books on the coffee table. "You come here a lot. It's downright rustic compared to your penthouse."

"Hmm."

I lead her into the kitchen. "It's twenty-five-hundred square feet with three bedrooms and a rooftop. I come here for a change of scenery—more since Jasper moved in."

"Who watches Cherry when you're gone?"

"Dog walker, one of Herman's relatives."

"Is that who kept her while you were in Virginia?"

I stop, my hands twitching as I wrestle with a bald-faced lie or . . .

"I didn't go. I stayed home instead." I glance away from her.

"You were alone over Christmas?"

"Don't feel bad for me. I could have gone to see Ronan and his family, but . . ." I pause, frowning. "It would have felt like an intrusion on their family time. He's got a kid now."

She watches me. "I get it. I've spent plenty of holidays with no one. Whether you're rich or poor, it's hard."

I set down two different types of ice cream, and she squeals and picks chocolate. I dish out a large portion in one bowl, spray whipped cream over it, grab two spoons, and lead her to the couch. She takes a mouthful and groans.

She talks around a glob of ice cream. "I remember you saying you didn't ever eat in the bed, but the couch is okay?"

"Don't make fun of me because I'm picky. The bed is for sleep and fucking." Then I tell her about Jasper and his cheese puffs on my couch.

"You've really got a sweet tooth," I say when she asks for more whipped cream.

"I never did much before . . ." Her words stop. "Anyway. I love the art you have." Her eyes trace the room, taking in the pieces I've collected. I tend to buy art from every place I visit, and I never know where to put it. The penthouse was decorated by an interior designer, so most of my personal purchases end up at the loft.

After we finish, I give her an old practice shirt, boxers, and a pair of white tube socks. I change into my oldest, most comfortable flannel pants and a T-shirt with holes. We lean back on the fluffy chaise in the den.

She snuggles into my arms, her head fitting under my chin as we talk about our favorite paintings. I tell her mine is *The Starry Night*.

"Van Gogh painted it from the view of his room in an asylum in France. It's dark, but there's light in the sky."

"Hope, maybe," she says. "He came from a religious family, and there's a church in the painting, as if he's clinging to God."

My fingers trail over her shoulders as I recall her compass. I add, "I like to think the stars are there to guide him back home to his brother, Theo. Vincent struggled with mental illness—that no one knew how to treat—religion, poverty, loneliness. He was there for a year, even took over an entire floor as a studio. He painted a hundred and fifty paintings in a year at the asylum."

"Then, a year after he left, he walked out to the wheat fields he loved to paint and shot himself in the chest. He walked back to the inn and got in his bed, and when his brother arrived, he told him that his sadness would last forever." She pauses. "Maybe today, he could get help."

"I like that you know who he is. Most people just know that he's the guy that cut off his ear."

She smiles. "And I like that you know who he is."

I ease her up. "Speaking of art, I still haven't shown you the surprise. Come on."

We hold hands as I guide her to my master bedroom. Before I open the door, I say, "This place doesn't get a maid. Prepare yourself . . ."

She sees the unmade bed I slept in a few nights last week and the floating bookshelves, then peers out at the floor-to-ceiling view of the rooftop. Outside is a retro yellow patio set with different-colored chairs, a hot tub, and a small pool that needs cleaning.

She nods. "Quaint. Not what I expected."

"The surprise is over there." I nudge my head to the charcoal sketch that hangs over the dresser, and she rushes toward it, nearly tripping over a pile of sneakers.

"It caught my eye years ago at an arts festival."

She looks from the sketch to me. Tears pool in her eyes.

"Sweetheart . . . ," I start, and she huffs under her breath.

"No, no, it's okay. I'm fine. Just crazy emotional right now. Sorry. I swear I never cry." She bites her lip as she studies the drawing of Wickham. "You got this at the art fair in Greenwich. You bought it." Her hand covers her chest. "Tuck . . . this means something, yes?"

Not replying to that, I close the space between us and stand behind her with my hands on her shoulders. "I bought it several years ago, yes."

"I drew it from a bench across the street," she continues. "I even sketched Herman at the door and Darden on his balcony. There's Cece talking to Brogan on the sidewalk."

My arms encircle her waist. "It got my attention because it was my building. And it's a good piece. See her?" I point to the woman leaning against the building.

She melts against me. "Me. In my harem pants with my satchel . . ."

"Wearing your locket."

She turns around in my arms. "Decadence? You recognized it? So you knew I lived or was familiar with Wickham outside Café Lazzo?"

I shake my head emphatically. "No. I recognized the locket as being familiar, but things moved so fast that night there wasn't time to figure it out. I realized it when we were in the elevator together after one of our walks."

"Fate is crazy."

"Hmm." We sway together to a song that isn't playing.

She looks up at me. "Just throwing this out, and keep in mind it's late and my thoughts tend to get more fanciful the later it gets . . ."

"Okay?"

"Some cultures believe in reincarnation, like a wheel of rebirth, and then there's the whole karma thing. Basically, your next life may depend on the way you lived your past life. When you're reborn, whether it's ten years later or a hundred, the people around you might be past family members or lovers, and you'll be faced with the same struggles. If you've been horrible, you might be an animal or a plant."

"Are you saying Cherry could be my dead ancestor that fucked up?"

She rolls her eyes. "Some say you're destined to meet the same person over and over until you get it right."

"Ah." I sweep her up and settle her in my bed, then plop down next to her. I lean up on my elbow as I gaze down at her. "So fate keeps pushing us together because we never got it right in our past lives?"

She rolls on top of me and smiles. "I hear skepticism. Do you believe in anything?"

I pause at the seriousness in her eyes, choosing my words carefully. "I believe in today. I believe the sun's going to come up with us together in this bed. There's no force pushing me around a chessboard. I create my own destiny. I'm not at the whim of the stars."

She tsks as her fingers trace my eyebrows. "You're a cynical man. I'm a cynic too, but . . ." A troubled expression flits over her face. "There must be purpose; otherwise what's the point in tragedy and suffering?"

"So our lives are prefixed? We can do nothing to stop the outcome?"

"We have free will. We choose the path. That's why it keeps happening over and over." She chews on her bottom lip. "I'm just a dreamer, Tuck. I'm not a Buddhist or Hinduist or a Christian. I'm not anything;

I'm still figuring that out. But I keep asking questions. Why did I feel driven to live in Manhattan? My dreams? Why did Wickham accept foster kids and I get in? Why did I meet Darden and Cece and Brogan? Why do I have this locket? Why have I seen you for years? Why did you buy my sketch? Why did we feel drawn to each other at the club? I bet if you made a map of Manhattan and took yarn and traced your steps and mine, they'd overlap over and over. It all piles up, layer by layer. Little pushes. Nudges. Leading us in a certain direction. Sometimes there are too many coincidences to call it a coincidence, yes?"

"Am I your fate?" I frown. I'm not good enough for her. I'm flawed. Ugly on the inside.

"Maybe." She rests her cheek on my chest as the sun slowly peeks over the horizon. Her finger traces my bicep. "How did you grow up in Virginia?"

"Normal. Typical. Lots of football." I card my fingers through her hair.

"But not perfect, right?"

I pause. "No."

"If there's a perfect family out there, then they're aliens masquerading as humans to take over the world, or they're robots. I like the robot idea. It reminds me of that book, what was it . . ."

"*Stepford Wives*? I watched one of the movies or TV shows."

Her nose scrunches. "That's it. Murdering husbands who replace their Connecticut feminist wives with docile, perfect robots." Her voice takes on a dreamy quality. "In spite of how I was in and out of foster homes, I want my own family. Not just Darden and Cece and Brogan."

A chill washes over me. "Not anytime soon, yeah?"

She's quiet, and my hands still. "Francesca?"

"Maybe sooner than I realized."

My throat tightens. "Shit." I ease her off me, stand, and pace around the room, my head tumbling. Why is she talking about fate, then family?

She hasn't moved from the bed, not an inch, her body strangely still as she looks at me. "You've always had this air about you, carefree and happy go lucky. I can see you as a dad—"

"Stop," I say sharply, adrenaline rushing through my veins as she hits a nerve.

She plucks at the comforter. "Ah, yes. I presume too much, and it's too soon for such talk. You were all I thought about in California." Her chest rises. "There's something I should tell you—"

"No, don't," I say, interrupting her. "Don't bring emotions into this."

She gets a puzzled look. "That's not—"

"I've been honest with you, Francesca. I don't want . . . ," I say, cutting her off, then trailing off, unsure how to continue. How do I say that I *can* love but I'm also a monster with sharp teeth?

Emotionally, I'm broken.

And physically? Jesus. What if I *am* my dad?

Part of me doesn't trust Francesca—not about the stalking; that's long gone.

She's hammering on the steel walls around my heart.

I can't let her in.

Can't.

Can't.

Jesus, there's such a long list of why I can't commit!

I rake both hands through my hair. "Don't you think this is a conversation for down the road?" Most girls wait months before poking at the idea of family.

"I guess when I know what I want . . ." Her shoulders shrug. "I kissed you. That means something . . ." Blue-green eyes flash up at me. "It's a big fucking deal."

"I'm not sure where we're going, okay? Let's date, yeah—I really like you. You're different. Beautiful. Special. I'd like it if I'm the only guy you're fucking, and I'll do the same. That's what I offer. Is that enough?"

The air crackles with tension.

She nudges her head at the door, and I see my hand on the knob. My knuckles are white. "Are you sure about that?" A wan smile flits over her face. "If you want to leave, go. I'm familiar with the experience."

Exasperation, mixed with uncertainty, surges over me.

I want light. Fun. Easy.

Not serious.

"You have me, okay? You played hard to get and won. I haven't been with anyone since Decadence. I want *you*, Francesca; I've never made that a secret. When I came to your door, when I saw you in the bookstore . . ." Pressure tightens in my chest. "I fucking need you, okay? I'm sorry I don't dig this fate thing."

"I didn't play any games. There was no 'hard to get' going on. I had doubts about you. I still do." She looks down at her hands. "As far as fate is concerned, you didn't have to agree with me or believe in it; I didn't expect that, but it bugs you—which I find telling. I don't understand our coincidences, but that isn't what this is about. I want to know who you really are. I want to know about your normal childhood. It only seems fair since you had someone look into my life."

There's an edge to that last sentence.

"I won't ever do that again," I tell her. "I swear."

"Too late now."

I let go of the doorknob and stalk to the window. My head dips as I ponder.

She's here, the most real thing I've had in years. So why can't I open up to her?

My fists clench. Self-preservation.

Because my mother taught me that love can be yanked away at any moment.

I learned to protect myself, to hide parts of myself.

I hear the shuffle of the sheets as she stands. "Tuck, I need to tell you—"

"Wait." I whip around and rush to her before she can say something that ends us. It's what I let my past girlfriends do. They get fed up; then finally, they give up and walk out.

"You're the only girl I've brought here; I want you to know that. This is me trying, but I'm fucked up, okay?" My teeth tug on my bottom lip; then out rush my words. "You want to know why I was alone over the holidays? My mother hates me because my dad killed himself on my birthday. He got in his car and drove it straight into a tree. He'd been drinking, and they'd argued. Maybe he'd given up on her. Maybe he was disgusted with himself, his life, her—I don't know."

I yank out the bottom drawer of the nightstand and pull out photos. She takes one. "Your parents?"

"At a society thing they were at." I sit on the bed with her as we gaze at the picture. It's like art, capturing a moment in time, a slice of emotion from my parents. Wearing a slinky gold evening gown with her hair swirled up, my mother stares up at my dad with adoration, maybe desperation. Dressed in a tux, he clasps her hand in his. His jaw is clenched as he glares at the photographer.

"You look like him," she murmurs.

I grunt. "Fuck that."

"Okay, you do, but he seems cold." She traces her fingers over his face.

"Never to her. He was mad with love. They didn't intend to have me. I was a mistake. I made things worse."

"Tuck . . . I'm so sorry."

I exhale long and hard. "He hit her, she hit him, and he hit me when I got between them. She covered her bruises with makeup and kept telling me to smile. Her love for me depended on that smile." My teeth grit at the emotion clawing at my chest. "And yeah, I still pretend like none of that happened. It's easier than dwelling on shit I should be over."

"It doesn't work like that, Tuck. Scars on the inside are still there."

"Her love had conditions; he never showed any. The thought of family terrifies me. I can only be responsible for myself. At least then, I'm not hurting anyone. Maybe I'll inherit her issues. It's genetic. You want to know me? Really? You want the stuff that's underneath?"

"Tuck—"

I can't stop. "I didn't grow up normal. I grew up tense and scared. With chaos all around me. I didn't know what would set him off—or her. I crept around our house on eggshells. Football was my only reprieve. The summers in high school when I went to Texas for football camp were the best months of my life. I've spent the last few years thinking I was good, you know, but now I'm dealing with open aggression issues. That's from my therapist. I rage. I fly off the handle at shit that wouldn't have bothered me five years ago. I'm worried about my future in football. I'm worried my mother will never forgive me. I'm worried I am my father deep down. I pick fights. I drive too fast. I'm so worn down and desperate that I take walks and give out coats to lower my stress."

"You do it for other reasons too."

"Do I? Maybe I'm just a real asshole and the only reason I'm doing it is to feel better about myself. Maybe I don't care about homeless people. Oh, and here's a tidbit for you. I take meds for depression and anxiety. Mash all that together, and what you get is a man on a razor's edge. Is that the guy you want to be with?"

She swallows. "Yes."

"Well, shit. Baby. That's not what I expected you to say." I brush a tear off her face. "Then stay. Just don't go, okay? People leave us, Francesca. Give me, us, a chance. Please."

Her breath hitches. "I will. I am."

"Patience?"

She nods. "Kiss me."

Relief soars in my chest, and I take her in my arms.

We fall back down to the bed and kiss until our lips are swollen. I keep my hands above her waist. Sweet. Gentle. Her face rests next to mine on the pillow, and I trace my fingers over her widow's peak, the curve of her cheek. "This is crazy. I should be exhausted, but you're here, and I'm not."

Her lashes drop, her voice fading. "Hmm, you're not sleepy?"

"I'm half-afraid you might disappear." The words are barely a whisper, and I'm not sure she hears.

I watch the slow rise of her chest as she drifts off. I'm in deep with her, and I've got no idea where we're going.

My fear?

This is gonna hurt when it's over.

Chapter 14

TUCK

I wake up a few hours later, my arm curled around her waist. I kiss her shoulder and head for the shower. I pass by the sketch of Wickham and don't realize I'm smiling until I glance in the mirror. I blink. Fuck. When's the last time I woke up looking forward to the day? A damn long time.

I bought the sketch around nine years ago, after the death of my father and when my mother went missing. Some of those days are blurry, cloudy, as if I were stoned. The truth is I was hurt and lost. Still, I put on my smile and played football. Pretending. I feel like shit for the women I went through in those years. And just when I was starting to find my footing, my mom showed up for help.

The hot water spills over me, and I hum Bia's "Can't Touch This" as it plays on the shower speaker. I dance. Shake my ass. And when "Come and Get Your Love," by Redbone, comes on, I'm singing.

"Wahoo! Can I join the party?" Francesca says as she sashays into the room, wearing nothing but my mask from Decadence. Her dark hair is mussed, her lips curled in a pouty smile. I laugh, the sound layered with joy and liberation.

With her hand on her hip, she blows a kiss at me. "Hey, sexy pantyhose slayer. Wanna open the door and let me in?"

"Hell yeah."

She removes the mask, puts it on the counter, and then giggles as she darts into my arms. I gaze down at her, and clarity tingles over me. She gets me and accepts me, and she *kissed* me. I know what that means. She's all in—and it doesn't even scare me right now.

Was it fate or coincidence that we met on my birthday, the anniversary of my dad's death? Don't know, but she feels right.

Like a gift from the heavens to make up for the bad shit.

Herman opens the door for us at Wickham. "You two look happy."

We murmur our hellos, then smile at each other.

"Okay, so what's the surprise today?" I ask as we get in the elevator. After our shower, she said she wanted to show me something today but wouldn't say what.

"There's no fun in telling you. First, I need to put on warm clothes, 'kay? Ones that fit me."

She's wearing a pair of my sweats rolled under at the waist a few times and a baggy Pythons sweatshirt. I'm wearing a thick cream fisherman sweater and jeans. I feel ready to take on the world.

The elevator door opens as Darden comes out of his apartment.

"Good morning," I say, and he grunts, his craggy face flattening.

"Are you two just getting in?" He glares at Francesca's clothes.

Francesca nods, her voice demure. "Yes, Mr. Darden."

He harrumphs. "Did any talking get done?"

"Uh, yeah?" I say uncertainly at his tone. I don't know what he's referring to, but perhaps Francesca has confided in him about us?

Francesca waves him off. "You look handsome today. Where are you headed, Mr. Darden?"

He points his cane at her. "Where do you think? Widow Crane has blackmailed me into her ridiculous book club. I'm going. A prisoner of war."

"Don't be dramatic. It doesn't suit you," Francesca coos as she walks to him and straightens his bow tie.

He lets her, arching his neck. "I'm about to undergo torture by a man-eater. For you, Miss Lane. I'd hardly call me dramatic. Perhaps if you'd been home last night, you could have come up with a solution to get me out of this predicament." He pats her arm. "Of course, you could end my suffering with just a few sentences." He gives her a meaningful look, and she brushes her lips over his cheek, then whispers something in his ear.

He rears back. "You *are* my business, young lady, and I want what's best for you. Communication is key. Stop pussyfooting around!"

He stomps off, and Francesca sighs as we walk inside her apartment.

"What was that?" I ask as I shut the door.

"Nothing really."

"Nice place," I murmur as I take in her art, the colorful decor. It's small but cozy and warm, and her view of the park is spectacular.

I follow her as she goes into the kitchen, stares at the coffeepot for a few moments, pours a cup, takes a long drink, and then groans in relief. I offered her coffee at my place earlier, and she said no.

"Is there something special about your coffee?" I ask.

"I just don't indulge often, but . . ." She shrugs. "Anyway, Darden is upset about joining the book club. It might be my fault."

Before I can ask more questions, Brogan comes out from where I guess is his bedroom. Wearing pajama pants and an NYU sweatshirt, he gives me an incredulous, almost happy look, then laughs. "Morning! Good to see you, Tuck—you know, outside of Decadence."

"And there's no British accent," I say as we clasp hands.

"Morning. Fancy a cuppa?" He grins as he moves to pour a mug for himself, then puts in sugar.

"Sure."

She tells us she needs to get dressed as Brogan and I chat about Decadence and the Vegas game.

"What are you guys up to today?" he asks as he gets me a cup of coffee.

"She wants to show me her favorite place."

Brogan's eyebrows rise. "Oh shit." A small laugh comes from him. "Where do you think it is?"

"In New York? I figured we're going to a museum or a gallery."

He shakes his head. "Here's the thing about Francesca. She's tough, but there's a sappy side . . ." He smirks. "Meh, I'll let her show you the place."

I inch closer. "Is she gonna take me to the Empire State Building for a kiss?"

He smiles slowly. "Not telling, but know this: she's read *The Notebook* and would have loved to be part of that book club but doesn't like Widow Carnes."

"Do I need to read this book?"

He laughs. "Maybe. But she loves that stuff. Ever see *Titanic*?"

"God, no."

"Right? She has. A hundred times. Just because I'm gay, they want to foist it on me." He flexes a bicep at me. "I'm a tough guy who enjoys thrillers and horror, but they force movies on me. *The Last of the Mohicans*, *To All the Boys I've Loved Before*, *La La Land*, *The Fault in Our Stars*. Sad shit. Her and Cece—Jesus, it's a wonder I haven't started a menstrual cycle living here."

"You said you loved *The Last of the Mohicans*!" Francesca calls from down the hall.

"I said I liked the booming orchestra music!" Brogan calls back, then half smiles, half grimaces. "She's got bionic ears."

"So she's taking me to the cinema to watch her favorite movie?"

"Worse. At least she won't be making you go to the catacombs under Saint Paul's. She cornered us into that one night. Freaky as hell. She loves all the tourist tours in the city." He pauses. "So, um, did you guys talk?"

I pause midsip. Darden asked the same thing. "Is there something I should know?"

"Nope. Just checking." He looks away from me and begins to clean up the kitchen.

She walks in the room and rushes up to me wearing a clingy black sweater dress with black heeled boots. She slips on her moto jacket, and when her hand takes mine, I try to forget about the tingle of unease I got from Brogan's question.

We walk down Fifth Avenue to Seventy-Fifth Street, cross over to the sidewalk, and enter Central Park. Holding hands in a companionable silence, we pass the playground, then *Alice in Wonderland*, a large bronze sculpture. Not crowded at this hour, the park is sparsely populated, the trees stark as they stick up into the sky.

We reach the lake and pass the boathouse, then the Bethesda Fountain. "Do you want to make a wish in the fountain?" I wait for her to tell me it's her favorite place.

"No."

"Well then, that leaves Bow Bridge up ahead," I murmur as we continue down the path.

Her hand tightens in mine. "Yep. One of New York's iconic landmarks."

I laugh at the glow that emanates from her smile.

"Is that your favorite place in New York?"

She nods. "Cliché, right? Made of cast iron—the second-oldest one in the US—it's the crown jewel of the park. The shape is a cupid's bow. I mean, come on—how cool is that? Doesn't it make you gooey?"

"No." I snort. "I mean, yeah, I appreciate how old it is, the style."

She nods. "Victorian, Gothic, and Renaissance styles. Plus you have the Manhattan landscape. Where's your favorite place, then?"

"No clue."

"Come on; you must have one!"

"Hmm, maybe the stadium? I won three Super Bowls there." I take in the couples on the bridge. "Don't people propose here a lot?"

"There's no ring in my pocket, so don't freak," she says with a smirk. "Let's get to the center and look out over the lake. I love the walkway, the way it slowly rises up. It's like a surprise at every step."

"Jesus. You are really, really silly," I say teasingly as I kiss her hand clasped in mine.

"Growing up, I always dreamed of seeing the landmarks here. This one *is* my favorite. Our city is full of grit, but here's the heart."

"Hmm."

We gaze out at a boat paddling by, and my arm goes around her.

She looks over at me, and our eyes cling. Hers are full of uncertainty. Questions.

I touch her face. "Hey. I like your favorite place. It's cool. I get it. Our city has magic. New York gets dinged for crime and scandals and homelessness, but it's home. Yours."

She lifts her hand, her fingers carding through my hair. Her words are shy. "And it's where I want you to kiss me."

Warmth fills my chest as I turn her to face me and press my lips to hers. "You and me, little princess. Kissing on Bow Bridge."

Chapter 15

FRANCESCA

I check my appearance in the mirror. My eye shadow is shades of gold, my lashes long and thick. I pivot for a side view—my tiny bump barely noticeable in a red miniskirt and a cropped pink sweater with a fuzzy red heart on the front. I smile, pushing down my anxieties.

It's celebration tonight. For two things. One is Valentine's Day, and the other is Darden, although he doesn't know it. I step out of Tuck's master bath and into his bedroom. He's already gone out to the den, and I pick up the room, folding my clothes I washed earlier. We barely spend time apart. Either I'm here, or he's at my place. Sometimes we go to the loft when we want time away from Jasper.

My gaze snags on the selfie I printed of us at the Bow Bridge, taken with his phone. Our faces are next to each other, and we're laughing. We look like cheesy tourists, and it makes me smile—until my throat tightens. The night before at the loft, I planned to tell him about the baby—even attempted it twice but pulled back as I realized he needed to vent. He shared his insecurities, and I couldn't pile more on top when he was being so vulnerable. Besides, I always had the next day. Only the next day was at Bow Bridge, and we were so happy I decided to wait until the next day.

And the next.

And the next.

I'll tell him today, I said after my last doctor's visit two weeks ago; only when I got back to his penthouse, he'd planned a carriage ride through the park at night for us.

We were a bubble of happiness, a magic spell, and why on earth would I break it?

The following night, I psyched myself up all day, going over the words and how to deliver them gently—only that night as we lay in bed watching TV, Cherry curled up next to me instead of him. She rested her head on my leg while Tuck pouted.

I have had a litany of excuses, but the crux of it is simple.

He is something I never imagined I needed.

And I don't want to lose him.

He is air. Life. And his flawed edges? His chaos? I love them the most. The struggle on his face when Jasper talks about football, the torment in his voice when he speaks to Nella on the phone, the nights he kisses me, then goes to the third floor and works out for hours.

In the back of my mind, a part of me is praying he'll fall so deep in love with me that the prospect of a baby wouldn't be that bad. I just need a bit more time.

The clock is ticking, my head says as I walk down the hall. I pause when I hear Cece's sugary voice. "The weak can never forgive. Forgiving is an attribute of the strong. You should remember that. It will keep your relationship with Francesca healthy."

"Isn't that a Gandhi quote?" Tuck asks.

"It's a Cece quote. Who's this Gandhi?"

He laughs, the dark rumble making goose bumps rise. "I never know if you're serious."

"Serious is for the dead. Now that is a Cece quote."

"Hmm. Tell me how you met Francesca."

I hear Cece exhale. "On the first day of class, she walked in in these outrageously stacked Converse. I giggled, and she gave me a dirty look. We ignored each other for weeks; then one night, I was out at this bar with a guy I was totally in love with. I know, me, right? Anyway, Francesca plopped down next to me on a barstool and said, 'Your boyfriend is having sex in the bathroom with a girl. Let's go kick his ass.' No *hi* or anything."

"Did you?"

Cece snorts. "Who do you think you're talking to? I kicked down the stall, slapped him, then stalked away. Best night ever. Then, she and I got trashed, maybe high, and ended up at Coney Island on the Ferris wheel. No clue how we got there. We vowed our friendship was forever."

"But you laughed at her shoes?"

"No—I mean, yeah, but it was more about hey, look at the balls on that chick. She's got something about her that people love—even old Darden." Her face turns serious. "He was her first friend, not me or Brogan. There's a pecking order. It's Darden, me, Brogan, then you."

I can feel Tuck bristle from here. His voice is silky. "I'm fourth? Fuck that."

"Whatever. I'm spilling no secrets tonight, but you know how she feels. Just don't mess with her, 'kay?"

I roll my eyes, turn the corner, and drink them in, my girl bestie and the man who's swept me off my feet.

The thought stalls as he turns and brings his whiskey to his lips as I walk. I take it slow, swinging my hips. Green eyes blaze with heat, and just like that, my insides quake. Happiness hits my brain, and my smile must be huge because Cece makes a gagging face behind Tuck's back.

It's going to end soon, a voice whispers.

He eyes me up and down. "You are fucking gorgeous."

"She's my boo," Cece murmurs.

I inhale his spicy male scent, and my body hums at the memory of us this morning, his maddening tongue tracing circles on my nipples as he pumped inside of me in his shower.

"Do you want a drink?" he asks.

"Just club soda."

"It's Darden's birthday, and we're probably going to give him a heart attack when he walks in. You might need alcohol."

"I'm good."

"I'll grab you a water." He kisses my cheek, then whispers in my ear. "You're mine later."

He strides off, and I let out a shaky breath, then turn to Cece, who's eyeing me.

"What?"

"You're in a bad spot, honey. You've caught feelings."

"I've got this," I lie as I head to the den.

Fifteen minutes later, Jasper, Cece, Brogan, Herman, and I wait in the dark for Darden. Tuck's mission was to ask him up to discuss a business venture. We hear the doorbell ping, Tuck's signal that he's got him. I wanted a party for Darden but knew he'd know if I planned it at my place; then Tuck offered to do it here.

"The package is arriving," Jasper whispers over by the light switch. "Remember he's eighty. So no shouting."

The door opens in the foyer, and Darden grumbles, "I don't understand why we couldn't talk at my place."

"I thought you might like to see the view from here and try a glass of this new Scotch I got."

"I only drink peppermint tea these days," he grouses. "Why is it so dark in here, Avery? It's a cave."

Jasper flips the lights on and cranks up "In da Club," and Cece releases a banner from a string that Brogan rigged up that says **Go For 100 Darden** on it. Herman and I call out, "Happy birthday!" Then someone starts the song.

Darden stands there stoically, glaring at all of us. "Who's to blame for this atrocity?"

I raise my hand, and he glowers. "Miss Lane. You should be out celebrating a holiday invented for flower shops and card companies. Can I go now?"

I smile. "There's birthday cake and ice cream."

"And applesauce if you don't have your teeth in," Brogan says.

Darden scowls. "Full of jokes, aren't you?"

"Don't be a grouch, Darden. We've got Hula-Hoops, am I right?" Jasper says, busting out the circular toys and passing them around.

"Is this a kindergarten party?" Darden asks.

I smirk. "We tried to come up with a theme. Cece wanted a 1940s thing, Brogan wanted to do all black, and I suggested we just have fun. You can laugh at us, yeah?"

His eyebrows bristle as he watches Herman slip a Hula-Hoop over his doorman suit, then swivel his hips. A small twitch lifts his lips when the hoop falls and Herman's face reddens.

Cece puts a birthday sash on him, and he grunts. "Bring me some cake. No ice cream. It makes me gassy."

"Sure," I say.

"Hey, man, would you like a margarita?" Jasper asks as he whips off his shirt, slips a Hula-Hoop over his head, and circles his hips. "I'd bet anyone in this room that I could make one and Hula-Hoop at the same time."

"I'm in," Tuck says and slaps down a dollar on the coffee table.

"Same!" Cece calls.

"Me! Don't forget me," Herman says and puts down a dollar.

Darden waves his hands at Jasper. "Can someone turn off that awful music and put on the nature channel?"

"It is your birthday, sir." Tuck kills the music, finds the channel, and gives Darden the remote.

Jasper fails at making margaritas while Hula-Hooping. He can't get close enough to the bar to hit the button as he swivels his hips, and we dissolve into laughter.

Cece and Jasper get into a Hula-Hoop contest, and Darden is the rule decider. Herman has a Slinky, and Brogan gleefully decorates Tuck's fireplace mantel with Silly String. I'm laughing as I look around, then miss Tuck. Easing away, I find him in the hallway, standing in front of the Pollock.

He wraps an arm around my waist when I appear. "I like your family," he murmurs.

"Thank you. Why are you over here? Come join us?"

He slides his hand under my hair and cups the back of my head, massaging. "Sorry. Sometimes I can't help but get pulled into this painting."

I exhale. "You could donate it to a museum?"

"Maybe." His fingers dance along my back and outline my tattoo by memory. "I have a gift for you."

"I have one for you." A sketch I did of him.

He laces our fingers together and tugs me to his room.

"Tuck, we can't—"

"It won't take long; I promise."

We end up at his dresser. He pulls out a drawer and opens a velvet case, and I gasp.

He holds up a glittering diamond necklace, and the center is huge, at least five carats—

"Tuck! This is too much." The diamonds' facets shine under the light.

"Shh." He turns me to face the mirror as he puts the necklace around my throat.

Our eyes hold in the mirror; then he dips his face to my neck. "Francesca, I'm not a man with pretty words, but . . . you've given me something. Hope, maybe? Trust? I want to give you the prettiest jewels, the best of everything. Just let me, okay?"

I melt against his frame as he kisses my neck. Lust rides me as his hands skim my waist. I reach behind me to his groin and unzip his pants.

"We have guests," he drags out in a rough voice.

"Don't care. Let's be quick. I'm already wet for you."

"Let me see, hmm?" He lifts the skirt of my dress in the front and palms my lace panties. He moves aside the elastic and rubs a slow circle, edging closer and closer until he groans, then sinks a finger inside. My hips move with him, my head thrown back in the crook of his shoulder. His cashmere sweater rubs my face, the softness of the fabric erotic against my cheek.

He lifts my sweater, exposing my bra. He pinches my nipple, and my pussy throbs as I moan.

"Shh, I'm not going to let you come. Later."

I whimper, and he kisses the shell of my ear as his fingers slip out of my panties. He tugs down my sweater and arranges the jewels around my throat. My face is flushed as he brushes his fingers over my mouth. "Rosebud lips. Such a beauty, Francesca."

He leaves the room as I try to catch my breath.

Fifteen minutes later he tugs me into the guest bathroom, sets me on the counter, spreads my legs, and tongues my core through the lace. With my knees bent up to my breasts, I try to slide my underwear aside, but he stops me. "Wait a little longer," he purrs as he fixes my hair, pure male satisfaction on his face as he walks out the door.

Later, I tug him into the kitchen pantry, unzip his pants, and suck him hard and fast, my tongue flicking his head. When his hands fist in my hair and he pushes me down to where my throat tightens around him, I ease back, then walk out.

It takes a full five minutes before he leaves the pantry.

When Herman says he needs to head home, we walk him out. After the elevator closes, Tuck picks me up in his arms and presses me against the wall. He shoves my skirt up and grinds his pelvis against my center. His zipper rubs against my clit, and I tug on his hair, tilting his head to kiss him deeply.

Darden leaves after Herman, and we repeat it, only going further, me pumping his dick as he fingers me.

When Cece and Brogan leave, he adds two fingers and whispers all the dirty things he wants to do with me.

We walk back in the penthouse, and Jasper is cleaning up. He takes in my tousled hair and the tent in Tuck's slacks and announces he's going to Courtney's.

The door shuts, and I'm unzipping my skirt in the den. I unhook my bra, and my breasts swing free. I cup them, brushing them against the diamonds. "Take off your clothes," I demand, an edge to my voice. If I don't get him inside me soon . . .

He takes it slow, first easing off his sweater and undershirt, then slowly unzipping his pants and shoving them down. His underwear is next, and his length springs free.

He prowls to me, a fierce look in his eyes. He stares down at me, searching my face. "Want to come, Princess?"

I turn around, brace my arms on the back of his couch, and wiggle my ass. "Yes."

He palms my breasts, then slides his hand down my back as fire licks where he touches. He rips my panties in pieces, and when I tell him how much they cost, he says he'll buy me more. I hear the crinkle of a condom; then he lines up behind me, his arms alongside mine, the tingle from his skin giving me goose bumps. He teases me with small strokes, then gives me more, then more.

I turn my head and hold his gaze. It's our thing. Intimate. He needs it. To be seen. I gasp and arch my back while he strums my clit like an instrument.

"I want to see your face," he says in a guttural voice from deep inside his chest.

We end up on the fur rug in front of the fireplace. He covers me, hooking my knees under his hands as he slides in.

The diamonds jiggle around my breasts as we fuck.

And fuck.

And fuck.

The feel of him; the protective, possessive gleam in his eyes; the excitement of the edging—I'm coming undone.

I combust around him, calling his name as my hands dig into his skin. My pussy clenches and vibrates as he pauses and rotates his hips, digging into me, groaning at the feel of me tightening.

His hand cups my face as our breaths mingle. He stares at me, holding me captive as he reaches closer to the top. There's a question in his gaze, a need for something. His lush lips part. "Jesus. Baby. Sweetheart. You. You. I lo—"

He stops and breaks apart in ecstasy, his head dipping to take possession of my lips in a savage, open-mouthed kiss. I ride the wave with him, my hands stroking his shoulders frantically, rubbing his face, pushing the hair out of his eyes.

"Mine," he murmurs as he rolls me on top of him.

The fire crackles as I rest my face on his chest, listening to the thump of his heart.

Tomorrow. Tomorrow.

I'll tell him.

Chapter 16

TUCK

I walk into Coletta's Italian Bistro and see Coach Hardy, the head coach for the Pythons. A tall and distinguished man with gray hair, he played quarterback for Virginia Tech back in the day. Being from the same home state bonded us in a way. I'm not so sure about that now.

He takes my hand. "Good to see you, Tuck. It's weird not seeing everyone around all the time, huh? First playoffs we haven't made in years."

I wince, but he doesn't seem to notice.

"Where the hell is your coat? Aren't you cold?"

"Nah." I nod to the maître d', who tells me that Ben, my agent, is already waiting for us at a quiet table in the back.

We stroll through the restaurant and take our seats. Ben is there, dressed in a killer suit with his dark hair slicked back. We share pleasantries as our whiskeys are delivered. Seemed like the right thing to order. I need something to calm my nerves.

Coach Hardy adjusts his tie and clears his throat as he looks at me. "Tuck, you and I have spoken in my office about the upcoming year. I've met with the owner, and we've had some discussions. I want you to know that I wanted you to stay, but with the losses we took this year, the overall feeling is we need a fresh start. You're the hardest-working player, and you've been with the franchise since you were drafted. We respect that. We admire your tenacity and dedication. But you're older, and you've had some personal issues. Perhaps it's time for you to take a break, maybe figure out what you want. We, the team, want to go in a new direction." He exhales.

My chest burns.

I take a sip of whiskey, forcing my hand not to tremble.

I knew this was coming. My gut twisted and rolled with it for eighteen weeks of football. I went out on that field each time with the thought that it might be my last time.

They're deserting me. Letting me go out to the farm because I'm old.

I wait for a wave of rage to hit, the anger that boils underneath, and it's there, but my head is stuck in other places too.

Cece's comment that forgiving is an attribute of the strong and that I should remember it with Francesca.

What the hell did she mean?

Why have I never seen Francesca drink alcohol since Decadence?

There's other hints. The worry on Darden's face when he sees us together.

A cold sweat breaks out over my skin, and the muffled sound of the other patrons dims even more.

"Tuck?"

I look at Hardy, my jaw tightening. "You're moving on to younger players. My contract won't be renewed. Got it."

"What's the spin on this, Coach?" Ben asks. "We'd want Tuck to announce he's retiring before you release a statement."

"I wouldn't do it any other way." Hardy takes his glasses off and wipes them. "I hate doing this, Tuck. I really do. I wouldn't be surprised if you ended up on another team and breathing life into them. You've got what it takes."

Another sip of whiskey hits my lips. "No. Apparently, I used to have what it takes."

He grimaces. "I'm one of the longest-running coaches in the NFL. You're one of the longest-running wide receivers. We're not that different. At some point, we move on."

A kid from the restaurant, maybe ten, appears at my side.

"Can I have your autograph, Tuck?" he asks nervously, his hand twitching with a napkin and pen.

I smile. "Sure, kid. Who do I make it out to?"

He tells me, and I sign it with numb fingers.

Coach hands over papers for me to initial, and he gives me a deadline to announce my retirement, says his goodbyes, and then shakes our hands.

Ben puts a hand on my shoulder after he leaves. "That was brutal."

Another sip. "Yeah."

It's over for me and the Pythons.

Again, I wait for the rage, but it's muted.

I accept it. It's time to move on. I roll my neck. "What's next?"

"First, you release a press statement to the media, via email or however you want. I'll draft one and send it over. But now, today, we can talk about other opportunities. If you want to keep playing . . ." He arches a brow at me.

"Maybe."

"Tennessee needs a veteran wide receiver. They've got rookies and not a lot of talent."

I tap my fingers. Besides the team, my mother was another reason I stayed in New York. Now I have Francesca. I shelve that thought as he continues.

"There's Kansas City. I've quietly inquired, and they've expressed interest."

Both decent teams. Not as good as the Pythons, but . . .

"Salary?"

"Twelve million—I know, less than you're making now, but there's a bonus for making the playoffs."

It's not really about the money . . .

"Okay, what else?"

"Let me be frank as a friend. You've had a tough year. You're a free agent, and who says you have to decide right away? Take some time away; take your yacht out, and let it simmer. If you don't do football, we can check in with broadcasting. You're damn pretty, you speak well, and people like your charm. You'd do well in front of the camera."

"Broadcasting?" I scoff.

"Less stress while still being part of the world; feel me?"

"I'm starting a nonprofit." I lay out the framework I've been working on and how I'd like to see it run.

He nods. "That's a huge undertaking to fund. Are you sure you can handle that and play football?"

"I have more money than I know what to do with. My dad left me two billion. I can use it to help others."

His eyes blink. "Fuck."

I smirk. "Drinks are on me, right?"

He whistles under his breath. "Tuck, you can *buy* a football team—or invest in one at least."

"Nah, if I'm not playing, I don't wanna watch some other guys."

"Okay, circling back to the nonprofit. We need a needs assessment, a market analysis, a board of directors, fundraising. There's legal, accounting, and technical issues to tackle. I can put you in touch with some lawyers who specialize. Meet with them, maybe touch base with other similar people who've started big foundations." He frowns. "I don't know, Tuck . . ."

I finish my drink. "Yeah. It's a lot to think about."

He gathers his things. "So when are you taking your boat out? Going to the Caribbean or the Mediterranean?"

Once again Francesca pops in my head—her lying in the sun on my yacht. Jasper said he's in for a couple of weeks, and Deacon too. I told them to invite whomever they wanted, but I haven't talked to her about it. She has her job, and while it's flexible, I'm not sure she can afford to take weeks off at a time.

"Not sure yet," I tell him.

Just as the valet is bringing around my car, he stops and pushes a brown manila envelope in my hands. "Oh, almost forgot. Here's the latest from the investigator. Sorry. I meant to drop it off at your place last week."

I frown. "More? I thought I had it all?"

"Apparently, he dug a little deeper. I gave you an initial report, and this is the last of it." He slaps me on the back. "Keep your head up. We're gonna figure out this football thing."

I look down at the envelope.

A terrible unease washes over me as I rub my fingers across it. Things between Francesca and me have been great. I'm not hiding my anxieties or worries about football. She sees the real me.

But this envelope, coupled with this niggling in my brain . . .

I shake it off. This is nothing.

So why do I feel as if an axe is about to fall?

I take a seat on the couch in Dr. Newman's office. A psychiatrist in her late forties, she wears her hair in a ponytail that never looks quite straight. Potted greenery is scattered everywhere: in her windows, on her desk, on the floor.

She sits in the club chair adjacent and smiles as she pulls out her notes.

"Thanks for seeing me."

She nods. "I had a cancellation."

"I was canceled too." It's been a day since the team dropped me.

She glances down at her notes. "Have you been experiencing any aggression about the loss of your team?"

I recall dinner last night with Francesca, then making love in our bed. "No. I feel a sense of relief that they told me. I just went home to my girlfriend."

"Let's talk about her. What attracted you to her?"

I clasp my hands and lean forward. "Her eyes. She bumped into me, and they . . . sort of took my breath. I don't know; is that weird?"

She smiles. "No, we're all drawn to different things in another person. Tell me about how you met."

"NDA there, but I couldn't *see* all of her face, but yeah, there was this sort of instant vibe between us. I liked her tattoo, her lips, the scar on her hip. She said unexpected things, about how I was dark, and it . . . stuck with me. It felt like she knew me, but she didn't. Well, she had seen me before—wow, this is confusing. She calls us fate. I call it coincidence." I fiddle with my thumbs. "It's just, I have strong feelings for her, but I feel as if she's keeping secrets from me."

"Why?"

I shrug, not able to grasp on to anything concrete. "Her friends will be talking, then stop when I come in the room. She'll start to say something, then stop. She stares at me with fear in her eyes; I mean, I can *see* it, but I'm too scared to ask her what it's about. What if she's actually afraid of me?" I stare at my hands. "I keep waiting for her to give up on me. She wants . . ."

"Yes?"

"More of me." I take a shaky breath.

"That makes you afraid because . . ."

"I'm always waiting for everything to implode. Maybe I'll hit her. Maybe she'll quit us."

"Do you want to hurt her? Ever fist your hands at her? Threaten? Curse at her?"

"Jesus, no! Never!"

"Are you your father, Tuck?" Her voice hardens, as if she's goading me.

"Fuck no!" I stand up and pace around the room.

"Hmm, have you ever hit a woman?"

"No."

"Ever want to?"

"Never." I sit back down and rake a hand through my hair.

She watches me. "Perhaps you use this self-talk of being like your father to protect yourself from caring. It's a good argument in your head, a reason to push people away. You watched your parents' relationship implode—so you don't take chances. You don't know what a healthy relationship looks like."

I nod. "Understatement." I tug on my bottom lip with my teeth. "She's fucking amazing. Talented. Beautiful. Funny." A small laugh comes from me. "What's cool is I bought one of her sketches before we met. It's like she's been coming and going in my life for years, and I didn't even know."

She pauses. "What I find interesting is she's the main thing we're discussing—and not the end of your time with the Pythons. True, I brought her up, but she's what's on your mind. Is it possible she's more important than your career?"

The world turned on its axis when my career ended. It's still carving a scar inside of me, but if she left, how many scars would I have? I shrug.

"Since the breakup with the team, have you had any chest pain or anxiousness?"

"No." I shake my head, and she quirks an eyebrow.

"You've had only a few close relationships. Ronan, your coach from high school, and now Jasper. So perhaps some of your mistrust for others has lessened? You seem to have made new friends, Darden, Brogan, and Cece?"

My lips twitch at the memory of a game night we had at Darden's. Cece stole a ceramic angel, Brogan used a Russian accent all night, and Darden bossed everyone around with his cane. Francesca laughed the entire night, her face lit up.

"You seem calm for a man who lost his job recently."

I inhale a deep breath. "Yeah."

"You're making inroads, learning to balance your life with the emotional upheaval of your childhood, along with your father's suicide and your mother's rejection. Those aren't easy roads, Tuck, yet you're sitting here and you're not the same man from last year."

"The meds?"

She inclines her head. "They can certainly help your brain chemistry, but some of this is you opening yourself up. This is the right path for healing."

My stomach flutters. I want that. I do.

"And your mother? There's no contact since her manic episode?"

"She's on new medication and back to her normal routine. According to the director, she's enjoying life."

"How does that make you feel?"

Emotion claws at my throat every time I think of her.

"Abandoned. Angry."

"Do you need her forgiveness? Is your happiness dependent on her love and acceptance?"

"I have no other family that I care about."

"What if she calls you tomorrow and says she never wants to see you again and she'll never forgive you?"

A wave of grief hits, and I lean over and scrub my face. "Devastated."

Compassion flits over her face. "I suggest you write a letter to confront her with your feelings, then move on with whatever her choice is."

My jaw clenches. "And that's all it takes? A letter?"

"I don't know. That's up to you. But you need some kind of closure with her." She pauses, her pen tapping against her pad. "Let me ask you this: What if you could live a perfect life? What would it look like?"

I swallow and look out the window.

Me playing ball, my mom and I reconciled, and . . . I rub my chest. Francesca.

How long will she stick with me before she wants a *real* family . . . ?

"A new team? Your relationship with your mother? Your girlfriend? Your nonprofit?" She stands, signaling the end of the session. "Envision your ideal life five years from now. Who are you? What have you accomplished? What makes you happy?"

I leave, thoughts churning. When I get in my car, the packet from yesterday is still on the passenger side. I pick it up to open it, then put it back down, my chest rising.

I told her I'd never investigate her again, but . . .

Chapter 17

Francesca

My place tonight. Jasper has plans so it's just us is the text that Tuck sends. I frown at the lack of endearments he usually includes.

Okay. You want to cook or me?

You. The media is releasing my retirement news today.

Alrighty. Chinese delivery for the win. 8:00?

Yep. Later.

I stand up from Darden's office and stretch my arms out, then yelp in surprise.

He hobbles in wearing a Yale sweatshirt and jogging pants. "What's wrong, Miss Lane? I've fed you, watered you, left snacks by my laptop, and turned the heat up for you. What did I miss?"

"Nothing. The carrots were yummy." My laptop crashed this morning, and I popped over to his place to borrow his. Instead of me taking it to my apartment, he insisted I stay.

"Well?" He hobbles over to me and glances at the computer. "I don't see anything strange. What is it?"

My eyes widen again, and I laugh with my hand on my stomach.

I take his hand and put it there. "She kicked hard, Mr. Darden. Feel! It wasn't just a flutter."

He gasps as she gives another one, then blinks. "How big is she?"

"About the size of an eggplant." I'm not as big as I should be, but she measures normally. Sadness washes over me as I think of Tuck not being with me at my doctor's appointments.

"Eggplants are disgusting."

"I didn't say she was a vegetable. She's kicking, checking out her reflexes. She's got a little nose and is probably sucking her thumb now. Her brain is developing at superspeed, and she responds to voices. Go ahead and say hi."

He blanches. "Hi."

"Boring. Put some feeling in it like Cece and Brogan do."

"No."

"Do it!"

"Fine! Hi, eggplant! Your mom is being a pest!"

I snort as he eases down in one of his club chairs. "How are the clients?"

"I've got another referral from the Wall Street couple. I—I don't know what I would have done without you, you know . . ." I struggle with a wave of emotion. "A true friend. I don't have a dad or grandparent, but I can't imagine them being better than you. Did you buy my paintings?"

"For the tenth time, I didn't buy your paintings. You aren't that talented."

I stick my tongue out at him. "I only asked once! Now twice. Chill."

"As if I'd send my man of business in that place."

I make a face at him. "I still like you. You're like a warm hug on a cold day." I mimic hugging myself as he narrows his eyes.

"Warm hug, my ass. That's your hormones talking. Last week you cried when I let you watch *Twilight* after you lost at chess . . ."

I come from behind the desk. "Don't play us down, you cantankerous old man. You're the one who rooted for me when I applied to live here. It gives you hives to talk about feelings, but I love you. We're not blood but better."

He gets flustered and fumbles around as he cracks open the *Times*. "You know I'm leaving all my money to charity, right?"

He peers over the newspaper, and I smirk. "I don't care about your wealth. I do care a whole hell of a lot about you."

He harrumphs.

"Since I have you here, I was wondering if I could pick your brain about the Russo family. All the rich people seem to know each other . . ." I asked him earlier in the week, and he said he'd make some phone calls for me.

He keeps reading the paper. "Valentina is an artist. Gianna is engaged. You told me that. I bought some land from their father, Lorenzo. Don't recall his wife's name. Their family made their money in construction, mostly building skyscrapers. One of my cronies told me they died in a car crash in the Catskills. They're treacherous roads there . . ." He rattles his paper between his legs. "Dammit, what was the name of the town where they died? Something about singing—oh yes, Wren's Song. It was the birthplace of Lorenzo and his siblings."

"Wren? You're sure?"

"I'd use the internet, but someone has it."

I whip around and type in *Wren's Song*, and a small town in the Catskills comes up, population 593. It doesn't say anything about the Russo family. I type in *Lorenzo Russo* and find an article about a bridge his company was contracted to build and his obituary last year, but nothing that gives me a clue about why the sisters were infatuated by my locket.

"Give me thirty seconds," I call out to Mr. Darden as I run through his den, out his door, and into mine; grab my locket; and then dash back to his place. I'm panting when I enter his study. "Was that thirty?"

"Did you go somewhere?"

I huff and hold out the necklace. "Here, does that look like a wren to you or just a bird?"

He pulls it up close to his face, then inspects it by turning it over. "It's small and short, but lots of birds are, so I guess."

I exhale noisily and lie down on the floor.

"Are you okay, Miss Lane?"

"Just thinking. I've always thought it was a wren. I paint wrens. I know my freaking wrens. It's a wren." I draw one in the air—the curved beak, the long tail. "You know what was super weird about meeting Valentina?"

"Her flashy red dress?"

I laugh. "No, but damn, I'm glad you do listen to me."

"Hmm."

I look over at him, but he's still reading. "It was weird that she looked like me. Same hair, our lips, but her eyes don't have the green that mine do. The first time I saw her, something, like . . . pricked at me, but it wasn't until later that I realized we looked alike."

"Don't you think you might be getting your hopes up? Or seeing things that aren't there? Your locket is unusual and expensive, a collector's piece—"

"Wait!" I sit up and straighten my pink sweater.

He drops the paper. "Did the eggplant kick?"

"No! I just remembered something Gianna said when she came in to get the tattoo. She said her friend had bought my dollhouse painting, that her friend was an artist and she collected everything, even jewels . . ." My heart races as I stand up.

"Don't leave me hanging," he mutters.

"She lied, Mr. Darden. It wasn't her friend. It was Valentina! Why would she say a friend bought my painting, unless it was to be secretive?"

"People lie for many reasons." He goes back to reading. "You."

I grunt. "You're no help." I pick up my phone and dial East Coast Ink. When Harlee answers, I say hi sweetly and "Thank you for not telling me about my paintings" and ask if she would put me through to Donny to discuss.

"Francesca?" Donny answers.

"Donny, hi. Thank you for the commission check. I need a favor, and you owe me. Can you look through your receipts and see who bought my dollhouse painting about six months ago?"

I hear the slide of his metal filing cabinet, the rustling of papers, and then his voice. "Tina Russo. She used an American Express. Total was fifteen hundred. I like that piece—"

I hang up. "I was right! It was her! But why?" I pace around the room, my adrenaline rising. "It makes no sense to lie."

"Yet people do . . . some people in this room."

I stop and glare. "I don't want to talk about Tuck. I'm going to tell him. I swear."

He shuts his paper. "Fine. Let's talk this out. What do you know? Give me the details."

I sit on the floor at his feet, crossing my black leggings. "One, Gianna sought me out because of her sister, not friend. Two, they stared hard at my locket. Three, there's a wren on my locket, and their parents were from Wren's Song. Four . . ." I chew my lips.

"What?"

I heave out a breath. "I have nothing but gut instinct."

"You looked them up online and found nothing, no address?"

"They keep their heads low, and your cronies didn't know."

He takes a sip of his peppermint tea, then sets it down to pick up his phone. He appears to send a text, then gives me a look, the one that says we need to talk. "Why don't we table this and move on to something else?"

I manage to push up a smirk. Tuck. It's all he wants to discuss.

"Are you itching for a new honey badger painting?"

He mutters under his breath, and I catch a "Stubborn woman," then, "When are you going to tell him? How long can this go on? What is your plan? He's going to see the changes in your body." His face reddens.

My fingers pluck at my sweater, and my throat prickles.

Tuck doesn't want kids.

He's going to be angry.

And commitment? He's not even close to that.

His voice softens. "Miss Lane . . ."

My teeth dig into my bottom lip as I turn and look out the window. Central Park is covered in two feet of snow, the first good snowfall we've had this year. My mother left me in such a snow, but I won't leave my child—I want her so much. If only he'd feel the same.

I admire his struggle to find strength in tackling his childhood traumas, the kindness he shows people that he isn't even aware of. I love how he laughs with his whole face—the dimples, the crinkling of the skin at the corners of his eyes. The way he wraps his whole body around me at night as if I might slip away any moment. Emotion clenches at my chest. I love the intimacy I feel when he holds my eyes. As if it's just me in his world.

I take a sip of tea, fighting to keep my eyes from leaking. "Do you think there are any honey badgers in New York State? Funny. I wish I knew more about them."

"You should have been a lawyer. No, my dear, the American badger is found in the Great Plains region of the US, but I saw a honey badger on a trip to Africa."

"Did it run at you?" I bare my teeth and growl. "Were you scared?"

"Pah! Nothing scared me, but they're the meanest animal in the world, and their only enemy is man. They've killed buffalo, lions, wildcats, even men. They go for the balls first."

"Phew. I was worried I might see one on the subway."

He nods, in the groove now. "Honey badgers would decimate a subway. They have thick muscles and sharp claws. If they attack a beehive, they release a noxious fume that flushes them out."

"Just out of its ass?"

He gives me a look. "Scent glands, Miss Lane."

An hour later, we've watched YouTube videos of honey badgers in the wild and brainstormed a trip to Africa. No talk of Tuck. I win.

His doorbell rings, and I move to answer it. "I'll get it."

"If that's Widow Carnes, tell her I'm dead already," he calls out.

"With pleasure. Maybe I should tell her all your money is going to charity."

I swing the door open and blink. "Levi? What are you doing here?"

"Francesca? I thought Mr. Darden lived here."

"I do." Mr. Darden comes into the foyer. "Do you two know each other?"

Levi's eyes widen, and I give him a quick shake.

No, I didn't tell him you were a fake client, nor did I tell him about our past.

"I'll explain later," I tell Darden, knowing I won't go into detail. Darden has enough to worry about when it comes to me being pregnant.

"What are you doing here?" I ask Levi.

He holds out an envelope. "I wanted to give Mr. Darden an invitation to the exhibition next week."

"Personally?"

He smiles at me. "He did send the email about you to me."

"And?"

"Your address was on the email, so I knew you lived in the same building."

Dammit. "Okay."

He smiles. "I left your invitation at the front desk. They wouldn't let me come up. I texted Darden yesterday, and he said I could bring his upstairs. The doorman let me up." He rakes a hand through his blond hair, then gives me a sheepish look. "I admit I hoped I might see you. I didn't realize you two lived next door to each other."

Mr. Darden wears a bored expression on his face. Clearly, he's not good at undercurrents. He murmurs a thank-you to Levi, then places the invitation on a salver on a table in the foyer. He pats my arm. "I'm going to go call a few more friends about that other thing we were discussing. I'll let you two catch up." His cane taps on the hardwood as he ambles away.

I turn back to Levi, pushing aside his tenacity in seeing me. "I have a client who's asked me to look at a few of the artists at the exhibition. Thanks for the invite."

Satisfaction settles on his face as he leans forward. "It would be pointless if you weren't there."

Apprehension tingles over me. "What do you mean?"

A wry smile lifts his lips. "Francesca, my muse, my best art, it's always been about you."

Chapter 18

FRANCESCA

Tuck walks in his door at ten. The Chinese has been tossed, and I switched my clothes out for joggers and a flannel shirt of his. He flicks on the light to the den and stops when he sees me on the couch.

He looks beautiful, and even though I've gotten used to seeing him day after day, he takes my breath. His suit is navy and sleek, his tie a purple paisley. I could eat him up if I wasn't pissed.

Cherry barks, jumps out of my lap, and dashes to him. He scoops her up in his arms. "I didn't think you'd still be here." His eyes capture mine.

"The only reason I'm still here is because Jasper texted me and said you guys ended up at the Baller with some of the team—"

"It was spur of the moment. I didn't know they wanted to go out. They hijacked me to stay longer. I'm sorry I missed dinner. I saw your texts, but . . ."

Yeah, I sent him several.

Where are you?

Dinner is up.

Ilsa Madden-Mills

This wonton is so good.

Tuck?

Hey, I'm worried. Where are you? Are you okay? Call me.

"You could have replied. Were you busy?" Shawna pops in my head.

His lips tighten. "I wasn't with anyone, Francesca. I needed some space."

Hurt ripples over me, and I look away from him. "Did you eat?" I ask quietly.

He shakes his head. "I kept meaning to but never did. I didn't feel like it."

"If you want Chinese, it's in the trash."

He puts Cherry down and tosses his keys on the island in the kitchen. The sound clangs in my ears. There's a thick tension in the room, and it isn't because he didn't text me. He brought it in with him. I see the tense line of his shoulders, the slight tremor of his hands.

I soften. He's been through hell for the past few months, wondering when his last game would be, and now it's over. He lost his team and feels rudderless. Today must have been awful.

On the other hand, he's been at ease these past two weeks. He's smiled more. We've giggled at movies. We danced on his rooftop when it snowed. We toured the Met and watched people gaze at art, seeing them experience it. We've bought books together at Lottie's. We've gone to Café Lazzo to pick up our food. We went to the bakery, and I gagged on the way home as he chowed down on chickpea cookies. We had game night at Darden's.

He's fit in seamlessly with my life.

But . . .

Tonight something is different.

When he walks to the Pollock and stands in front of it, I follow.

214

"Are you okay?"

He cocks his head. "Pollock was talented, but his personal life was insane. He was an alcoholic, depressed, couldn't keep relationships. I never asked for it as a gift, didn't even see it until after the funeral. It's chaotic. Like me."

"You're the good kind of chaos." I fidget. "I have a client in the morning. Do you want me to stay or go?" I hear the neediness in my tone and cringe.

More tension fills the space between us, heavy with words he isn't saying.

We rushed headlong into this, not staying one night apart, and now he isn't replying.

A breath comes from me. I'm such a fool. Maybe this is it. Someone told him.

A cold sweat breaks out, and I clench my fists as I steel myself for rejection.

Of me. Of our child.

He whips off his jacket and lets it fall as he stalks to the kitchen, opens a drawer, and pulls out a brown manila envelope. Coming back into the den, he plops it down on the coffee table.

"What's that?"

"Look at it. Your name is on the front. It's meant for you."

He puts his back to me and looks out his windows at Manhattan.

Fear coils tighter, snaking around my chest. "More investigations?"

He turns to the bar and makes himself a whiskey. His profile gives nothing away. "I didn't ask for it. I thought the initial report was all. Ben's guy is a super PI. Used to be a cop. He delivered this the day of the meeting."

"And you've read it?"

He takes a drink. "I promised I wouldn't do that to you."

"Yet here it is," I say sharply, jabbing my finger at it.

He turns. "Why don't you tell me what might be in it."

"I . . ."

"No, Francesca." A long emotional exhale escapes his lips. "The thing is maybe I should have tossed this in the trash, but I didn't. I've been mulling it over, trying to figure out what to do. There's this instinct that knows something is off. Today it dawned on me that I've let someone in—I've trusted you—but maybe you haven't been honest. What's in that envelope? Open it, and tell me. Then we'll throw it away."

"Tuck . . ." My words trail off as my fear closes my throat.

"I want what we have," he says, "but why is this envelope so thick? I can't stop thinking about it."

He sits in the chair across from me, facing me with his elbows on his knees.

I pick up the package, slide open the loop, and pull out typed pages and a wad of photographs.

"Photos?" My hackles rise. "That's an invasion." I thumb through them with lightning speed—pics of Edward and Harlee, one of Donny as he left the shop, me in Central Park, me with Brogan coming out of Dr. Lovell's office, me exiting galleries. A tear falls when I see one of me with Tuck as we pick out his Christmas tree. The final one is my last visit to the doctor. Cece laughs as she flashes her new engagement ring from Lewis.

"Here." I slide them over to him, but he doesn't pick them up.

"I'm in deep with you, Francesca, and I don't want to drown—feel me? The morning I walked out of Decadence, I wanted to stay. You scared me even then. You mean so much to me . . ." His voice catches. "Just don't let me lose that, okay? Tell me there's nothing important in there."

My hands clench around the pages as he captures my eyes. I want to tell him how I really feel about him, those three little words I rarely use, but it feels so wrong right now.

Loving Tuck is a shot of sunshine under a magnifying glass, sizzling hot and fiery.

And right now, he's simmering.

He has every right. His gut instinct is right.

I'm terrible. Awful. I should have told him long ago.

I break his gaze and stare down at the papers. My chest tightens at the first piece of information—I wasn't expecting it. I lick dry lips. "Cece is a former escort—you know that—but I worked for her agency for two dates before I got on at East Coast."

His expression doesn't change, and frustration makes my hands clench.

"Does that bother you?"

"It's not something I want to think about. Did you have sex with them?"

"It was up to me, and I didn't. I was jobless; then Donny called me."

"Fine. Go on." His words are cold.

"I know what you're doing," I say. "You're putting up walls. You're looking for a reason to ruin us."

"Do I have a reason?"

Yes.

A brittle laugh erupts as I turn the pages. "And he got access to my medical records. Every single visit with Dr. Lovell. Illegal as shit."

"Are you sick?"

"No." With a long breath, I wipe my face, meet his eyes, and shove out the words. Relief and fear mingle inside of me. I've waited too long for this, and now it's too late. "I'm pregnant. I found out the night we met at Café Lazzo. I was sick on the way home, and then . . . Tuck, I tried to tell you—I really did, twice. But the timing was off, and we were happy, but I wanted to—"

His face whitens as he interrupts me. "Who's the father?"

I put my hand to my chest and rub. "Yours. Decadence. She's yours."

"Impossible," he breathes.

A watery smile comes from me. "Who says? We were drunk. It happened."

He rakes both hands through his hair. "I don't want kids and you . . ."

"I kept the baby because she's mine."

"She?"

"Just a hunch. I don't want to know the sex." Trying to stay calm, I stuff the rest of the papers back inside the envelope.

His throat bobs. "And you've known all the time and didn't . . ." His voice cracks. "You lied to me. Jesus, this explains so much. Darden . . ."

I keep silent. This may take a minute. Hearing it, refusing to believe it, anger, and then the bargaining and acceptance.

How long will it take him to accept that he's going to be a father?

"I want a paternity test."

I shove down the pain that causes to my heart. It makes sense coming from him and how we met. He's a celebrity, and I'm just me. "Of course."

"What do you want from me? How much?"

Oh, if I thought his earlier comment caused pain, this one decimates me. Distrust and anger layer his voice.

"All I want is you." More tears slide down my face.

He gives me an incredulous look, his breathing uneven. "I can't do . . ." He dips his head and sucks in breaths, then exhales.

"Tuck?" My voice rises as I rush over to him. I touch his arm. "Are you okay?"

He shakes me off, his chest rising rapidly as he speaks. "Francesca. Leave. Please."

I can't. I sit on the floor next to his chair and look up at him. "I'm sorry. This wasn't to trap you. I was scared. I meant to. I tried—"

"How can I trust anything you say?" Fierce eyes blaze. "When you've been lying for months! I feel like a fool."

He stands, seeming to be more in control. He snaps up the envelope, not looking at me—as if he's already erasing me.

He doesn't want a family, and I'm foisting one on him. I get how I was in the wrong, but my heart is shattering.

"Do you think this is the first paternity issue I've had? It's not. And they were all false. My lawyers will contact you."

Dots dance in front of my eyes as a dizzy spell washes over me. I cling to the end of the chair and push up, bit by bit. He doesn't notice as he pours himself another drink.

"Don't let us slip away."

He closes his eyes. "Please, for God's sake, leave."

I grab my satchel and go.

Chapter 19

FRANCESCA

It takes two to three business days to get a paternity test back, but when you're Tuck Avery, it's only twenty-four hours. Two days after I saw him in his penthouse, his lawyer, Mr. Shapiro, called to schedule a lab visit for me. I went with Brogan and Cece, gave blood, and left. Mr. Shapiro attended. As I left the office, Tuck walked in. He wore no coat and wouldn't meet my eyes.

"Have some peppermint tea," Mr. Darden says as he sets a cup and saucer on his desk.

I blink, looking up. I'm still using his laptop. I ordered a new one, but it has been delayed and hasn't arrived. I'm glad. I don't want to be alone in my apartment.

"All right," I murmur.

All right. I've been saying it to everyone. When the baby bed arrived and Cece and Brogan put it together. When Widow Carnes saw me crying in the elevator. When Herman opened the door for me to take a walk.

The world is full of fog, and I have to squint to think straight.

"He knows he's the father." I glance out the window. "He's somewhere running scenarios through his head. He's rethinking the Brogan aspect, if he was part of a scheme. He's wondering if I tampered with the condoms. He's wondering if I've been stalking him for years, looking for an opportunity. He distrusts every single word I ever said to him, trying to see where he messed up—"

"Stop. What he thinks, you can't change. What he does, you can't undo. You made a choice to keep your baby, Miss Lane. He's grappling with it."

My voice wavers. "He's also scared. He never wanted kids because he had horrible parents. They blamed him for things he couldn't even control." I swallow thickly. "He fears he'll be his father. He fears he'll withhold love like his mother. He fears chaos and uncertainty because that's how he grew up. I upended his life with my pregnancy. He's wondering how to fix it." I bite my lip to hold in the tears.

He hobbles over to his seat. "I'm sorry, dear, but you need to buck up. You're made of stronger stuff."

"Am I?"

There's a knock at the door, and I rush up to get it before he gets his cane.

"If that's Widow Carnes, tell her *The Notebook* is the worst bit of drivel I've read."

"Blasphemy, but for you, I'll do it."

I stop at the mirror in the foyer. My hair is up, oily from lack of a shower this morning; my face is pale; and gray smudges are under my eyes. Whatever.

I open the door and stiffen. "Mr. Shapiro, what do you want?"

He inclines his head. Dressed in a dark suit, he has a slick air about him. "I knocked on your door, and your roommate said you were here. May I come in?"

My breath quickens. Do I want to hear what's going to come out of his mouth?

"All right."

He takes a seat in the den, and Mr. Darden comes in and points his cane at him. "I have a law degree I never used, so no funny business, young man."

"Of course."

Darden sits next to me on the couch.

Shapiro smiles. "First, Mr. Avery would like to not make this a public issue. No media. No interviews with magazines, television shows, etc. There's an NDA here"—he slides a piece of paper onto the coffee table—"to keep your relationship, the events of it, your knowledge of his personal life from public purview."

"Of course." I sign it without reading, and Darden grunts his displeasure.

"What else?" I ask.

He opens a leather bag and pulls out more papers. My throat prickles with unease.

"We can go to court, of course, to arrange your settlement, or we can agree here and keep it quiet. It's a generous offer. We spent time calculating the cost of a child, medical care for both of you, a nanny, private school, university—"

"I don't want anything from him."

Mr. Darden grunts again, and I send him a look.

Shapiro smiles. He's good at it. "Miss Lane, you might change your mind once the child is born, and Mr. Avery wishes to stay out of court. If we settle this now, things will go back to normal."

I laugh. "Normal?"

"You can get on with your life knowing your child will be well taken care of financially, and Mr. Avery can continue his, knowing you're both doing well."

I glance at the papers as if they're alive and evil. "Is he requesting any custody rights?"

"No."

I feel winded. Swallowing thickly, I find my voice. "Why isn't he here?"

He pauses. "Ah, he chose not to be."

"He needs to be here." My chest squeezes. I want to *see* him. I can explain. I can tell him how I was afraid, that I didn't want *this* to happen.

"You must leave," I say.

"Don't be foolish, Miss Lane," Mr. Darden murmurs. "Let's hear him out."

"No. Tell Tuck I'm not interested in his money. You have your NDA. He can go fuck himself."

I walk to the foyer and open the door and cling to it, hands white with the effort.

He's not here.

He doesn't want rights.

He'll never see her.

That, *that* is nearly unbearable.

The walks we took.

The harmony.

He doesn't want it.

Or me.

Or her.

A tear falls.

And another.

And another.

Rejection claws at me.

Cruel.

Harsh.

Distrustful.

If he's my fate, then I don't want him.

Shapiro heaves out an exhale as he stands and straightens his jacket. "Miss Lane, I have two daughters. It's expensive. Perhaps, now, because of your feelings, you're angry and not thinking clearly."

"Don't patronize me."

"You'll need financial security. It's important to him that you're happy with the settlement. Today he's offering you five million a year. In court, it might be different. Take this, and become a wealthy woman."

My jaw grinds. "Tell Tuck that I don't want one cent from him. Goodbye."

He leaves, and I slam the door. My hands fist and I yell, "Motherfucker!"

"Francesca," Mr. Darden says, then takes my shoulder. "My dear . . ."

I turn to him, and he wraps his arms around me. "My eyes are leaking again," I whisper.

He gives me his handkerchief.

A few moments later his phone rings, and I ease away so he can answer it.

When he disappears to the study, I dash out, hit the elevator button, and punch in the code for the penthouse. He didn't change it at least, I think. I could have tried to see him earlier, but the distance between us felt too big, insurmountable. He said he needed space.

But now . . .

I bang on the door, and it flies open.

Jasper is there; he sees me and blinks.

I push past him. "Where is he?"

He follows me, grabbing a shirt off the back of the chair and slipping it on.

"Are you okay? You're—"

"I'm fine! Where's Tuck?"

I walk downstairs, into the library, into his bedroom. The bed is made, the bathroom clean.

"He hasn't been here since you left. You're pregnant," he murmurs with a wondering expression on his face as he looks at my stomach. "I mean, now that I know, I see it. Are you doing all right? Taking your vitamins? Eating good? I have sisters."

I hug him fiercely, and he grunts and wraps his arms around me. "He sent his lawyers, Jasper. He doesn't want to see her."

He pets my hair. "Darling, I don't know what to tell you. He's crazy about you."

I sniff. "But where is he? Is it the loft? A hotel?"

He steps back, a look of unhappiness on his face.

"Tell me!"

"He's at the marina, where the yacht is. He's getting it ready to take out."

A gust of air comes from me. "He's leaving."

Jasper winces. "Yeah. He saw his mother, and whatever happened, it was bad. I think he wants to leave it all behind." He stops. "Not you, though. You know he cares about you."

But maybe he was always looking for a reason to end us?

"It's really over for him."

He reaches for me, but I step back. I look at the Pollock, and anger boils. I wish I could set fire to it and destroy everything that hurts Tuck.

But this is his choice.

Just like I had a choice.

I chose her and me.

He chose himself.

Chapter 20

TUCK

I get off the phone with Shapiro and walk around the deck of my yacht. Called *Lost at Sea*, she's stark white with teak trim. She's over a hundred feet long with five staterooms and space for four crew members, the captain, a chef, a maid, and an engineer. She cost thirteen million several years ago. I don't regret one penny spent. My head clears at sea. I leave the pressure of football. Life.

It's the one place I can forget everything.

Will this trip do that? Doubtful.

The cold wind whips at my hair as I stride into the 360-degree-vision sky lounge and take in the pilot seat, the L-shaped couch, the forty-two-inch TV, the stereo system, the teak tables, the wet bar with a subzero ice chest. Gorgeous.

My shoulders slump. There's no anticipation here. No excitement.

Where is she? my heart demands.

Have I fucked up with her?

I am fucked up.

My lashes fall.

I'm flawed.

I'm not fit to be a parent.

I look like my father; I am my father.

I don't deserve love. Or a family.

I don't deserve any comfort.

I shouldn't have been born.

All words my mother said yesterday when I saw her. My eyes fill with water, and I blink it back. Fuck that.

The captain, Bruce, gives me a salute. I nod and tell him that I've already checked in with the others. Rooms are clean, the galley is stocked for a couple of weeks, and the engine is primed for sea.

"How's it going?" he asks.

"Good." Fucking terrible. There's a wall of stones on my chest, and I can't push them off.

I can't sleep. Or eat. I'm standing still, and the world goes on without me.

Francesca is my love, the only one I want.

I kick that down. I opened myself up. I trusted, and she let me down.

I cringe as I recall her walking out of the lab. I hadn't been able to meet her eyes. Mistrust, mixed with shock and anger, rode me. Then, I went to see my mother. Uninvited. I read her a letter I'd written about the hurt and damage of my childhood, about how much I care about her in spite of it.

Bruce speaks, bringing me back. "Sailing is a majestic thing, yeah? Two more days, and we'll hit the water."

I lick my lips. "That's what I wanted to check on. I thought there was another nor'easter coming in?"

He frowns. "We're headed south. Our first stop is Fort Lauderdale for supplies and fuel. The storm shouldn't impact us."

Anxiousness rises. Can I really leave her in New York? "Should we take another look at the radar?"

"I checked it an hour ago, spoke to Channel Three, and called the weather station. We're good, sir."

"Check again."

He starts. "If we wait, it might be several days before—"

"Just do it."

I step out of the sky lounge and lean over the rail, my head churning with thoughts as I gaze at the sea. It reminds me of Francesca's eyes. Then I picture her rosebud mouth. The widow's peak I love to trace. My hands clench around the railing.

She's gone. And it's on me. I pushed her away.

A clammy sensation tingles over my skin as I sway on my feet. The truth is I'm facing my biggest fear: harming a child with my own destructive past. Me, with my rough hands, holding another person's future. It feels terrifying. Mind boggling.

A wave rises like an arm and crashes up the side of the boat, then ebbs away. Another does the same, hitting the hull. My breath catches.

Can I rise? Be a good father? Let fear go and accept love?

My eyes close as my throat tightens with emotion. There's a secret side of me that I'm scared to look at, the part of me that yearns for someone to accept the shadows inside of me, for real love, for family.

Only I've been too scared to allow myself to ever dream of such a possibility.

I stare out at the Atlantic.

Reaching in my pocket, I tug out the letter I wrote to my mother, rip it into pieces, and toss it into the water. It floats for a moment, rides a wave, and then ebbs away.

I watch the pieces sink beneath the sea. My mother is who she is. I can't change her. I can't make her forgive me—or love me.

My clarity rises stronger, and my head feels clearer than it has in days. My childhood has trapped me for years, creating a hollow man who didn't know how to let others in.

Then a princess came along, tore down my defenses, and stole my heart.

A ragged sound comes from my lips.

Who says this has to be my life? Only me.

I think of the compass Francesca gave me. *To guide you home safely,* she said.

Is my penthouse home without her? The loft? The yacht?

Nowhere will be home without her.

She knows my chaotic past, how it shaped me.

She accepts me and embraces me for who I am.

And when she gazes at me, Jesus, I see her love for me—and it doesn't come with strings. She doesn't want my money. She doesn't want the celebrity footballer.

Her love is steadfast. Solid.

"She only wants me," I murmur to the sea in a wondering tone.

Yeah, surprising things have happened. I'm going to be a father.

But being part of a family doesn't have to be about anger, guilt, or blame.

Having a child doesn't have to be full of fear. With her next to me, we can climb each mountain together; we can battle the chaos that might come.

In my heart there's still a flicker of faith in her, in us.

It's not over yet. It can't be.

My hand slaps against the railing.

I have to make amends, and I'm going to come out swinging.

Chapter 21

Francesca

I stand in front of an Upper West Side brownstone where the Russo sisters live. It's four stories and a rich chocolate color with a wrought iron door. Green winter ivy grows up the front. It's like a dream house in Manhattan. Several steps lead up to the landing, and I worry about Darden getting up there.

I tighten the scarf around his neck. "You didn't have to come with me."

"I'm the one who's been working on this since yesterday. I'm invested." He grimaces, giving me a careful glance. "Plus, we don't know what they'll say. You need backup."

"You're the bad cop, and I'm the good cop?"

He huffs out a laugh. "We'll see."

Last night, he found the information he was looking for: their address, plus a little more. The Russos' grandmother's name was Francesca. She went by Frances and came from Sicily to marry into the Russo family.

We move carefully up the steps. I ring the bell, and a housekeeper opens the door. "May I help you?" she asks as she takes in my thick hoodie, joggers, and coat.

At least Darden thought ahead and put on a suit.

She sees an elderly man with a cane, and her bland expression softens.

I can't find my voice, so Darden speaks—and puts some sweet in his tone. "Hello. How are you? Are the Russos in today?"

"Are you expected?"

He smiles. "Sorry, no. I knew their father, Lorenzo." A gust of wind whips his hat off, and I dash to get it. Darden fakes a dramatic shiver as I set it back on his head.

She lets us in the foyer area that opens to a formal living and dining room. The ceilings are at least fifteen feet tall; heavy gold chandeliers glitter in the air. The walls are covered in a gold damask wallpaper, the wooden furnishings ornate.

Darden removes his coat and hands it to her. I do the same.

"Who was it?" Gianna appears in the hall, sees me, and blinks. It's early, and she's in a lounging two-piece sweater-and-pant set. There's a cup of coffee in her hand. "Francesca? What . . . why are you here?"

I brush past the housekeeper. "We need to talk."

"You could have texted?" she says.

"I could have, but it seemed imperative that we do it in person."

She glances at Darden. "Who's he?"

"Family," I say.

She gives me a surprised look as I introduce them. She says she recognizes his name from around Manhattan.

Darden wobbles on his cane, and I'm not sure if it's for effect or real. I steady him, then look at Gianna. "May we sit and chat? If your sister is here, we'd like to talk to her as well."

Gianna's back straightens, and her eyes gleam—whether with excitement or fear, I don't know. "Sure. Lori, escort them to the study."

Half an hour later, Valentina and Gianna appear in the study, a large room with two desks near the windows and more damask wallpaper, this time in green. A velvet lounger and chairs are arranged around a muted Oriental rug. It's all very plush but uncomfortable.

Valentina is dressed in a black suit. Gianna wears red. I take in the widow's peak on Valentina, and my breath quickens.

"So how are you, Francesca?" Valentina says formally.

"Great." I take off my locket and hold it out. "My mother left this for me, and you know who she is."

Gianna looks at her sister, and Valentina gives her an imperceptible nod. Gianna clears her throat. "Francesca, we believe your father left it for you, our uncle. His name was Dante, after the poet."

What? My heart thunders. Dante was an Italian poet known for his *Divine Comedy*, an epic poem that questioned evil, human nature, and redemption. We studied him in art school because so many artists were influenced by his *Inferno*, the first part of the poem.

I swallow thickly. "Not my mother?"

Valentina picks up as her sister winces. "We didn't know about the possibility of you until our father passed last year. We were going through his desk and found a few letters from Dante. One said that he'd become a father. No name or sex was given, just that he'd given the baby up. We didn't know where. The letter was postmarked in Kentucky, but he never lived there, we think. Now that we know more, it seems he may have posted it on his way to Florida." She sighs. "Lorenzo was our father, and there was no love lost between him and Dante."

"I see." I really don't. My head races with questions. "Who was my mother?"

Valentina looks down at her hands. "Perhaps I should start at the beginning. Our uncle—your father, Dante—was older than our father by three years. He was all set to inherit his part of the company and work for the family, but he had a rebellious streak. He was handsome, and everyone adored him. That's what our mother told us, anyway." She points to a portrait to the right of a fireplace. "That's him."

232

As in a dream, I rise up from my seat and float to the painting, the type someone probably commissioned. He's laughing, a glint in his blue-green eyes. There's a widow's peak in his dark hair. Tingles ghost down my spine.

"He grew up in this house?"

They nod.

I gaze around, searchingly, imagining I can hear male laughter in the background; I picture a broad-shouldered man with dark hair walking through the door of the study, spreading his arms wide and hugging his parents.

"What happened?" I ask as I turn around.

"At Harvard he got in with a rough crowd, drinking and partying. He got into a motorcycle accident and became addicted to painkillers; then it was meth, then heroin. One night he had a fight with our grandfather about getting his inheritance early. He didn't want to settle down and do the family business. He wanted to strike out on his own. Our grandfather told him no and that if he didn't go back to school and finish, he'd be disinherited. This may seem drastic, but Dante had just returned from a rehab facility, and with his drug issue, our grandfather refused."

She continues. "So while the family slept, Dante opened the safe and took money, the family jewelry, then the candlesticks and silverware from the pantry. It was the last our family saw of him; then our grandmother, Frances, died a week later. She and Dante had a special relationship. He was her firstborn, and she doted on him."

My head reels with stories of their family. My family?

She sighs. "My grandfather and father never forgave Dante for what they believed caused her death. Your father learned of her death a few months later when he called to ask for money."

"Oh."

She nods. "To answer your earlier question, through our investigation, we learned that a woman gave birth to you in Albany at a house they rented. She died from blood loss."

My eyes close. I mean, I suspected she was dead. Still, my fingers feel chilled, and I rub them together. "And Dante?" The syllables feel foreign on my tongue.

"He died from an overdose of heroin in Florida a year after you were born."

My fists clench. He's gone.

Valentina watches as I struggle with my emotions. Her voice turns gentler. "He left you behind because he couldn't care for you. He wrote in the letter that he was despondent over your mother's death but didn't want you to grow up with us. I'm sorry. We have the letter, copies of it . . ."

"My mother? What do you know? Who was she?"

Gianna winces. "We assume she was someone he met along the way. The name he gave the coroner was Katherine May, but there's no strings to follow from that. The trail ends there."

A dead end, but so much more on my paternal side.

I rub my forehead as the moments tick by on a grandfather clock. "So we're first cousins?"

Gianna nods with a soft smile. "Dante was the oldest. Lorenzo was our father; then there's two sisters, Margarete and Amelia, who have two children each. You have six cousins."

"Oh," I say, my chest rising. I lick dry lips. "So you two read the letter, then set out to find me?"

Valentina says, "Our investigators discovered you."

Rich people and their PIs.

I look at Valentina. Their dad died a year ago; later they found the letters, then proceeded to find me. Then she bought my paintings. "You came in and bought a painting but didn't meet me; then Gianna shows up for a tattoo and talks my ear off. Why didn't you tell me?"

Valentina leans forward. "How do you approach someone you don't know and inquire? It felt like an overstep and very intrusive. I bought your painting because I liked it; it wasn't planned, but it spurred Gianna on." She throws a look at her sister. "It wasn't my idea for her to get the tattoo, but my sister does her own thing."

I study Valentina. I can believe she'd want to take baby steps.

"Did you know about my foster care? How I went from home to home?"

Gianna takes over. "We don't know much, Francesca. We focused on getting your name and where you were. It felt wrong to dive into your life." She pauses, her face softening. "I'd like to hear about how you grew up. If it was good or bad. If you were happy. I pray that you were."

I shake my head. This isn't the time or the place. "I'm still wrapping my head around this. Why haven't you contacted me since then?" I direct my gaze at Valentina. She's obviously in charge.

She nods. "We've been working up to it—"

Gianna flicks her hair. "Valentina was scared you might cause a scandal."

Valentina sighs. "That's not the whole truth. Scandals blow over these days, but we do care about the family business and have a reputation to maintain. We weren't ignoring you. We'd been grieving for our parents, and the letter—well, it kind of blindsided us. We were mulling over how to approach you, and then we saw you at the gallery wearing the locket, and it hit home for us. We were planning to approach you after that, but—"

"My fiancé broke up with me a week later," Gianna interrupts. She sniffs. "I've been a mess these past few weeks."

"Gianna, I'm so sorry," I say. "Your tattoo . . ."

She waves me off. "I'm keeping it as a reminder not to fall for jerks again. I'm doing better. Trust me. I'm just sorry we took so long and now you're here finding us." She walks over to me, stares at my locket, and smiles. "That was a wedding gift to our grandmother, Frances. He may have pawned everything else, but he made sure he left it with you, the eldest grandchild."

"I'm not giving it up," I say wryly.

She smirks. "I am a little jealous that it's an heirloom, but it's yours. I prefer diamonds anyway. You're also entitled to an inheritance from our grandfather. Even though your father was cut out of the will, his descendants were not."

Mr. Darden rubs his hands. "Now we're getting to the nitty-gritty. How much is it?"

I glare at him, and he shrugs.

Valentina pops an eyebrow at him. "If the DNA fits, our lawyers and accountants will figure it out."

Gianna scoffs. "Come on, Tina; look at her. She's you! But way more fun!"

I blink as Gianna crushes me in a hug. "I enjoyed my time in your tattoo chair. And that Edward—I wanted to kill him." She pauses as she considers my face. "Would you like to get to know us better, Francesca?"

There's silence in the room as everyone looks at me.

I hear the hushed tinkle of dishes as the housekeeper brings in coffee and croissants.

Darden's breathing. Mine.

Theirs.

Dante was my father. I know it in my soul.

He was a wreck but left his mother's locket with me. He never sold it, so maybe his family did mean something to him. Why else would he write the letter to his brother to let him know about me? Maybe he never came back home because of blame and guilt over his mother.

He walked away because he was an addict. Perhaps he was devastated with grief. Perhaps he would have been a better man if she'd lived and they'd raised me. Or perhaps I was always meant to walk a harder journey. Or maybe my life was the better journey.

I inhale sharply, connecting a faint similarity between Tuck and Dante. Dante may have wanted a family with my mother—I'll never truly know until I read his letter—but he gave me up because he didn't think he was good enough to take care of me. In a way, Tuck feels the same.

After a hellish last few days, a sense of peace settles around me. I reply to Gianna's question. "I have family. We all live on the Upper East Side in the same building for the moment. Cece is moving to California soon." A breathless laugh comes from me as I hug Gianna. "I'm also pregnant, so you have a cousin coming, and yes, I'd love to get to know you and Valentina."

Valentina watches us stiffly from her chair, but I see a sheen of tears in her gaze. A smile, a very small one, crosses her face.

I glance over at Darden as he dabs his eyes with his hankie.

"Allergies," he grumbles under his breath, and I smile.

Chapter 22

FRANCESCA

My eyeliner wings out, creating a sweeping, exotic look. It's dark navy, like my eye shadow. My dress is bold and modern, a gift from Cece. Knee length and cut tightly, the cream fabric is covered in lace and small beads. It accentuates my baby bump. In the past few days, it's become obvious. Or maybe I'm just into showing it off.

I turn my body from side to side in the mirror. "Looking good, little Frances," I whisper.

"I heard that!" Cece yells from the den.

"What happened to Cecelia Ivy?" Brogan bellows.

"Just thinking out loud," I yell back.

My hair is stick straight and long as it frames my face. I slip on four-inch clear stilettos and march out to the den.

Cece gasps. "Oh, Fran, you look so gorgeous."

I blush. "The baby makes my hair shiny, yeah?"

She gives me a hug, careful not to mess with our dresses. "It's more than that. Since you met the Russos, you've been radiant. You found your family."

"You and Brogan and Darden are family. They are the cherry on top." I smile.

She pouts. "I'm happy for you, but what if I don't like these girls? Are they prettier than me?"

I snort. "Just be sweet to them tonight."

"I'm already jealous. I want a sexy Italian name."

I kiss her nose. "You're the prettiest girl in Manhattan, boo bunny."

"I know, right?" She simpers. "I wish Darden was coming."

I nod. "He's found a show on the nature channel he didn't want to miss, something about a harpy eagle."

Brogan takes some pics of us with his phone, then heads out to Decadence. Herman buzzes up to let us know that our limo has arrived.

We get inside with Gianna and Valentina, who greet Cece warmly. Our DNA tests, again in twenty-four hours, came back yesterday. I'm officially a Russo. The limo gets into traffic and heads to the gallery in Brooklyn near the Greenpoint waterfront.

The line outside the gallery is long but moves fast. A red carpet has been laid out from the entrance. Cece tells me to be careful to stay on the carpet. She's spied black ice and is worried about my heels.

We move into the three-story converted warehouse. The first floor has been set up to allow for large groups to congregate. A quartet plays string instruments in the back, there's several bar areas, and servers carry trays of champagne and finger foods.

It's a throng of people, and the Russo sisters introduce me as their cousin. An hour after we arrived, we finally head up to the second floor. We're on the stairs when my cell pings. I pull it out of my navy clutch. It's Jasper.

Where are ya? We're here at this dumb gallery. Darden told us where to find you.

Him and Tuck? My heart skips. I type out our location, then stuff my phone away. I don't want to get my hopes up. Jasper might be with Courtney.

We meander through the second floor, then head to the third, where Levi's exhibit is.

Levi looks up from a group of women, smiles at us, and walks our way. He's dressed in a crisp dark-gray suit paired with a matching tie. I introduce him around but don't include him in the news that I'm their cousin.

He leads us to his display.

"Oh." My hand drops from Cece's as I take it in.

"It's as if the statue is alive, isn't it?" Levi murmurs to me. "As if you're really there."

"Me?" I frown at a female nude in white marble. Life size, her body lies on a bed as she gazes up. A single tear rests on her cheek. Ghostly white hair frames her heart-shaped face. She looks heartbroken.

Blood rushes through my veins as I recognize the arch of my widow's peak, my lips, my breasts.

She's me, a depiction of beautiful agony.

Pain makes the best art, right? Pollock, Van Gogh . . .

"This is how I recall you," he says.

In pain? I remember our love, but it seems so unimportant now.

My heart twinges for Tuck, and I glance around, as if expecting him to appear.

"Do you remember?" Levi says, and I finally turn to him. Yes, this. I focus on this . . . art.

I nod. "She's very real. Quite a statement piece. What's it called?"

"Virgin."

"Original," I mutter. "Is there more?" I hope not. While I appreciate his talent, I feel as if everyone in the room knows it's me. It's as if he peeled me open, and I've had enough of that lately.

He lets out a laugh, a frustrated sound. "Isn't this enough? It's what I've been working on for over a year. Painstakingly. It's taken up all my time."

I shake my head. "But why immortalize me? I don't get it."

"Because I took your innocence, then deserted you. I ruined you."

He pauses and clears his throat, maybe at what's on my face. "Although you've recovered quite well."

"That's right." I nod.

"I created this for me to remember." He gives me a puzzled look. "I truly adored you, Francesca. I was in pain too. I messed up with you. If I hadn't listened to my mother, we could have made it."

I keep my face expressionless. Dude. Not in a million years . . .

Gianna does a hair flick. "This all sounds truly awesome, and the fake Francesca is gorgeous, but my feet hurt, and I need some champagne. Where's a waiter when you need one?"

"Waiter, waiter, we need you," chimes in Cece as she waves her champagne glass.

Valentina snaps her fingers, and a server rushes over. Gianna squeals and hands a champagne glass to Cece.

"What do you think, Francesca?" Levi says, still hanging on my sleeve. "Do you love it?"

It is beautiful.

And I hate it.

"How much is it?" Valentina inquires. Wearing a red sheath dress, she inches closer to us, sliding between me and Levi.

He tells her an exorbitant sum with six zeros, and my eyes bulge.

She doesn't even twitch. "I'll take it." She leans into my ear. "Don't worry. I'll find somewhere to store it so no one ever sees it. After all, it does look a lot like me too."

My eyes want to leak. I smile at her. "You really don't have to."

"No, it's a baby gift."

I laugh. "Odd, but . . ."

"Francesca," says a husky voice behind us.

I whip around, and there's Tuck.

It takes a moment to catch my breath as my eyes drink him in.

He looks pale, with dark shadows under his eyes. His hair is a mess, his scruff is now a beard, and his dress shirt is halfway buttoned up. There's a bandage on his chest, and I gasp. Before I can ask him what it is, he rushes toward me, his gaze lingering on my face, then landing on my stomach. He weaves on his feet, finds his footing, and then takes my hands.

"What's wrong with you? Are you okay?" I ask.

"Just dizzy. I'll be fine."

"What happened to your chest?"

"It's nothing." His throat bobs as he swallows.

The moments tick by as we stare at each other. A warm feeling pulses through my veins as his eyes refuse to let mine go. It feels like forever since I saw him.

"Why are you here?" I ask.

He licks his lips as he gathers himself. "Francesca. I thought that losing my career would be my zero hour, but . . ." He leans his head forward and inhales.

Unease washes over me. He looks ill. "You're *not* okay. Are you drunk?"

He shakes his head. "No, sweetheart. Listen to me. It's you; you're my zero hour. I can't lose you. Jesus. I'm wrong. I'm fucking wrong. I'm messed up, and that's forever, but you make it okay. I'm scared, but you're the optimist, the yin to my yang, peas and carrots—sorry to be lame, but it's something Jasper says, and it fits for me and you. I don't know what the future is, if I'll go down a dark road, but I need you in my life. I don't deserve you, but I'll try. I'll try; I'll be good for you; I'll be the best man I can. We know what darkness looks like. We lived it, but we won't—we'll be the best fucking parents in the fucking world . . ." He stops to breathe, and his eyes sweep the crowd and land on Levi, then the sculpture.

A growl comes from his chest as he glances down at me. "Is that statue supposed to be you?"

"Yes."

Red rushes up his face, and his eyes glitter. He drops my hands. "Stay here."

"Tuck. Let it go." I follow him as he stands over the sculpture. His nostrils flare, and his fists clench. Levi shrinks back as Tuck stalks to him.

"This is a gallery, Mr. Avery. It's just art," he says as he backpedals. "No need to get physical."

Tuck leans into his face, their noses nearly touching. "I'm not touching you. You're the dirt on the bottom of my shoe." He raises his fist and slams it into his palm, and Levi's eyes bug out.

Jasper parts the crowd that has gathered, running as he calls Tuck's name. He trips over someone's shoe and shoves into Tuck. Tuck teeters, trying to find his footing, and falls toward the sculpture. Jasper's shoulder hits the stone; then Tuck falls on top of him, his head connecting with the marble.

I run over to him, pushing people out of the way as they try to help. He was already sick, and now this? Jasper groans and moves away from Tuck and rubs his arm, holding it at the elbow and close to his chest.

"Dammit. My shoulder is dislocated," he grunts, and I tell him to move as I reach for Tuck.

His left temple and cheek hit the edge, and blood drips down his face. His eyes are shut, his mouth parted.

"He's knocked out," Jasper rasps, kneeling down with me.

The crowd murmurs under their breath, and I shout, "Someone call 911!"

Without moving him, I check him for other injuries. "Tuck, darling," I whisper. "I'm here; I'm not leaving you, I promise . . ." I push away my scream, striving for calm.

"Is he okay?" I ask Jasper.

He checks his pulse. "He's breathing. It's a head injury. He's used to those."

"He hit a rock, Jasper," I snap. "Not another player."

He winces. "I was moving too fast; I'm sorry. I thought he was gonna pummel that dude."

"He wasn't."

I lean down to his face. "Tuck, can you hear me?"

His lashes flutter. He swallows and nods. "I love you, Francesca. I'll love our little girl. I'll be the best . . ." And then he's gone, his eyes closing.

I'm pacing the ER waiting room when the doctor comes out and heads our way.

Gianna, Valentina, Cece, and Darden are with me. Brogan has called a few times to check in. Jasper has already been treated, his arm in a sling. He's currently slouching in one of the hard chairs in the waiting room.

We've been here for two hours to see how Tuck is. We followed the ambulance to the hospital as soon as he was taken away.

They all walk with me as we meet the doctor halfway.

He smiles. "Hi, all. I'm Dr. Milson, and I've been in charge of Mr. Avery's care. It seems he has a lot of family."

"He does," I say. "Tell me how he is, please." Now. Look at me. I'm in charge.

He does. "Well, the MRI is good. No trauma to the brain, but he does have a serious concussion. Mr. Avery mentioned a pain in his ankle, and after a scan, we saw a fracture on his fibula."

Dammit. Two injuries. I frown.

Darden points his cane at Jasper. "You broke his moneymaker!"

The doctor shakes his head. "It's a minor fracture, but it will need to heal. I'd like to keep him overnight for monitoring." He goes on to tell me he'll need to see a sports orthopedist for more detail about his ankle, and I nod, my head racing as I take notes mentally.

"Is he awake?" I ask.

"We gave him pain meds, and he's resting." He gives us a sweeping glance. "He's lucky it wasn't worse. From what I understand, most of his weight hit Jasper." Dr. Milson smiles at Jasper, clearly a fan.

"That's me!" Jasper says. "See, I might have screwed up, but I saved him!"

"You pushed him, moron," Cece corrects, and he pouts.

He huffs. "I've explained it a hundred times. I was trying to protect him from losing his temper. I got clumsy." He moves to cross his arms, then growls when he realizes he can't. "And I'm thirsty. Cece, can you go get me some juice or soda? Pretty please."

I turn back to the doctor. "Anything else I should know?"

"After his release, watch for unusual behavior, vomiting, or severe headaches. He needs to rest mentally and physically. The ankle will take a little longer. Before he goes, I'll give you a packet on how to treat it."

"He was already sick before he fell," I say. "Did you check him out for that?"

The doctor smiles broadly. "Ah, yes, he has a phobia of needles and was experiencing agitation after getting a tattoo."

Jasper snorts. "Pining. The man was pining."

I look at him. "What tattoo? Why are you just now telling us?!"

Jasper smiles knowingly. "'Cause it's not my story to tell."

"How romantic," Cece says on a sigh. "He's deathly afraid of clowns and needles. Francesca, I'm wondering if you need a new baby daddy. Tuck is scared of a lot."

I shake my head. "But . . . why would he get one?"

Jasper winces. "There was bourbon involved beforehand and a story about how if you'd had fifty dates, would he get a tattoo of you on his body. Apparently, he said never. Then the more we drank, a grand idea was born. He wanted to prove he's in this with you." Jasper looks at my stomach.

"Would you like to see him?" the doctor asks me. "We've moved him to a VIP room."

Hospitals have VIP rooms?

I nod quickly and follow him on the elevator to the fifth floor. He tells me the room number, and I walk inside. It's dim, lit by a lamp from the desk illuminating the area. His large frame rests on the white bed. His ankle is elevated and wrapped, and his head is bandaged.

I take in his pale face and breathe out a long sigh of relief.

"Tuck," I say softly. "What were you thinking?"

Being quiet, I pull a chair over to the side of his bed and take his hand. I trace the scars on his knuckles, the ones on his wrist. I press my lips to them.

"Hi there," he murmurs, and I look up at him.

His voice is groggy. "I hit my head."

I let out a small laugh and squeeze his hand. "Jasper went rogue."

"Jay Bird. He worries about me."

Tears pool in my eyes. "I was too."

"I've missed you," he murmurs.

He inches over as I lie on the edge of his bed, my arms around his waist.

He reaches for the remote and raises up the bed. "Help me get out of this gown."

I frown. "What? You'll be naked."

"I have underwear on, and you need to see my chest."

Oh. I help him slip his arms out, then tuck the covers around his abdomen.

"Go ahead," he mumbles as he lies back on his pillow. "Look at it. Four hours of agony."

I peek under the wrapping, and my eyes flare. *Francesca* is written in a fancy script directly over his left pec.

"I love the font you chose, and . . . wait, what is that tiny little thing underneath . . ." I sigh softly at an image of Bow Bridge drawn at the end of my name. "My favorite place."

He grasps my hand and clings. "I'm so cliché, right?" He tries to laugh and ends up wincing. "I found some random tattoo parlor. I didn't have a picture of your face—remember your question was if I'd get your face?"

I nod.

"I have one of us on my phone, but the artist said it would take too long to do the detail anyway. He offered to sketch something, and I talked about you in a masquerade mask and a wedding dress, and he got confused."

"Too much bourbon."

He grimaces. "Trust me; I was sober when he started inking. I passed out twice, and Jasper slapped me awake."

"Jesus."

"I wanted a gesture—shit, and this one is all screwed up. It should have been your face."

"It's my name and the bridge. It's perfect. I love you, Tuck."

His eyes mist. "You asked me once where my favorite place in New York is, and I couldn't really give you a true answer, but . . ."

"Yeah?"

"It's you, Francesca. You. Nowhere is good if you aren't there. I canceled the yacht. I'm not going to play pro."

"But you love the game . . ."

He swallows. "I'm too old to play. And I'm good with that. No more aches and pains. No anxiety about my performance. It's been a relief to spend the past few weeks with you and not think about football." He shuts his eyes, then opens them, his words getting groggier. "I'm sorry I made you leave and didn't talk to you. I needed the space, but I could have been kinder." Then he mumbles an apology about the paternity test and lawyer.

"I'm sorry I didn't tell you sooner," I say softly.

He shakes his head and winces. I tell him to stay still and stop talking, and he nods. I hide my smile as joy takes over. He's okay. We're okay.

"I'll tell you about my mom later, what happened when I saw her, but the important part is I've chosen to move forward with you. Our family."

"Tuck, shh. Rest, darling." I card my fingers through his hair.

A few moments pass; then his eyes open wide, and he turns his head to me. "Francesca, we're going to have a baby. I hope you know all the things because I don't know shit about kids. I'm still trying to imagine her. I'm scared—not gonna lie. I never thought it would happen to me . . ." A vulnerable look flashes over his face.

"When I get scared, I do this. Give me your hand again."

I place his hand on my stomach and talk to her, telling her I adore her and her daddy does too. The baby kicks against him, and he starts, then smiles. I gaze up at him and see the wetness in his eyes. I scoot up and brush my lips over his.

He cups my scalp. "Thank you. Thank you for believing in me. For not giving up. We're going to give her everything she needs. Two people who love her—"

Jasper sneaks into the room. He exhales. "Sorry to interrupt this touching moment, but I had to put my eye on you. Big T, you look like shit. Meh, I've seen worse. What about my arm, huh?"

"You pushed me," Tuck grumbles.

"Sorry." He puffs up his chest. "So if the baby is coming in June, I'll still be around, yeah? Instead of moving out, you know, I'd be a great nanny until camp starts."

Tuck narrows his eyes at him. "She won't need a nanny. I'll be there."

"But I like babies!"

"She's my daughter," Tuck growls, and I hold up a hand.

"Okay, you can both change diapers and feed. It's not a contest. Jasper, I don't care if you stay until your place is ready. Now get out of here so I can kiss my baby daddy."

He leaves, and I stare down at Tuck, taking him in. Harmony settles in my gut.

His gaze softens. "My brave little princess."

"Yours. All yours."

His arms wrap around me, and we hold each other. "Me and you and baby makes three," he says softly. "Will you stay with me? Marry me?"

"You have a concussion." I press my face into his throat and giggle. "You're on meds, Mr. Avery, and while I love your ideas, we'll chat later."

"Jasper!" I come flying out of my and Tuck's bedroom and into the den. "Where's Tuck?"

"He left for a meeting with some investors." He doesn't take his eyes off the women's volleyball game on TV. "You need me to make a french fry run?"

I stop in front of the screen, the only way to get his attention.

He peers around me. "Can you move a little to the left? Your ginormous belly is in the way."

"That's because I'm nine months pregnant and ready to give birth."

He leans over to see the screen. "Uh-huh. Is everything all right? You aren't due for another week."

I take in a calm breath. "This is true, but a baby comes when it wants to. And this is a determined child."

He tosses a Cheeto in his mouth.

"Jasper, I think I'm in labor."

He munches. "Did you see how high that player jumped? Dude, these female volleyball players are kick ass."

My hands clench. "Jasper! Stop watching TV! My mucus plug is out!"

His face scrunches up with disgust; then realization dawns. He jumps up, and his Cheetos and Pop-Tarts tumble to the floor. Cherry snatches some of it and darts off down the hall. I would chase her down, but this feels a little more important.

He rakes both hands through his long hair. "Shit! Call Darden. Call Brogan and Cece! Call the cousins! That's my job when you go into labor. Right?"

"Calm down, and yes. I called Tuck, and he's not answering."

"What? How could he not be answering? He's in charge! Are you okay?"

I nod. Thankfully, I was in the shower when it happened, and there wasn't a mess to clean up.

He wrings his hands. "What's a mucus plug anyway? Are you sure you're in labor? You had those fake contractions last time—"

"It's a wad of gooey stuff that's been protecting my cervix."

He pales. "Cervix?"

I demonstrate with my hands like Dr. Lovell showed me. "The cervix is the door to the uterus, and when the plug comes out, it means the door is opening for the baby." I don't have time for an anatomy lesson, but every man should know the wonderful, complicated parts of a woman.

He gags. "Was it gross?"

"Nothing about my baby is gross," I call out.

A contraction starts, new, and I groan as it ripples over my body. Breathing through it, I try to time it as I jog back to the bedroom and change out of my robe for joggers, a soft thermal, and a cardigan Tuck picked up one day while out shopping with me for maternity clothes. I stick my feet in flip-flops, then think better of it and put on Converse. I wince as the contraction continues. That was at least over sixty seconds.

Stalking around the penthouse, I try Tuck's cell again. Still no answer, but I hear a buzzing in the hall bathroom. I pop in and stop. "Well, at least I know why he isn't answering." I grab his phone.

Jasper comes flying out of his room, hair tamed, dressed in Pythons gear. "Got the bug-out bag. I left him a text to meet us at Saint Mary's."

"Yeah, I read it. He left his phone at home."

Another wave hits, and Jasper pants with me. Labor is coming soon.

"That's it; breathe, Francesca, breathe."

"I want Tuck," I growl. "You're supposed to tell me you love me, how beautiful I am, and how wonderful our life will be."

"Do you want me to?"

"No! It's not the same," I call out, then waddle to the den and grab the bag by the door.

Jasper grunts and takes it from me and slings it over his shoulder. "How long are they apart?"

"Maybe five minutes? I don't know. I'm trying to time them in my head, and Tuck was supposed to be here for that part. When they hit, I just hurt."

He whips to me. "Five minutes! We have to go. Right now!"

"That's what I've been saying!"

He escorts me out the door and into the elevator. We stop at my floor, and Darden gets on, a spring in his step. He cackles as he takes in my red face and damp hair. "Looking mighty pretty today, Miss Lane. Being pregnant with an eggplant suits you."

I stick my tongue out at him. "Where's everyone?"

Darden nods. "Called Brogan, and he's en route. He was in a summer class. Cece and Lewis popped out for breakfast. They're also coming."

I pant. "All right." I glance up, then smack at Jasper's hand. "Put your phone down and stop videoing. You are not the moviemaker of this event, no matter what you've been asking."

"You're flush with womanhood, and you're bringing baby Jay into the world. Someone needs to commemorate it for prosperity when she becomes an Olympic volleyball player," Jasper replies but sticks his phone back in his pocket.

By the time we get inside Saint Mary's, I've had three more contractions, and I can physically feel my cervix expanding. I don't know if that's even true, but it sure as hell feels like something is trying to pop out of me.

"Bring the drugs," I tell my nurse when I'm finally in the bed and hooked up to the monitors. Brogan feeds me ice chips, Cece paces, Jasper calls people who are at the meeting with Tuck, and Darden sits next to my bed and holds my hand. He keeps talking about financial stuff, the stock market, the current political climate, the latest honey badger show he watched—all of it to distract me. Valentina sits calmly in a club chair near the window, casually scrolling on her phone while Gianna keeps doing nervous hair flicks as she gives me terrified looks.

The pain relievers hit my system, but by the time the next contraction arrives, it's as if they gave me absolutely nothing. I scream out and shake my head on the pillow. "That's it. I'm done. I'm not doing this. Cece, pack up. Jasper, give me a hand. Let's go take a baby from the nursery and call it a day."

There's a tense silence, and I rise up and yell, "Jeez. I was kidding!"

Dr. Lovell sweeps in the room, all calm and serene, and I beg her to give me more drugs. She pats my hand and reminds me that I didn't want the epidural, and I groan.

"How much longer?" I ask her.

She checks me, then looks at me, her eyes big. "Everyone out but . . ."

"I'm here!" Tuck yells as he sprints into the room. He runs his eyes over the group, taking in our family. He rushes over to me and presses his forehead against mine. "Darling. Sweetheart. I forgot my phone . . . I'm so sorry. Are you all right?"

I give him a steely look. "No, Tuck, I am not all right. This is all your fault. You got me into this, and then you weren't there when my plug came out . . ."

He chuckles, the lines around his eyes crinkling. He kisses the five-carat emerald on my ring finger. He asked me to marry him half a dozen times, but I kept telling him no. I wanted him to be certain that it wasn't because of the baby.

You are my soul, he said. *The light that guides me home. So why does it matter if it was sooner than we might have anticipated?*

I gave in last month on my birthday. I walked in my apartment, and he was on his knees. He'd asked Darden for my hand. And Cece and Brogan and my cousins. He bought me a gallery, with which I could do whatever I wanted. He even said he'd get another tattoo—which made me laugh.

"Maybe you can tell me about that plug later? Let's have a baby," he murmurs as he kisses my nose.

He takes my hand when I stiffen at the new contraction.

For some reason, no one leaves, and Dr. Lovell doesn't seem particularly concerned. Maybe because she keeps barking orders at me, like "Push now" and "Stop pushing" and then "Again" until I'm so tired.

"Here she comes!" Brogan yells, and I don't even care that he's watching.

"Stitch me up, and make it pretty afterwards," I mutter as pressure fills my abdomen, and I push, straining, my hands clenching around Tuck's.

The world turns on its axis as life enters. There's a shift in my heart. Hope, family, and so much love.

Sounds come and go as my body relaxes. "Is she okay?" I mumble as my muscles tremble.

"Welcome to the world, baby boy," Tuck breathes down at the bundle in his arms. There's awe and amazement on his face as he places him on my breast.

I push out a laugh. He has a widow's peak and Tuck's lips.

A tear runs down Tuck's face, and I smile up at him, my own eyes wet.

"He's beautiful," I say.

"You both are."

I gaze around, realizing the room has emptied of our friends and family. Thank God.

"Our little bundle of fate. Franco?" Tuck murmurs.

I laugh. "We barely thought of boy names."

Tuck gazes into my eyes. "I love you, and I love this journey."

I repeat the words back, our little mantra we say to each other.

"Franco Tucker Avery," I say and grab his hand.

"Perfect." He kisses me softly with a heart that is true.

Epilogue

Tuck

Several years later

It's the tickling on my face that wakes me up. I glance over at Francesca's form as she sleeps splayed out on her side of the bed, hogging the covers. She snores loudly. I turn back and see my son standing next to the bed. Cherry sits at his feet, wagging her tail.

I check the clock. Four in the morning. Jesus.

Franco peers at me, his four-year-old face scrunched in concentration. It's the same look he gets when he plays checkers with Darden. He inherited Francesca's widow's peak and artistic intelligence. From me, he got his tall frame and kind nature—or that's what Francesca says. I never would have described myself as kind, but she believes in me. I'm definitely mellow, living my best life at forty. Funny how I always worried about what came after football, and you know what? Happiness came. Oh, it's not always perfect. There's always a dab of chaos here and there, but it's the way you handle it that makes life beautiful.

Franco's tawny hair is mussed, his football pajamas wrinkled from sleep.

"Hey, little dude. Did you wake up too early? Wanna crawl in with me?" My voice is groggy with sleep as I tug the duvet down for him to get in the bed. He sleeps with us sometimes. After a bad dream or during a storm. Cherry too.

He shakes his head.

"Okay, did something happen? You all right?" I scrub my jawline as I sit up. He had a stomach bug last month. Vomit. Diarrhea. Crying. Record-breaking awful. Francesca and I got it next. That whole week feels like a blur. See, chaos.

He smirks, an expression straight from Francesca.

I glance at his hand—the one he just put behind his back. "Is that a Sharpie?" I grunt. "Ah, so that was the tickling. What did you draw on me?"

"A smiley face. A race car."

He doodles on everything. His body, his toys, his closet wall.

Getting out of the bed, I grab my plaid pajama bottoms and slide them on. I take his hand, and we tiptoe out of the bedroom so we don't wake Francesca. His feet pad softly against the marble as I stop in front of the mirror in the master bath.

I sigh. I can't even be mad about it. I mean, yeah, it's in permanent marker and will be a bitch to get off, but the detail and clean lines are damn good. The car is on my forehead, complete with him inside of it, his hands on the wheel. Like me, he loves fast cars. There's a tiny smiley face on my nose.

I ruffle his hair. "You're gonna help me get this off later when I'm awake. You ready to go back to sleep?"

He pauses, his lips quivering. "I got up to pee, then heard something in the house. So I made art."

I ease down and rub his back. "Hey. I'm here. It's okay. I like your art, just not on my skin."

"Can I draw on Mama's?"

A conspiratorial laugh comes from me. "I'd love to see it, but best to ask first. Go ahead and pee."

He slips onto my toilet, does his business, and then comes back out and gazes up at me with adoration in his aquamarine eyes. "Will you check the house, Daddy?"

Daddy. I take a deep breath. That word never gets old and still gets to me emotionally, especially in his sweet voice.

"Sure thing. Let's walk it together, yeah? We can figure out what woke you up. Big-boy stuff."

Holding his small hand in mine, I walk through the modern-style two-story house, our beach home in the Hamptons. With most of the walls made of heavy glass and concrete, the space is about three thousand square feet, with a small cottage and a heated pool. I bought it for Francesca's birthday four years ago, right after we got married. It came with ten acres of land and 250 feet of private beachfront. It's an oasis. Manhattan is her true love, but this is our escape from me running the nonprofit and her gallery. Plus, it's bigger than the yacht. It's become the hub for our get-togethers with the family. We throw a Christmas party, celebrate our birthdays, and have a huge spring event, complete with an egg hunt and me as the Easter Bunny. Cece and Lewis come in from California, Darden sits in a chair and points his cane at us—well, except for the kids who attend. He adores those. Brogan and his current love interest attend, and Ronan and Nova and their brood come.

With Cherry on our heels, we stroll the state-of-the-art kitchen. I check each pantry and closet, then turn on ambient lights as we walk into the den. Everything is quiet—just the lulling sound of the ocean in the distance. Invariably, my gaze goes to Francesca's painting of our family over the fireplace. My heart swells. I married her a few months after Franco was born in a small ceremony in Central Park. We stood in front of each other on Bow Bridge and made vows. Mine was to always love her and put her first, to support and lift her up, to be the shoulder she needs if she cries. I promised to be her family, to take her people into mine and build something beautiful.

After checking the entire first floor, we head upstairs and walk the hall. We stop outside one of the bedrooms. I hear a soft clicking sound.

"Maybe it was that?" I ask. "The room is right next to yours."

He looks up at me. "Should we check?"

Gladly. We ease into the pink nursery, then peer into the baby bed. Darryn (for Darden) Cecelia Ivy is over a year old, with dark hair and a Cupid's bow mouth. She sleeps on her stomach with her butt in the air, her face to the side. Her hand is wrapped around her pacifier. In her sleep, she alternates between putting it in her mouth, then knocking it against the rail of her bed.

"Is that the noise?" I whisper to Franco.

"It's just the paci." He blinks up at me, all innocence. "I like her better when she's sleeping."

I smother a laugh. Since she started walking, she has turned into a little tornado on feet. She rushes headlong into each room, discovering new things, chasing the dog, begging Franco to let her play trains with him. "She's fun to have around, though, right?"

He sighs, his expression softening as he looks at her. "She's all right."

"Think you can go back to sleep, little dude?" I heave him up in my arms, and his head goes to my shoulder. He nods, soft air brushing against my ear as he breathes.

"All right." I carry him to his room next to hers and put him in his big-boy bed. His favorite sleeping partners are lined up on the pillow next to his. A small bear in a Pythons outfit from Darden, a yellow duck in an elaborate white dress from Cece and Brogan, and a plush clown from Jasper—yes, I allowed it—plus a stuffed unicorn from the Russo girls.

Cherry jumps up to crawl under the covers with him.

"When it's time to get up, I'll make you waffles, yeah? Then we'll hit the beach and play."

He nods, his eyes already fluttering closed.

I kiss his forehead, my heart full of love for him, for Darryn, for Francesca. Sometimes I feel so grateful that I'm terrified, like something awful might whisk them away from me. I know the root of that fear, leftover trauma that may never disappear. And when that happens, I remind myself that Francesca and I aren't my parents. We're special. We're, well, fated, written in the stars. And I'll cherish each moment we share.

I walk back to my bedroom and slide back in the bed as I grab my phone from the nightstand.

"Francesca," I sing softly. "I'm recording you snoring. The kids will laugh for days. Hell, I'm already laughing."

She grumbles under her breath and flops over to face me.

"Franco woke me up, and now I'm wide awake," I murmur, mostly to myself. I tap my fingers on the duvet. I could get up and work out, but . . . "Ugh. No."

Francesca grumbles under her breath. "Tuck, you're talking in your sleep, darling . . ."

She flips back over, and I snuggle in behind her, my hand curling around her waist. "No, I'm talking while I'm awake. Long story, but you should see my face. There's a race car on it. He's gonna be good, Fran, like incredible in art—"

"If you wanna have sex, boo, just roll me over . . . ," she says around a yawn as she turns to snuggle into my arms.

"Sex wasn't what I had in mind, but . . ." My voice trails off as she melts closer to me, brushing against the tent in my boxers.

"Do that thing with your lips," she says, her voice still lulled with sleep as her hands go to my hair, carding through the strands.

"What thing?"

"You know . . ."

"Yes?" I tease.

"Where you kiss me like I'm your everything. You want me to brush my teeth first?"

I chuckle. "No, Mrs. Avery. You always taste like fresh dew in the morning."

She grunts. "Funny."

I kiss her softly, then smile against her lips. "You are, you know. My everything. Always will be."

"Mmm, I love your dirty talk."

"Oh, I can get dirtier." Easing on top and straddling her on my knees, I wrap the covers over us like a cocoon. "I love you, Princess," I tell her. Moments pass into slow, languid minutes as I express with my body how deeply she's ingrained in my soul.

She tells me she loves me back, and the world—ah, it's the perfect chaos.

TURN THE PAGE FOR AN
EXCERPT FROM
BEAUTY AND THE BALLER.

Chapter 1

RONAN

"Hey, didn't you once buy some poster of *Star Wars* for like . . . twenty grand?" Tuck asks as he plops down next to me where I'm alone at a table for eight. It's after dinner, and most of the players have wandered off to dance with their partners.

"I have two, *The Phantom Menace* and *The Last Jedi*. Why do you ask?" I say, then drain my fourth or fifth whiskey, embracing the burn of the bourbon. The room isn't spinning yet, which means I'll need more. It takes a lot to forget that my NFL career is over, my fiancée gone.

"Dude . . . are you listening?"

I focus back on Tuck, faking normal. "Yeah, sure."

He grins. "Good. Your perfect woman just walked into our party. Like a gift from heaven. We must make a plan."

"Really." I arch a brow.

"I hear your sarcasm, but come on, would I lie to my best friend?"

"Is water wet?"

He says something else, probably some wisecrack, but I miss it when a woman laughs in the ballroom, light and airy. I close my eyes, inhaling a sharp breath. For a second, she sounded like Whitney. See, the body can be numb, but little things trickle in and haunt me. And football? Not playing cuts like a razor blade, sharp and vicious. I can barely breathe when my team takes the field without me.

I signal the server for another drink.

The waiter gives me a nod, pours it, and then rushes over and hands it to me. I take a hearty sip under Tuck's gaze.

"You never used to drink, Ronan. Don't you think you've had enough?"

Ha. This is nothing compared to those mornings when I wake up and can't recall details from the night before. "The girl? What's it about her that makes her perfect for me?"

"Look for yourself," he says, nudging his head toward where she must be. "You won't believe what she's wearing. Behind you and to your left. Check it."

With a heavy exhale, I loosen my tie and swivel in my seat and peer around various players. I focus in on the girl about twenty feet away and inhale as I get the full effect.

Whoa.

There's no way anyone could miss her. Not with that getup.

What the hell was she thinking?

"She's lost, yes?" he murmurs.

"Hmm," I say as my eyes brush over her.

Tall with pale-blonde hair, she's wearing a costume, legit, like Princess Leia—slave-girl version, the one where she was captured by Jabba the Hutt. It's a gold bikini with a red filmy loincloth over her hips. She's even got the sleek plaited high ponytail and golden knotted necklace. From the metal snake cuff around her upper arm to the green lace-up boots, the costume isn't one of those cheap knockoffs from a Halloween store. It's damn perfect, and she wears it better than Carrie Fisher did in *Return of the Jedi*.

A low whistle comes from Tuck. "She waltzed in the fanciest hotel in the city and crashed a Pythons party. Right in the middle of all these

Beauty and the Baller

suits and dresses. Everyone's staring at her. Wait a minute . . . looks like someone isn't happy . . ."

His voice trails off as a black-clad security guy approaches her, clipboard in hand, headset on his head. A scowl settles on his face as he snaps out words to her. Security is tight at our events. Fans, crazy ones, will do anything to get a glimpse of their favorite team.

She doesn't look like a weirdo fan. Those are usually wearing black-and-gold Python gear and shouting players' names.

She *is* lost.

Tuck lowers his voice. "She's about to get thrown out—or arrested. They've done it before. She needs a Han Solo to save her."

I turn back to him. "Subtle."

He shrugs. "She's your type—into *Star Wars*, blonde, *and* a damsel in distress."

"Not interested."

"Liar," he says. "Bet you can't get her digits."

I lean back in the chair and shake my head at him. Before I got serious with Whitney, we used to compete at bars to see who could get the most numbers. Jesus. That feels like a million years ago.

"You wanna play that, huh?" I ask. "Is this you trying to motivate me to move on?"

"It's been almost a year since . . ."

"The wreck," I finish, my voice thickening. "The anniversary of her passing is in four days."

"I'm sorry." He sighs and glances away, then comes back to me, leaning his arms in on the table, an earnest expression on his face. "Look. I miss you, okay? Dammit. I sound like a silly schoolgirl. It's just . . . you're avoiding *me*, your best friend. You're drinking. A lot." He rakes a hand through his messy sandy-brown hair and sighs. "I'm sorry, man. This isn't about me, and I've got no clue what you're going through, and Whitney, the way it went down—it sucks . . ."

I stare at the table as his words ping-pong around in my head. He's not wrong. I'm in a dark place, a pit of hell, and I crave to crawl out. Some days it feels as if there's nothing left inside of me. No spark. No hope. No joy.

I sat out the season on the injury list, and that was mostly out of respect for my history with the team. Everyone knew I'd never play. I didn't even want to come to the end-of-the-year celebration, but I dragged myself here anyway. I just need something, *anything*, to numb this ache in my chest.

"Our team won't be the same without you," he says. "Maybe if you rehab another season, try different physical therapy—"

"I've done it all, Tuck." I endured two surgeries and rehab from some of the best doctors in the world—and that was just for my knee. I had a whole other round for my face.

He exhales noisily. "But you know I can't shut up, right?"

I tip my glass up at him. "Nine years together, and you never once stopped running your mouth."

An eager expression crosses his face, his words coming in a rush: "Let's play. 'Kay? Like old times? You rescue her from security, chat her up, and get her number, and I'll wash your Porsche and let you take pics of me and brag about it, post it on Insta, whatever. Anything else that happens"—he flashes a grin—"I'm talking maybe kiss her, will be icing on the cake; feel me? You don't need a lesson on how to woo a woman, do you?"

My lids lower. "No." I've been a phenom quarterback since I was fourteen. Women have always gravitated to me.

Or they used to.

I catch my reflection in the mirror behind him and see the scars on the left side of my face. Jagged and pink, the longest one starts at my temple, traces past my ear to my jawline, and ends midneck. Sixteen inches long, that cut was a quarter inch from an artery. Other scars, like jagged spiderwebs, slice into my cheek on the same side, then disappear into my dark hair. Last year, my hair was shaved around my ears and longer on top in a classic pompadour, but it has grown out, the longer length brushing my chin. Still, they're visible. Last week, one of the trainers dropped off some personal equipment I'd kept at the field. When I opened the door, he saw my face . . . and flinched. Might as well get used to it. They aren't going away. I rub the long one, my thumb brushing over it.

"They give you a dangerous vibe," Tuck says.

"Frankenstein—yeah, that's a good look." I drain my glass and set it on the table.

"All right, buddy, let's get you moving," he says as he tugs me up.

I weave on my feet—whoa—then straighten and frown. "What's the rush?"

He waves that off. "Listen to me. Go talk to that girl. For your best friend in the whole wide world. *Please.*" He bats his lashes at me.

"You're an idiot," I say as I glance back over at her.

While we were talking, the security guy called another one over. They moved her to a corner near the entrance, and she's got her chin tilted, a defiant look on her face as they question her. In a flurry of her loincloth, she nudges past them and gazes around the room, her eyes landing on me and sticking. Her face transforms, a radiant smile curving her lips.

Tuck lets out a surprised sound. "Huh, will you look at that? She knows you! This is perfect! You've got this!" He slaps me on the back. "Go get her, tiger. Go, go!"

"No," I mutter.

Then the security guard puts his meaty hand on her arm and half drags her to the door.

"Dammit," I breathe as a twinge of protectiveness rises. I heave out an exhale, shake off Tuck, and jostle my way through the crowd, leaning slightly on my right side to compensate for the prickle of pain on my left.

"That's what I'm talking about!" Tuck calls out. "Save the princess!"

Whatever. I flip him off over my shoulder.

I'll see what she's about, and that's it.

Maybe get her out of here without causing her any embarrassment. I grew up with two younger sisters, and there's a long list of escapades I've saved them from. Hell, I half raised them. What's the harm in helping the princess? It'll be a good story *and* get Tuck off my back.

As I approach, she's having words with the guy holding her arm. She fights free of his grasp—again—then rushes toward me, the slits of her skirt showcasing her long, toned legs. Security is hot on her heels, but she never looks back, her posture straight, her steps sure, as she keeps that "I know you" smile directed straight at me.

We meet in the middle of the ballroom underneath one of the chandeliers among the dancers, and I send a head nudge to the duo behind her.

"Ease up, guys. She's with me."

They shrug and leave. I'm sure crazier shit has happened at an NFL party.

My breath hitches as I take her in. I didn't appreciate her before at the table, but this close, it's as if someone created everything I love in a woman: tall, blonde, heart-shaped face, sapphire eyes, luscious tits. Toss in the costume . . .

My teenage fantasy in the flesh.

She takes both of my hands in hers, and the touch sends a buzz of awareness racing over my skin. I didn't expect that.

"Ronan," she murmurs.

Okay, she knows my name—not surprising.

"Hey, um . . . ?" What are you doing here?

"Help me," she implores dramatically. "You're my only, um, salvation . . . and stuff like that . . . to save the universe."

I huff out a rusty laugh. "Well, that's almost Leia's first line in *Star Wars*."

She leans in, and her fingers dance up my jacket and land on the lapels, stroking the black fabric. "I love this suit. You like my outfit?"

My gaze tangles in the soft curves of her body, lingering on her bikini-clad breasts. Gradually, I move up to the smooth line of her throat, to the dark winged eyebrows that contrast with her hair and frame her face. Even without the kick-ass costume, she's the kind of girl you see on the street and do a double take. Hourglass shape, classic features, and a perfect pouty bottom lip.

"Yes," I murmur.

"I could get used to this skirt." She moves her hips, swishing the fabric.

"Loincloth."

"You don't say? I'll make a note of that." With a sly yet sweet smile, she does a little twirl, then stops in front of me and places a hand over her heart.

"What?" I ask.

"It's sinking in. You really came to help me."

My lips twitch. "To save the universe. And stuff like that." I glance around the room. "Can I escort you somewhere?"

Disappointment flickers over her face before she quickly hides it. "No. I'm fine. Really. It was nice of you to come over. I'll go. I just wanted to pop in and see . . ." She stops, seeming to think about her words, then smiles ruefully. "Never mind. Thank you. Goodbye, Ronan."

When she turns, I grab her hand. "Wait."

I don't know why I stop her, but . . .

My eyes lock with hers, several breathless moments passing as our hands cling. Acting on instinct, my thumb caresses her palm.

Her lips part, heat flashing in her irises.

A long breath comes from me. I miss *this*. Desire, not pity, in a woman's eyes.

I swallow thickly. There's been no one since Whitney. I've had opportunities, mostly Tuck dragging me out to dinners and get-togethers, and girls have offered, but my body—and my heart—wasn't ready.

It's been forever since I flirted with a girl, but . . .

Lowering my lids, I tug her closer to me until our chests brush. "Who are you, gorgeous?"

Silence, thick and sweet, stretches between us. "Yours."

A shot of lust, fueled by her whispered words, hits me. The lizard part of my brain, the primitive side that reacts on instinct to fighting and fucking, rears up. *This one,* it demands. *Take it.*

She's not the right girl, the other side of my head shouts, even as my index finger strokes her cheek. She turns her head into the touch, sighing softly, and my chest seizes at her automatic response.

You wanted something to push that grief back.

"Dance with me," she murmurs and doesn't wait for my reply but leans her forehead on my shoulder, her body starting to sway to the slow song the DJ plays.

I dip my head and sway with her, slow and easy. My hands slide around her waist, almost tentatively. Moments tick by, heavy with expectation, as if waiting to see what happens next. My thumb finds the small of her back and circles the soft skin there. It's my favorite part of a woman, and I can't resist. My breath snags as her fingers trace designs on my shoulders, then press harder, her nails dragging down my back, then up. I bite back a groan. Touch. It's one of the things I've missed, the smooth glide of hands over skin, the feeling of connection.

We go from one song to another, the music bleeding together as the DJ spins slow tracks. I keep my eyes shut, my body relaxing against hers. Even my knee feels better. A long exhale comes from my chest as the tension from the last few hours vanishes. It was hard to walk in here. To sit at a table with couples, recognize their sorrow-filled glances, and realize that once again, I'm alone.

The truth is it's the nights that eat at me the most. I'm sick of spending them by myself.

Vaguely, as if from a distance, I'm aware that "Say You Won't Let Go," by James Arthur, is on the speakers, a song about two people connecting . . . maybe it's a message.

Her lips brush against my neck, almost hesitantly; then, braver, she moves back and kisses my throat. Electricity flares, and I toy with the top of her loincloth, rubbing the fabric. I ease my hand underneath it, my fingers grazing the curve of her ass. My heart hammers as she responds by swishing her leg in between mine, brushing against the bulge in my pants.

Powerful and greedy, desire slams into me.

I stop our dancing and slide my hands up her arms to her neck, tilting her face up. Need soaks her features, eyes dilated, cheeks flushed.

She isn't one of Tuck's party girls who flirts with me to be nice.

And I'm not misreading her signals.

I didn't see this (her) coming, but . . .

"You wanna get out of here?" I ask in a gravelly voice. "Maybe do some role-playing, hmm?"

She knows what I mean. Her. Me. One night.

Her pink tongue dips out and dabs at her plump lower lip. "All right."

"Good," I purr as my thumb brushes her mouth.

I crook her arm through mine and lace our hands together. We move through the dancers as we leave the ballroom. Outside, the foyer is crowded with people, and we dodge past them with heads bent. I'm doing it to not be recognized; she seems to understand.

With each step, the air thins, my chest tightening. I'm not sure if it's because this is an impulsive decision I'll probably regret tomorrow or if it's her. We get inside the elevator, and I slap the button for the top floor, then ease her against the wall. Words don't feel necessary as I run my nose up her throat. She smells fresh and tart, like apples, and I'm rushing, totally—I don't know this girl, even her name, but I don't care. Nothing has stemmed the darkness, even alcohol, but I'll sink myself into a beautiful woman to bring on oblivion.

She looks up at me. "I—I don't normally, um—"

I stop her with a finger to her lips. "I'm going to kiss you. Is that okay?"

She nods.

I slant my mouth across hers, our breaths mingling as I part her lips. She melts against me. A shudder ripples over me as lust, long banked and hungry, strains to be unleashed, to crush her beneath me. I hold it back, for now, and learn her mouth, the shape of it, the dips and valleys. Her breath hitches as I tug on her bottom lip with my teeth, then kiss it softly. I move from her cheek to her ear, my teeth biting on the lobe.

"I don't normally either," I breathe.

Later, she takes the card from me and opens my door. We walk inside the suite and pause in the foyer as she takes in the penthouse I booked. The decor is mostly white with a low-profile, black gas fireplace burning in the den. The views of Manhattan are glorious from the windows, which is where she drifts, but my gaze goes to the kitchen . . . and the whiskey bottle.

I offer her a drink, and she says no. I pour a glass for me; then we wander into the master bedroom, where an empty bottle already sits on the nightstand. Tuck was right about me not being a drinker. For years, I set high goals, studying how to be a great leader and quarterback for my team, pushing my body to its limits with training, eating right, rarely consuming alcohol. For me, it was the game I lived for.

I won three Super Bowls in a row.

Look at me now.

There's a moment of clarity, my mind debating if bringing the girl here was a good idea. I'm supposed to see Whitney's parents tomorrow—

I kick that thought away.

She gives me a heart-stopping smile and does a pirouette in front of the window, her loincloth billowing around her. She repeats her quote, correctly this time, then laughingly admits she doesn't know any more. I tell her I'll teach her all my favorites. I finish my drink, then another. Time passes fast, yet slow, as she flits around the room. She talks, telling me things, maybe her name, and I soak her in, the graceful way she walks, the way her overgenerous lips curl when she smiles.

Propping myself against the wall to keep steady, I find music on my phone, some slow pop song.

"You're incredible," I murmur in her ear when she glides over to me. *How did I get here with you? How did you find me?*

With our arms draped around each other, we sway as she sings along with Savage Garden's "I Knew I Loved You." Her voice is rich, each note perfect and clear. She's good. Or maybe I'm just trashed and anything sounds good.

When the song ends, there's a silence as we face each other.

The air thickens.

I brought her here, but she can walk out that door.

With that thought, I twine our fingers together and dip my face into her neck and inhale deeply, deciding this spot is my second-favorite part of a woman. I rest my hands on her clavicle with ownership, my thumb brushing against the goose bumps on her skin.

"It's game time. Are you staying, Princess?"

"Yes." Her gaze is steady and sure.

It's all I need as I try to remove her costume, but my fingers don't know where all the snaps and buttons are, and she does it for me, quickly, tossing her top to the floor, then her bikini bottoms, revealing a white lace thong. Sitting on the bed, she loosens her green boots, tugging at the laces. She undoes her hair, the curls from the braid spilling around her shoulders. My mouth dries as she stands unabashedly in front of me. There's no shyness. No pretention. She's lush and decadent, her tits heavy, her nipples a rosy red. The curve of her waist gives way to full hips and long legs. Her toes are painted a shimmery gold—

My thoughts halt as she jerks the duvet and blankets to the floor, leaving the sheet and pillows on the bed.

My adrenaline spikes. We're doing this. *I'm* doing this.

"Come to me," I demand softly.

She walks over and strips me of my jacket, then tosses it on a chair. She unknots my tie while I tear at the buttons on my shirt. They fly across the room. My pants are next, both of us fighting for the zipper as our breaths mingle. I shove down my underwear, and she takes my length in her hands. A long guttural sound comes from my chest as our bodies fall to the bed.

I shove down the pain in my knee and cage her in underneath me. She looks fragile and vulnerable, and my blood heats, the alpha in me rearing up to protect her. I capture her sapphire eyes, and something there is eerily familiar. Shadows of pain.

I nudge my nose against hers softly, then give her tender kisses as our scents mingle, my whiskey with her sweetness. I tell her she's perfect, that she's safe with me, that she's mine. "And I'm going to eat you up," I purr.

"Ronan . . ." She runs her hands through my hair, pulling on the ends and dragging me down for a wet, open-mouthed kiss that turns frantic. My hand cups one breast as I suck the other nipple into my mouth. I move between the two, my five-o'clock shadow brushing over her soft skin. She tastes like . . . I don't know . . . joy.

I kiss down her body, my hands following. I touch the curve of her waist, her inner thigh—then I'm at her center. I lick the nirvana there, my hands clenching on top of her thighs as I feast.

Moaning, she tugs on my hair, and I rise up.

An unexpected flicker of disconnect hits, almost choking the desire, as the chain around my neck, the one with Whitney's engagement ring on it, swings between us, glittering. I shove the ring to my back as guilt washes over me.

A dark road flashes in my head, the scratching swipe of windshield wipers, hail pinging, wind battering the car. I should have paid more attention to the storm and slowed down, taken a different road, insisted she put her seat belt on—fuck, how did I miss that? She hated wearing it, the one rule she refused to follow, and I wasn't paying attention; then a bolt of lightning hit the bridge—my breath shudders. No.

I don't want to think about that.

Not here. Not now.

I kick back the ache of those memories; I try, even as the condom gets rolled on. I slide inside her, all the way home, a primal roar coming deep from my chest. I stare down at the beauty in my bed, and finally, she's the only thing I see in my head.

We become a whirlwind of carnal need, straining to crawl into each other. We're wild, grasping, finding new positions, new places to touch. I'm voracious; she's ravenous. I grunt with every thrust, my eyes eating her up as the headboard clatters against the wall.

"Ronan . . ." Her head thrashes back and forth on the pillow.

"I'm there, Princess . . ."

My fingers circle her nub, and she explodes brilliantly, magnificently, her body undulating in sinuous waves.

My cock thickens, eager to follow, ecstasy a heartbeat away.

"Whitney," I call out as I come.

My body trembles as I rest on top of her before rolling off and falling to my back. I shove my damp hair off my face and suck in gulps of air. That was incredible. My hand reaches over the space between us and toys with her long blonde hair, carding it through my fingers. She's already flipped over, facing the other direction, the sheet around her shoulders.

Some of the blood returns to my brain.

Wait . . .

A sinking feeling trickles in.

Did I . . . did I call her . . . *Whitney?*

No way. Impossible.

My heart drops to my stomach as realization kicks in.

Jesus, I totally did, but . . . it wasn't like that.

It just wasn't.

I don't know what to say. She heard me, of course. Grimacing, I stare at the back of her head and wrestle with how to explain about Whitney's death, how she died in my arms, how it was my fault . . . but those memories are full of thorns.

I search for words, but my tongue feels thick, my brain sluggish, fighting through the haze of bourbon. I should say I'm sorry, I should ask what her name is, I should tell her that she's the best thing that's happened to me in a year . . .

Exhaustion wins and drags me under.

When I wake up, my head is stuffed with cotton balls. Sunlight glints in through the blinds, and I rub at the grit in my eyes. Tensing, I turn to look at the pillow next to me. There's no one there, not even an indentation. The room is dead quiet except for the blaring horns from the traffic outside. A heavy feeling settles in my chest, and I can't decide if I'm relieved or disappointed she left. I rake my hands through my hair, frowning, as I try to piece the night together. It might take a while.

I hiss when I see that it's two in the afternoon, and I've missed lunch with Whitney's parents in Connecticut. Cursing under my breath, I yank my pants off the floor, fish out my phone, and then fire off a text apologizing.

I collapse back on the bed. One thing is clear. *I had sex.*

Guilt chews me with sharp teeth, then spits me out in disgust. Couldn't I have waited until after Whitney's one-year anniversary?

Doesn't she deserve that? I loved her with my whole heart, with everything inside me, yet it feels as if I betrayed her.

Swallowing thickly, I get up and grab my clothes, when a golden arm cuff rolls out of my shirt. I rub my fingers over the thick metal, my head flashing to last night. I recall us dancing, the sex, yet . . . I frown, squinting. She was blonde, yes. She had blue eyes, yes, but the rest is vague and blurry.

Sure, I've been blackout drunk, but how can I remember the awe in her eyes when we met, her bubbliness, the smell of her neck . . . yet *not* her features?

Maybe I don't want to? Guilt over Whitney? I exhale. I don't know.

Another memory trickles in, ugly and harsh, and a curse escapes my lips. I called her Whitney. A fresh wave of remorse settles over me. Jesus. No wonder she left without a word.

My insides twist as I glare at the whiskey bottle on the nightstand as if it's to blame.

Deep breaths come from my chest as I pace around the room, my head churning. I pick up the bottle and toss it in the trash. Something has to give. I can't keep doing this to myself, to my body. The truth is I'm numbing myself, wallowing, spiraling closer and closer to destruction. This isn't me. I'm not a drunk. I'm a former superstar. I'm Ronan Smith and . . . I pause as clarity runs through my head. I want my life back, no matter what that may be.

Closing my eyes, I touch the ring around my neck.

Today is when everything changes.

ABOUT THE AUTHOR

Wall Street Journal, New York Times, USA Today, and number one Amazon Charts bestselling author Ilsa Madden-Mills pens angsty new adult and contemporary romances. A former high school English teacher and librarian, she adores all things *Pride and Prejudice,* and of course, Mr. Darcy is her ultimate hero. She's addicted to frothy coffee beverages, cheesy magnets, and any book featuring unicorns and sword-wielding females. Feel free to stalk her online.

Please join her Facebook readers group, Unicorn Girls, to get the latest scoop and to talk about books, wine, and Netflix: www.facebook.com/groups/ilsasunicorngirls. You can also find her on her website, www.ilsamaddenmills.com. Sign up for her newsletter at www.ilsamaddenmills.com/contact.